PENGUIN BOOKS

741

TROUBLE IS MY BUSINESS

RAYMOND CHANDLER

Raymond Chandler was born in Chicago of an American Quaker father and an Irish Quaker mother. At an early age he went to England, and attended Dulwich College, completing his education in France and Germany. After that he had many professions: teacher, book-reviewer, poet, paragraph writer, essayist, soldier in a Canadian infantry regiment, student pilot, accountant, oil executive, and 'pulp writer'. For twenty years until his death he lived in the United States, his home being in the southern California area which forms the background of his books. He died in 1959.

RAYMOND CHANDLER

Trouble is my Business

AND OTHER STORIES

PENGUIN BOOKS

Penguin Books Ltd, Harmondsworth, Middlesex
AUSTRALIA: Penguin Books Pty Ltd, 762 Whitehorse Road,
Mitcham, Victoria

—

The stories in this volume first appeared in various American
magazines between 1933 and 1939. They were first issued in
book form in the U.S.A. in 1946, 'Trouble is my Business' in a
volume entitled *Spanish Blood*, the remainder in a volume
entitled *Red Wind*. This is the first volume publication in
Great Britain. First published in Penguin Books 1950.
Reprinted 1951, 1952, 1954, 1957, 1960, 1962, 1964

—

—

Made and printed in Great Britain
by Hunt, Barnard & Co, Ltd, Aylesbury
Set in Monotype Baskerville

Contents

I

Trouble is my Business

1

ANNA HALSEY was about two hundred and forty pounds of middle-aged putty-faced woman in a black tailor-made suit. Her eyes were shiny black shoe-buttons, her cheeks were as soft as suet and about the same colour. She was sitting behind a black glass desk that looked like Napoleon's tomb and she was smoking a cigarette in a black holder that was not quite as long as a rolled umbrella. She said: 'I need a man.'

I watched her shake ash from the cigarette to the shiny top of the desk where flakes of it curled and crawled in the draught from an open window.

'I need a man good-looking enough to pick up a dame who has a sense of class, but he's got to be tough enough to swap punches with a power shovel. I need a guy who can act like a bar lizard and backchat like Fred Allen, only better, and get hit on the head with a beer truck and think some cutie in the leg-line topped him with a breadstick.'

'It's a cinch,' I said, 'You need the New York Yankees, Robert Donat, and the Yacht Club Boys.'

'You might do,' Anna said, 'cleaned up a little. Twenty bucks a day and ex's. I haven't brokered a job in years, but this one is out of my line. I'm in the smooth-angles of the detecting business and I make money without getting my can knocked off. Let's see how Gladys likes you.'

She reversed the cigarette holder and tipped a key on a large black-and-chromium annunciator box. 'Come in and empty Anna's ashtray, honey.'

We waited.

The door opened and a tall blonde dressed better than the Duchess of Windsor strolled in.

She swayed elegantly across the room, emptied Anna's ashtray, patted her fat cheek, gave me a smooth rippling glance and went out again.

'I think she blushed,' Anna said when the door closed. 'I guess you still have it.'

'She blushed – and I have a dinner date with Darryl Zanuck,' I said. 'Quit horsing around. What's the story?'

'It's to smear a girl. A redheaded number with bedroom eyes. She's shill for a gambler and she's got her hooks into a rich man's pup.'

'What do I do to her?'

Anna sighed. 'It's kind of a mean job, Johnny, I guess. If she's got a record of any sort, you dig it up and toss it in her face. If she hasn't, which is more likely as she comes from good people, it's kind of up to you. You get an idea once in a while, don't you?'

'I can remember the last one I had. What gambler and what rich man?'

'Marty Estel.'

I started to get up from my chair, then remembered that business had been bad for a month and that I needed the money.

I sat down again.

'You might get into trouble, of course,' Anna said. 'I never heard of Marty bumping anybody off in the public square at high noon, but he don't play with cigar coupons.'

'Trouble is my business,' I said. 'Twenty-five a day and a guarantee of two-fifty, if I pull the job.'

'I gotta make a little something for myself,' Anna whined.

'O.K. There's plenty of coolie labour around town. Nice to have seen you looking so well. So long, Anna.'

I stood up this time. My life wasn't worth much, but it

was worth that much. Marty Estel was supposed to be pretty rough people, with the right helpers and the right protection behind him. His place was out in West Hollywood, on the Strip. He wouldn't pull anything crude, but if he pulled at all, something would pop.

'Sit down, it's a deal,' Anna sneered. 'I'm a poor old broken-down woman trying to run a high-class detective agency on nothing but fat and bad health, so take my last nickel and laugh at me.'

'Who's the girl?' I had sat down again.

'Her name is Harriet Huntress — a swell name for the part too. She lives in the El Milano, nineteen-hundred block on North Sycamore, very high-class. Father went broke back in thirty-one and jumped out of his office window. Mother dead. Kid sister in boarding school back in Connecticut. That might make an angle.'

'Who dug up all this?'

'The client got a bunch of photostats of notes the pup had given to Marty. Fifty grand worth. The pup — he's an adopted son to the old man — denied the notes, as kids will. So the client had the photostats experted by a guy named Arbogast, who pretends to be good at that sort of thing. He said O.K. and dug around a bit, but he's too fat to do leg-work, like me, and he's off the case now.'

'But I could talk to him?'

'I don't know why not.' Anna nodded several of her chins.

'This client — does he have a name?'

'Son, you have a treat coming. You can meet him in person — right now.'

She tipped the key of her call-box again. 'Have Mr Jeeter come in, honey.'

'That Gladys,' I said, 'does she have a steady?'

'You lay off Gladys!' Anna almost screamed at me. 'She's worth eighteen grand a year in divorce business to me. Any guy that lays a finger on her, Johnny Dalmas, is practically cremated.'

'She's got to fall some day,' I said. 'Why couldn't I catch her?'

The opening door stopped that.

I hadn't seen him in the panelled reception-room, so he must have been waiting in a private office. He hadn't enjoyed it. He came in quickly, shut the door quickly, and yanked a thin octagonal platinum watch from his vest and glared at it. He was a tall white-blond type in pin-striped flannel of youthful cut. There was a small pink rosebud in his lapel. He had a keen frozen face, a little pouchy under the eyes, a little thick in the lips. He carried an ebony cane with a silver knob, wore spats and looked a smart sixty, but I gave him close to ten years more. I didn't like him.

'Twenty-six minutes, Miss Halsey,' he said icily. 'My time happens to be valuable. By regarding it as valuable I have managed to make a great deal of money.'

'Well, we're trying to save you some of the money,' Anna drawled. She didn't like him either. 'Sorry to keep you waiting, Mr Jeeter, but you wanted to see the operative I selected and I had to send for him.'

'He doesn't look the type to me,' Mr Jeeter said, giving me a nasty glance. 'I think more of a gentleman –'

'You're not the Jeeter of *Tobacco Road*, are you?' I asked him.

He came slowly towards me and half lifted the stick. His icy eyes tore at me like claws. 'So you insult me,' he said. 'Me – a man in my position.'

'Now wait a minute,' Anna began.

'Wait a minute nothing,' I said. 'This party said I was not a gentleman. Maybe that's O.K. for a man in his position, whatever it is – but a man in my position doesn't take a dirty crack from anybody. He can't afford to. Unless, of course, it wasn't intended.'

Mr Jeeter stiffened and glared at me. He took his watch out again and looked at it. 'Twenty-eight minutes,' he said, 'I apologize, young man. I had no desire to be rude.'

'That's swell,' I said. 'I knew you weren't the Jeeter in *Tobacco Road* all along.'

That almost started him again, but he let it go. He wasn't sure how I meant it.

'A question or two while we are together,' I said. 'Are you willing to give this Huntress girl a little money – for expenses?'

'Not one cent,' he barked. 'Why should I?'

'It's got to be a sort of custom. Suppose she married him. What would he have?'

'At the moment a thousand dollars a month from a trust fund established by his mother, my late wife.' He dipped his head. 'When he is twenty-eight years old, far too much money.'

'You can't blame the girl for trying,' I said. 'Not these days. How about Marty Estel? Any settlement there?'

He crumpled his grey gloves with a purple-veined hand. 'The debt is uncollectable. It is a gambling debt.'

Anna sighed wearily and flicked ash around on her desk.

'Sure,' I said. 'But gamblers can't afford to let people welsh on them. After all, if your son had won, Marty would have paid *him*.'

'I'm not interested in that,' the tall thin man said coldly.

'Yeah, but think of Marty sitting there with fifty grand in notes. Not worth a nickel. How will he sleep nights?'

Mr Jeeter looked thoughtful. 'You mean there is danger of violence?' he suggested, almost suavely.

'That's hard to say. He runs an exclusive place, gets a good movie crowd. He has his own reputation to think of. But he's in a racket and he knows people. Things can happen – a long way off from where Marty is. And Marty is no bathmat. He gets up and walks.'

Mr Jeeter looked at his watch again and it annoyed him. He slammed it back into his vest. 'All that is your affair,' he snapped. 'The district attorney is a personal friend of mine. If this matter seems to be beyond your powers – '

'Yeah,' I told him. 'But you came slumming down our street just the same. Even if the D.A. is in your vest pocket – along with that watch.'

He put his hat on, drew on one glove, tapped the edge of his shoe with his stick, walked to the door and opened it.

'I ask results and I pay for them,' he said coldly. 'I pay promptly. I even pay generously sometimes, although I am not considered a generous man. I think we all understand one another.'

He almost winked then and went on out. The door closed softly against the cushion of air in the door-closer. I looked at Anna and grinned.

'Sweet, isn't he?' she said. 'I'd like eight of him for my cocktail set.'

I gouged twenty dollars out of her – for expenses.

2

The Arbogast I wanted was John D. Arbogast and he had an office on Sunset near Ivar. I called him up from a phone booth. The voice that answered was fat. It wheezed softly, like the voice of a man who had just won a pie-eating contest.

'Mr John D. Arbogast?'

'Yeah.'

'This is John Dalmas, a private detective working on a case you did some experting on. Party named Jeeter.'

'Yeah?'

'Can I come up and talk to you about it – after I eat lunch?'

'Yeah.' He hung up. I decided he was not a talkative man.

I had lunch and drove out there. It was east of Ivar, an old two-storey building faced with brick which had been painted recently. The street floor was stores and a restaurant. The building entrance was at the foot of a wide straight stairway to the second floor. On the directory at the bottom I read – *John D. Arbogast, Suite 212.* I went up the stairs and found myself in a wide straight hall that ran parallel with the street. A man in a smock was standing in an open doorway down to my right. He wore a round mirror strapped to his forehead and pushed back and his face had a puzzled expression. He went back to his office and shut the door.

I went the other way, about half the distance along the hall. A door on the side away from Sunset was lettered – *John D. Arbogast, Examiner of Questioned Documents. Private Investigator. Enter.* The door opened without resistance onto a small windowless ante-room with a couple of easy chairs, some magazines, two chromium smoking-stands. There were two floor lamps and a ceiling fixture, all lighted. A door on the other side of the cheap but thick and new rug was lettered – *John D. Arbogast, Examiner of Questioned Documents. Private.*

A buzzer had rung when I opened the outer door and gone on ringing until it closed. Nothing happened. Nobody was in the waiting-room. The inner door didn't open. I went over and listened at the panel – no sound of conversation inside. I knocked. That didn't buy me anything either. I tried the knob. It turned so I opened the door and went in.

This room had two north windows, both curtained at the sides and both shut tight. There was dust on the sills. There was a desk, two filing-cases, a carpet which was just a carpet, and walls which were just walls. To the left another door with a glass panel was lettered: *John D. Arbogast. Laboratory. Private.*

I had an idea I might be able to remember the name.

The room in which I stood was small. It seemed almost too small even for the pudgy hand that rested on the edge of the desk, motionless, holding a fat pencil like a carpenter's pencil. The hand had a wrist, hairless as a plate. A buttoned shirt-cuff, not too clean, came down out of a coat-sleeve.

The rest of the sleeve dropped over the far edge of the desk out of sight. The desk was less than six feet long, so he couldn't have been a very tall man. The hand and the ends of the sleeves were all I saw of him from where I stood. I went quietly back through the ante-room and fixed its door so that it couldn't be opened from the outside and put out the three lights and went back to the private office. I went around an end of the desk.

He was fat all right, enormously fat, fatter by far than Anna Halsey. His face, what I could see of it, looked about the size of a basket ball. It had a pleasant pinkness, even now. He was kneeling on the floor. He had his large head against the sharp inner corner of the kneehole of the desk, and his left hand was flat on the floor with a piece of yellow paper under it. The fingers were outspread as much as such fat fingers could be, and the yellow paper showed between. He looked as if he were pushing hard on the floor, but he wasn't really. What was holding him up was his own fat. His body was folded down against his enormous thighs, and the thickness and fatness of them held him that way, kneeling, poised solid. It would have taken a couple of good blocking backs to knock him over. That wasn't a very nice idea at the moment, but I had it just the same. I took time out and wiped the back of my neck, although it was not a warm day.

His hair was grey and clipped short and his neck had as many folds as a concertina. His feet were small, as the feet of fat men often are, and they were in black shiny shoes which were sideways on the carpet and close together and neat and nasty. He wore a dark suit that needed cleaning. I leaned down and buried my fingers in the bottomless fat of his neck. He had an artery in there somewhere, probably, but I couldn't find it and he didn't need it any more anyway. Between his bloated knees on the carpet a dark stain had spread and spread –

I knelt in another place and lifted the pudgy fingers that

were holding down the piece of yellow paper. They were cool, but not cold, and soft and a little sticky. The paper was from a scratch pad. It would have been very nice if it had had a message on it, but it hadn't. There were vague meaningless marks, not words, not even letters. He had tried to write something after he was shot – perhaps even thought he *was* writing something – but all he managed was some hen scratches.

He had slumped down then, still holding the paper, pinned it to the floor with his fat hand, held on to the fat pencil with his other hand, wedged his torso against his huge thighs, and so died. John D. Arbogast, Examiner of Questioned Documents. Private. Very damned private. He had said 'yeah' to me three times over the phone.

And here he was.

I wiped doorknobs with my handkerchief, put off the lights in the ante-room, left the outer door so that it was locked from the outside, left the hallway, left the building and left the neighbourhood. So far as I could tell nobody saw me go. So far as I could tell.

3

The El Milano was, as Anna had told me, in the 1900 block on North Sycamore. It was most of the block. I parked fairly near the ornamental forecourt and went along to the pale blue neon sign over the entrance to the basement garage. I walked down a railed ramp into a bright space of glistening cars and cold air. A trim light-coloured Negro in a spotless overall suit with blue cuffs came out of a glass office. His black hair was as smooth as a bandleader's.

'Busy?' I asked him.

'Yes and no, sir.'

'I've got a car outside that needs a dusting. About five bucks worth of dusting.'

It didn't work. He wasn't the type. His chestnut eyes became thoughtful and remote. 'That is a good deal of dusting, sir. May I ask if anything else would be included?'

'A little. Is Miss Harriet Huntress's car in?'

He looked. I saw him look along the glistening row at a canary-yellow convertible which was about as inconspicuous as a privy on the front lawn.

'Yes, sir. It is in.'

'I'd like her apartment number and a way to get up there without going through the lobby. I'm a private detective.' I showed him a buzzer. He looked at the buzzer. It failed to amuse him.

He smiled the faintest smile I ever saw. 'Five dollars is nice money, sir, to a working man. It falls a little short of being nice enough to make me risk my position. About from here to Chicago short, sir. I suggest that you save your five dollars, sir, and try the customary mode of entry.'

'You're quite a guy,' I said. 'What are you going to be when you grow up – a five-foot shelf?'

'I am already grown up, sir. I am thirty-four years old, married happily, and have two children. Good-afternoon, sir.'

He turned on his heel. 'Well, good-bye,' I said. 'And pardon my whiskey breath. I just got in from Butte.'

I went back up along the ramp and wandered along the street to where I should have gone in the first place. I might have known that five bucks and a buzzer wouldn't buy me anything in a place like the El Milano.

The Negro was probably telephoning the office right now.

The building was a huge white stucco affair, Moorish in style, with great fretted lanterns in the forecourt and huge date palms. The entrance was at the inside corner of an L, up marble steps, through an arch framed in California or dishpan mosaic.

A doorman opened the door for me and I went in. The lobby was not quite as big as the Yankee Stadium. It was floored with a pale blue carpet with sponge rubber underneath. It was so soft it made me want to lie down and roll. I waded over to the desk and put an elbow on it and was stared at by a pale thin clerk with one of those moustaches that get stuck under your fingernail. He toyed with it and looked past my shoulder at an Ali Baba oil jar big enough to keep a tiger in.

'Miss Huntress in?'

'Who shall I announce?'

'Mr Marty Estel.'

That didn't take any better than my play in the garage. He leaned on something with his left foot. A blue-and-gilt door opened at the end of the desk and a large sandy-haired man with cigar ash on his vest came out and leaned absently on the end of the desk and stared at the Ali Baba oil jar, as if trying to make up his mind whether it was a spittoon.

The clerk raised his voice. 'You are Mr Marty Estel?'

'From him.'

'Isn't that a little different? And what is your name, sir, if one may ask?'

'One may ask,' I said. 'One may not be told. Such are my orders. Sorry to be stubborn and all that rot.'

He didn't like my manner. He didn't like anything about me. 'I'm afraid I can't announce you,' he said coldly. 'Mr Hawkins, might I have your advice on a matter?'

The sandy-haired man took his eyes off the oil jar and slid along the desk until he was within blackjack range of me.

'Yes, Mr Gregory?' he yawned.

'Nuts to both of you,' I said. 'And that includes your lady friends.'

Hawkins grinned. 'Come into my office, bo. We'll kind of see if we can get you straightened out.'

I followed him into the doghole he had come out of. It was large enough for a pint-sized desk, two chairs, a knee-high cuspidor, and an open box of cigars. He placed his rear end against the desk and grinned at me sociably.

'Didn't play it very smooth, did you, bo? I'm the house man here. Spill it.'

'Some days I feel like playing it smooth,' I said, 'and some days I feel like playing it like a waffle-iron.' I got my wallet out and showed him the buzzer and the small photostat of my licence behind a celluloid window.

'One of the boys, huh?' He nodded. 'You ought to of asked for me in the first place.'

'Sure. Only I never heard of you. I want to see this Huntress frail. She doesn't know me, but I have business with her, and it's not noisy business.'

He made a yard and a half sideways and cocked his cigar in the other corner of his mouth. He looked at my right eyebrow. 'What's the gag? Why try to apple-polish the dinge downstairs? You gettin' any expense money?'

'Could be.'

'I'm nice people,' he said. 'But I gotta protect the guests.'

'You're almost out of cigars,' I said, looking at the ninety or so in the box. I lifted a couple, smelled them, tucked a folded ten-dollar bill below them and put them back.

'That's cute,' he said. 'You and me could get along. What you want done?'

'Tell her I'm from Marty Estel. She'll see me.'

'It's the job if I get a kickback.'

'You won't. I've got important people behind me.'

'How far behind?'

I started to reach for my ten, but he pushed my hand away. 'I'll take a chance,' he said. He reached for his phone and asked for Suite 814 and began to hum. His humming sounded like a cow being sick. He leaned forward suddenly and his face became a honeyed smile. His voice dripped.

'Miss Huntress? This is Hawkins, the house man. Hawkins. Yea . . . Hawkins. Sure, you meet a lot of people, Miss Huntress. Say, there's a gentleman in my office wanting to see you with a message from Mr Estel. We can't let him up without you say so, because he don't want to give us no name . . . Yeah, Hawkins, the house detective, Miss Huntress. Yeah, he says you don't know him personal, but he looks O.K. to me . . . O.K. Thanks a lot, Miss Huntress. Serve him right up.'

He put the phone down and patted it gently.

'All you needed was some background music,' I said.

'You can ride up,' he said dreamily. He reached absently into his cigar box and removed the folded bill. 'A darb,' he said softly. 'Every time I think of that dame I have to go out and walk around the block. Let's go.'

We went out to the lobby again and Hawkins took me to the elevator and highsigned me in.

As the elevator doors closed I saw him on his way to the entrance, probably for his walk around the block.

The elevator had a carpeted floor and mirrors and indirect lighting. It rose as softly as the mercury in a thermometer. The doors whispered open, I wandered over the moss they used for a hall carpet and came to a door marked *814*. I pushed a little button beside it, chimes rang inside and the door opened.

She wore a street dress of pale green wool and a small cockeyed hat that hung on her ear like a butterfly. Her eyes were wide-set and there was thinking room between them. Their colour was lapislazuli blue and the colour of her hair was dusky red, like a fire under control but still dangerous. She was too tall to be cute. She wore plenty of make-up in the right places and the cigarette she was poking at me had a built-on mouthpiece about three inches long. She didn't look hard, but she looked as if she had heard all the answers and remembered the ones she thought she might be able to use some time.

She looked me over coolly. 'Well, what's the message, brown-eyes?'

'I'd have to come in,' I said. 'I never could talk on my feet.'

She laughed disinterestedly and I slid past the end of her cigarette into a long rather narrow room with plenty of nice furniture, plenty of windows, plenty of drapes, plenty of everything. A fire blazed behind a screen, a big log on top of a gas teaser. There was a silk Oriental rug in front of a nice rose davenport in front of the nice fire, and beside that there was Scotch and swish on a tabouret, ice in a bucket, everything to make a man feel at home.

'You'd better have a drink,' she said. 'You probably can't talk without a glass in your hand.'

I sat down and reached for the Scotch. The girl sat in a deep chair and crossed her knees. I thought of Hawkins walking around the block. I could see a little something in his point of view.

'So you're from Marty Estel,' she said, refusing a drink. 'Never met him.'

'I had an idea to that effect. What's the racket, bum? Marty will love to hear how you used his name.'

'I'm shaking in my shoes. What made you let me up?'

'Curiosity. I've been expecting lads like you any day. I never dodge trouble. Some kind of a dick, aren't you?'

I lit a cigarette and nodded. 'Private. I have a little deal to propose.'

'Propose it.' She yawned.

'How much will you take to lay off young Jeeter?'

She yawned again. 'You interest me – so little I could hardly tell you.'

'Don't scare me to death. Honest, how much are you asking? Or is that an insult?'

She smiled. She had a nice smile. She had lovely teeth. 'I'm a bad girl now,' she said. 'I don't have to ask. They bring it to me, tied up with ribbon.'

'The old man's a little tough. They say he draws a lot of water.'

'Water doesn't cost much.'

I nodded and drank some more of my drink. It was good Scotch. In fact it was perfect. 'His idea is you get nothing. You get smeared. You get put in the middle. I can't see it that way.'

'But you're working for him.'

'Sounds funny, doesn't it? There's probably a smart way to play this, but I just can't think of it at the moment. How much would you take – or would you?'

'How about fifty grand?'

'Fifty grand for you and another fifty for Marty?'

She laughed. 'Now, you ought to know Marty wouldn't like me to mix in his business. I was just thinking of my end.'

She crossed her legs the other way. I put another lump of ice in my drink.

'I was thinking of five hundred,' I said.

'Five hundred what?' She looked puzzled.

'Dollars – not Rolls-Royces.'

She laughed heartily. 'You amuse me. I ought to tell you to go to hell, but I like brown eyes. Warm brown eyes with flecks of gold in them.'

'You're throwing it away. I don't have a nickel.'

She smiled and fitted a fresh cigarette between her lips. I went over to light it for her. Her eyes came up and looked into mine. Hers had sparks in them.

'Maybe I have a nickel already,' she said softly.

'Maybe that's why he hired the fat boy – so you wouldn't make him dance.' I sat down again.

'Who hired what fat boy?'

'Old Jeeter hired a fat boy named Argobast. He was on the case before me. Didn't you know? He got bumped off this afternoon.'

I said it quite casually for the shock effect, but she didn't move. The provocative smile didn't leave the corners of her lips. Her eyes didn't change. She made a dim sound with her breath.

'Does it have to have something to do with me?' she asked quietly.

'I don't know. I don't know who murdered him. It was done in his office, around noon or a little later. It may not have anything to do with the Jeeter case. But it happened pretty pat – just after I had been put on the job and before I got a chance to talk to him.'

She nodded. 'I see. And you think Marty does things like that. And of course you told the police?'

'Of course I did not.'

'You're giving away a little weight there, brother.'

'Yeah. But let's get together on a price and it had better be low. Because whatever the cops do to me they'll do plenty to Marty Estel and you when they get the story – if they get it.'

'A little spot of blackmail,' the girl said coolly. 'I think I might call it that. Don't go too far with me, brown-eyes. By the way, do I know your name?'

'John Dalmas.'

'Then listen, John. I was in the Social Register once. My family were nice people. Old man Jeeter ruined my father – all proper and legitimate, the way that kind of heel ruins people – but he ruined him, and my father committed suicide, and my mother died and I've got a kid sister back East in school and perhaps I'm not too damn particular how I get the money to take care of her. And maybe I'm going to take care of old Jeeter one of these days, too – even if I have to marry his son to do it.'

'Stepson, adopted son,' I said. 'No relation at all.'

'It'll hurt him just as hard, brother. And the boy will have plenty of the long green in a couple of years. I could do worse – even if he does drink too much.'

'You wouldn't say that in front of him, lady.'

'No? Take a look behind you, gumshoe. You ought to have the wax taken out of your ears.'

I stood up and turned fast. He stood about four feet from

me. He had come out of some door and sneaked across the carpet and I had been too busy being clever with nothing on the ball to hear him. He was big, blond, dressed in a rough sporty suit, with a scarf and open-neck shirt. He was red-faced and his eyes glittered and they were not focusing any too well. He was a bit drunk for that early in the day.

'Beat it while you can still walk,' he sneered at me. 'I heard it. Harry can say anything she likes about me. I like it. Dangle, before I knock your teeth down your throat!'

The girl laughed behind me. I didn't like that. I took a step towards the big blond boy. His eyes blinked. Big as he was, he was a pushover.

'Ruin him, baby,' the girl said coldly behind my back. 'I love to see these hard numbers bend at the knees.'

I looked back at her with a leer. That was a mistake. He was wild, probably, but he could still hit a wall that didn't jump. He hit me while I was looking back over my shoulder. It hurts to be hit that way. He hit me plenty hard, on the back end of the jaw-bone .

I went over sideways, tried to spread my legs, and slid on the silk rug. I did a nose dive somewhere or other and my head was not as hard as the piece of furniture it smashed into.

For a brief blurred moment I saw his red face sneering down at me in triumph. I think I was a little sorry for him – even then.

Darkness folded down and I went out.

4

When I came to, the light from the windows across the room was hitting me square in the eyes. The back of my head ached. I felt it and it was sticky. I moved around slowly, like a cat in a strange house, got up on my knees and reached for the bottle of Scotch on the tabouret at the end of the davenport. By some miracle I hadn't knocked it over. Falling I had hit my head on the clawlike leg of a chair. That had hurt me a lot more than young Jeeter's haymaker. I could feel the sore place on my jaw all right, but it wasn't important enough to write in my diary.

I got up on my feet, took a swig of the Scotch and looked around. There wasn't anything to see. The room was empty. It was full of silence and the memory of a nice perfume. One of those perfumes you don't notice until they are almost gone, like the last leaf on a tree. I felt my head again, touched the sticky place with my handkerchief, decided it wasn't worth yelling about, and took another drink.

I sat down with the bottle on my knees, listening to traffic noises somewhere, far off. It was a nice room. Miss Harriet Huntress was a nice girl. She knew a few wrong numbers, but who didn't? I should criticize a little thing like that. I took another drink. The level in the bottle was a lot lower now. It was smooth and you hardly noticed it going down. It didn't take half your tonsils with it, like some of the stuff I had to drink. I took some more. My head felt all right now. I felt fine. I felt like singing the *Prologue to Pagliacci*. Yes, she was a nice girl. If she was paying her own rent, she was doing right well. I was for her. She was swell. I used some more of her Scotch.

The bottle was still half full. I shook it gently, stuffed it in my overcoat pocket, put on my hat somewhere on my head and left. I made the elevator without hitting the walls on either side of the corridor, floated downstairs, strolled out into the lobby.

Hawkins, the house dick, was leaning on the end of the desk again, staring at the Ali Baba oil jar. The same clerk was nuzzling at the same itsy-bitsy moustache. I smiled at him. He smiled back. Hawkins smiled at me. I smiled back. Everybody was swell.

I made the front door the first time and gave the doorman two bits and floated down the steps and along the walk to the street and my car. The swift California twilight was falling. It was a lovely night. Venus in the west was as bright as a street lamp, as bright as life, as bright as Miss Huntress's eyes, as bright as a bottle of Scotch. That reminded me. I got the square bottle out and tapped it with discretion, corked it, and tucked it away again. There was still enough to get home on.

I crashed five red lights on the way back but my luck was in and nobody pinched me. I parked more or less in front of my apartment house and more or less near the kerb. I rode up to my floor in the elevator, had a little trouble opening the doors and helped myself out with my bottle. I got the key into my door and unlocked it and stepped inside and found the light switch. I took a little more of my medicine before exhausting myself any further. Then I started for the kitchen to get some ice and ginger ale for a real drink.

I thought there was a funny smell in the apartment – nothing I could put a name to offhand – a sort of medicinal smell. I hadn't put it there and it hadn't been there when I went out. But I felt too well to argue about it. I started for the kitchen, got about half-way there.

They came out at me, almost side by side, from the dressing-room beside the wall bed – two of them – with guns. The tall one was grinning. He had his hat low on his forehead and he had a wedge-shaped face that ended in a point, like the bottom half of the ace of diamonds. He had dark moist eyes and a nose so bloodless that it might have been made of white wax. His gun was a Colt Woodsman with a long barrel and the front sight filed off. That meant he thought he was good.

The other was a little terrier-like punk with bristly reddish hair and no hat and watery blank eyes and bat ears and small feet in dirty white sneakers. He had an automatic that looked too heavy for him to hold up, but he seemed to like holding it. He breathed open-mouthed and noisily and the smell I had noticed came from him in waves – menthol.

'Reach, you — ,' he said.

I put my hands up. There was nothing else to do.

The little one circled around to the side and came at me from the side. 'Tell us we can't get away with it,' he sneered.

'You can't get away with it,' I said.

The tall one kept on grinning loosely and his nose kept on looking as if it was made of white wax. The little one spat on my carpet. 'Yah!' He came close to me, leering, and made a pass at my chin with the big gun.

I dodged. Ordinarily that would have been just something which, in the circumstances, I had to take and like. But I was feeling better than ordinary. I was a world-beater. I took them in sets, guns and all. I took the little man around the throat and jerked him hard against my stomach and put a hand over his little gun-hand and knocked the gun to the floor. It was easy. Nothing was bad about it but his breath. Blobs of saliva came out on his lips. He spat curses.

The tall man stood and leered and didn't shoot. He didn't move. His eyes looked a little anxious, I thought, but I was too busy to make sure. I went down behind the little punk, still holding him, and got hold of his gun. That was wrong. I ought to have pulled my own.

I threw him away from me and he reeled against a chair and fell down and began to kick the chair savagely. The tall man laughed.

'It ain't got any firing pin in it,' he said.

'Listen,' I told him earnestly, 'I'm half full of good Scotch and ready to go places and get things done. Don't waste much of my time. What do you boys want?'

'It still ain't got any firing pin in it,' Waxnose said. 'Try and see. I don't never let Frisky carry a loaded rod. He's too impulsive. You got a nice arm action there, pal. I will say that for you.'

Frisky sat up on the floor and spat on the carpet again and laughed. I pointed the muzzle of the big automatic at the floor and squeezed the trigger. It clicked dryly, but from the balance it felt as if it had cartridges in it.

'We don't mean no harm,' Waxnose said. 'Not this trip. Maybe next trip. Who knows? Maybe you're a guy that will take a hint. Lay off the Jeeter kid is the word. See?'

'No.'

'You won't do it?'

'No, I don't see. Who's the Jeeter kid?'

Waxnose was not amused. He waved his long .22 gently. 'You oughta get your memory fixed, pal, about the same time you get your door fixed. A pushover that was. Frisky just blew it in with his breath.'

'I can understand that,' I said.

'Gimme my gat,' Frisky yelped. He was up off the floor again, but this time he rushed his partner instead of me.

'Lay off, dummy,' the tall one said. 'We just got a message for a guy. We don't blast him. Not to-day.'

'Says you!' Frisky snarled and tried to grab the .22 out of Waxnose's hand. Waxnose threw him to one side without trouble but the interlude allowed me to switch the big automatic to my left hand and jerk out my Lüger. I showed it to Waxnose. He nodded, but did not seem impressed.

'He ain't got no parents,' he said sadly. 'I just let him run around with me. Don't pay him no attention unless he bites you. We'll be on our way now. You get the idea. Lay off the Jeeter kid.'

'You're looking at a Lüger,' I said. 'Who is the Jeeter kid? And maybe we'll have some cops before you leave.'

He smiled wearily. 'Mister, I pack this small-bore because I can shoot. If you think you can take me, go to it.'

'O.K.,' I said, 'Do you know anybody named Arbogast?'

'I meet such a lot of people,' he said, with another weary smile. 'Maybe yes, maybe no. So long, pal. Be pure.'

He strolled over to the door, moving a little sideways, so that he had me covered all the time, and I had him covered, and it was just a case of who shot first and straightest, or whether it was worthwhile to shoot at all, or whether I could hit anything with so much nice warm Scotch in me. I let him go. He didn't look like a killer to me, but I could have been wrong.

The little man rushed me again while I wasn't thinking about him. He clawed his big automatic out of my left hand, skipped over to the door, spat on the carpet again, and slipped out. Waxnose backed after him – long sharp face, white nose, pointed chin, weary expression. I wouldn't forget him.

He closed the door softly and I stood there, foolish, holding my gun. I heard the elevator come up and go down again and stop. I still stood there. Marty Estel wouldn't be very likely to hire a couple of comics like that to throw a scare into anybody. I thought about that, but thinking got me nowhere. I remembered the half-bottle of Scotch I had left and went into executive session with it.

An hour and a half later I felt fine, but I still didn't have any ideas. I just felt sleepy.

The jarring of the telephone bell woke me. I had dozed off in the chair, which was a bad mistake, because I woke up with two flannel blankets in my mouth, a splitting headache, a bruise on the back of my head and another on my jaw, neither of them larger than a Yakima apple, but sore for all that. I felt terrible. I felt like an amputated leg.

I crawled over to the telephone and humped myself in a chair beside it and answered it. The voice dripped icicles.

'Mr Dalmas? This is Mr Jeeter. I believe we met this morning. I'm afraid I was a little stiff with you.'

'I'm a little stiff myself. Your son poked me in the jaw. I mean your stepson, or your adopted son – or whatever he is.'

'He is both my stepson and my adopted son. Indeed?' He sounded interested. 'And where did you meet him?'

'In Miss Huntress's apartment.'

'Oh I see.' There had been a sudden thaw. The icicles had

melted. 'Very interesting. What did Miss Huntress have to say?'

'She liked it. She liked him poking me in the jaw.'

'I see. And why did he do that?'

'She had him hid out. He overheard some of our talk. He didn't like it.'

'I see. I have been thinking that perhaps some consideration – not large, of course – should be granted to her for her co-operation. That is, if we can secure it.'

'Fifty grand is the price.'

'I'm afraid I don't – '

'Don't kid me,' I snarled. 'Fifty thousand dollars. Fifty grand. I offered her five hundred – just for a gag.'

'You seem to treat this whole business in a spirit of considerable levity,' he snarled back. 'I am not accustomed to that sort of thing and I don't like it.'

I yawned. I didn't give a damn if school kept or not. 'Listen, Mr Jeeter, I'm a great guy to horse around, but I have my mind on the jog just the same. And there are some very unusual angles to this case. For instance a couple of gunmen just stuck me up in my apartment here and told me to lay off the Jeeter case. I don't see why it should get so tough.'

'Good heavens!' He sounded shocked. 'I think you had better come out to my house at once and we will discuss matters. I'll send my car for you. Can you come right away?'

'Yeah. But I can drive myself. I – '

'No. I'm sending my car and chauffeur. His name is George; you may rely upon him absolutely. He should be there in about twenty minutes.'

'O.K.,' I said. 'That just gives me time to drink my dinner. Have him park around the corner on Kenmore, facing towards Franklin.' I hung up.

When I'd had a hot-and-cold shower and put on some clean clothes I felt more respectable. I had a couple of drinks, small ones for a change, and put a light overcoat on and went down to the street.

The car was there already. I could see it half a block down the side street. It looked like a new market opening. It had a couple of headlamps like the one on the front end of a streamliner, two amber fog-lights hooked to the front fender, and a couple of sidelights as big as ordinary headlights. I came up beside it and stopped and a man stepped out of the shadows, tossing a cigarette over his shoulder with a neat flip of the wrist. He was tall, broad, dark, wore a peaked cap, a Russian tunic with a Sam Browne belt, shiny leggings, and breeches that flared like an English staff major's whip-cords.

'Mr Dalmas?' He touched the peak of his cap with a gloved forefinger.

'Yeah,' I said. 'At ease. Don't tell me that's old man Jeeter's car.'

'One of them.' It was a cool voice that could get fresh.

He opened the rear door and I got in and sank down into the cushions and George slid under the wheel and started the big car. It moved away from the kerb and around the corner with as much noise as a bill makes in a wallet. We went west. We seemed to be drifting with the current, but we passed everything. We slid through the heart of Holly-wood, the west end of it, down to the Strip and along the glitter of that to the cool quiet of Beverly Hills where the bridle path divides the boulevard.

We gave Beverly Hills the swift and climbed along the foothills, saw the distant lights of the university buildings and swung north into Bel-Air. We began to slide up long narrow streets with high walls and no side-walks and big gates. Lights on mansions glowed politely through the early night. Nothing stirred. There was no sound but the soft purr of the tyres on concrete. We swung left again and I caught a sign which read Calvello Drive. Half-way up this George started to swing the car wide to make a left turn in at a pair of twelve-foot wrought-iron gates. Then something happened.

A pair of lights flared suddenly just beyond the gates and a horn screeched and a motor raced. A car charged at us fast. George straightened out with a flick of the wrist, braked the car and slipped off his right glove, all in one motion.

The car came on, the lights swaying. 'Damn drunk,' George swore over his shoulder.

It could be. Drunks in cars go all kinds of places to drink. It could be. I slid down onto the floor of the car and yanked the Lüger from under my arm and reached up to open the catch. I opened the door a little and held it that way, looking out over the sill. The headlights hit me in the face and I ducked, then came up again as the beam passed.

The other car jammed to a stop. Its door slammed open and a figure jumped out of it, waving a gun and shouting. I heard the voice and knew.

'Reach, you — ! 'Frisky screamed at us.

George put his left hand on the wheel and I opened my door a little more. The little man in the street was bouncing up and down and yelling. Out of the small dark car from which he had jumped came no sound except the noise of its motor.

'This is a heist!' Frisky yelled. 'Out of there and line up, you — — — !'

I kicked my door open and started to get out, the Lüger down at my side.

'You asked for it!' the little man yelled.

I dropped – fast! The gun in his hand belched flame. Somebody must have put a firing pin in it. Glass smashed behind my head. Out of the corner of my eye, which oughtn't to have had any corners at that particular moment, I saw George make a movement as smooth as a ripple of water. I brought the Lüger up and started to squeeze the trigger, but a shot crashed beside me – George.

I held my fire. It wasn't needed now.

The dark car lurched forward and started down the hill furiously. It roared into the distance while the little man out in the middle of the pavement was still reeling grotesquely in the light reflected from the walls.

There was something dark on his face that spread. His gun bounded along the concrete. His little legs buckled and he plunged sideways and rolled and then, very suddenly, became still.

George said, 'Yah!' and sniffed at the muzzle of his revolver.

'Nice shooting.' I got out of the car, stood there looking at the little man – a crumpled nothing. The dirty white of his sneakers gleamed a little in the side glare of the car's lights.

George got out beside me. 'Why me, brother?'

'I didn't fire. I was watching that pretty hip draw of yours. It was sweeter than honey.'

'Thanks, pal. They were after Mister Gerald, of course, I usually ferry him home from the club about this time, full of liquor and bridge losses.'

We went over to the little man and looked down at him. He wasn't anything to see. He was just a little man who was dead, with a big slug in his face and blood on him.

'Turn some of those damn lights off,' I growled. 'And let's get away from here fast.'

'The house is just across the street,' George sounded as casual as if he had just shot a nickel in a slot machine instead of a man.

'The Jeeters are out of this, if you like your job. You ought to know that. We'll go back to my place and start all over.'

'I get it,' he snapped, and jumped back into the big car. He cut the foglights and the sidelights and I got in beside him in the front seat.

We straightened out and started up the hill, over the brow. I looked back at the broken window. It was the small one at the extreme back of the car and it wasn't shatterproof. A large piece was gone from it. They could fit that, if they got around to it, and make some evidence. I didn't think it would matter, but it might.

At the crest of the hill a large limousine passed us going down. Its dome light was on and in the interior, as in a lighted showcase, an elderly couple sat stiffly, taking the royal salute. The man was in evening clothes, with a white scarf and a crush hat. The women was in furs and diamonds.

George passed them casually, gunned the car and we made a fast right turn into a dark street. 'There's a couple of good dinners all shot to hell,' he drawled. 'And I bet they don't even report it.'

'Yeah. Let's get back home and have a drink,' I said. 'I never really got to like killing people.'

5

We sat with some of Miss Harriet Huntress's Scotch in our glasses and looked at each other across the rims. George looked nice with his cap off. His head was clustered over with wavy dark-brown hair and his teeth were very white and clean. He sipped his drink and nibbled a cigarette at the same time. His snappy black eyes had a cool glitter in them.

'Yale?' I asked.

'Dartmouth, if it's any of your business.'

'Everything's my business. What's a college education worth these days?'

'Three squares and a uniform,' he drawled.

'What kind of guy is young Jeeter?'

'Big blond bruiser, plays a fair game of golf, think's he's hell with the women, drinks heavy but hasn't sicked up on the rugs so far.'

'What kind of guy is old Jeeter?'

'He'd probably give you a dime – if he didn't have a nickel with him.'

'*Tsk, tsk*, you're talking about your boss.'

George grinned. 'He's so tight his head squeaks when he takes his hat off. I always took chances. Maybe that's why I'm just somebody's driver. This is good Scotch.'

I made another drink, which finished the bottle. I sat down again.

'You think those two gunnies were stashed out for Mister Gerald?'

'Why not? I usually drive him home about that time. Didn't to-day. He had a bad hangover and didn't go out until late. You're a dick, you know what it's all about, don't you?'

'Who told you I was a dick?'

'Nobody but a dick ever asked so goddam many questions.'

I shook my head. 'Uh-uh. I've asked you just six questions. Your boss has a lot of confidence in you. He must have told you.'

The dark man nodded, grinned faintly and sipped. 'The whole set-up is pretty obvious,' he said. 'When the car started to swing for the turn into the driveway these boys went to work. I don't figure they meant to kill anybody, somehow. It was just a scare. Only that little guy was nuts.'

I looked at George's eyebrows. They were nice black eyebrows, with a gloss on them like horsehair.

I said: 'It doesn't sound like Marty Estel to pick that sort of helpers.'

'Sure. Maybe that's why he picked that sort of helpers.'

'You're smart. You and I can get along. But shooting that little punk makes it tougher. What will you do about that?'

'Nothing.'

'O.K. If they get to you and tie it to your gun, if you still have the gun, which you probably won't, I suppose it will be passed off as an attempted stick-up. There's just one thing.'

'What?' George finished his second drink, laid the glass aside, lit a fresh cigarette and smiled.

'It's pretty hard to tell a car from in front – at night. Even with all those lights. It might have been a visitor.'

He shrugged and nodded. 'But if it's a scare, that would do just as well. Because the family would hear about it and the old man would guess whose boys they were – and why.'

'Hell, you really are smart.' I said admiringly, and the phone rang.

It was an English-butler voice, very clipped and precise, and it said that if I was Mr John Dalmas, Mr Jeeter would like to speak to me. He came on at once, with plenty of frost.

'I must say that you take your time about obeying orders,' he barked. 'Or hasn't that chauffeur of mine – '

'Yeah, he got here, Mr Jeeter,' I said. 'But we ran into a little trouble. George will tell you.'

'Young man, when I want something done – '

'Listen, Mr Jeeter, I've had a hard day. Your son punched me on the jaw and I fell and cut my head open. When I staggered back to my apartment, more dead than alive, I was stuck up by a couple of hard guys with guns who told me to lay off the Jeeter case. I'm doing my best but I'm feeling a little frail, so don't scare me.'

'Young man – '

'Listen,' I told him earnestly, 'if you want to call all the plays in this game, you can carry the ball yourself. Or you can save yourself a lot of money and hire an order-taker. I have to do things my way. Any cops visit you tonight?'

'Cops?' he echoed in a sour voice. 'You mean policemen?'

'By all means – I mean policemen.'

'And why should I see any policemen?' he almost snarled.

'There was a stiff in front of your gates half an hour ago. Stiff meaning dead man. He's quite small. You could sweep him up in a dustpan, if he bothers you.'

'My God! Are you serious?'

'Yes. What's more he took a shot at George and me. He recognized the car. He must have been all set for your son, Mr Jeeter.'

A silence with barbs on it. 'I thought you said a dead man,' Mr Jeeter's voice said very coldly. 'Now you say he shot at you.'

'That was while he wasn't dead,' I said. 'George will tell you. George –'

'You come out here at once!' he yelled at me over the phone. 'At once, do you hear? At once!'

'George will tell you,' I said softly and hung up – in his face.

George looked at me coldly. He stood up and put his cap on. 'O.K., pal,' he said. 'Maybe some day I can put you on to a soft thing.' He started for the door.

'It had to be that way. It's up to him. He'll have to decide.'

'Nuts,' George said, looking back over his shoulder. 'Save your breath, shamus. Anything you say to me is just so much noise in the wrong place.'

He opened the door, went out, shut it, and I sat there still holding the telephone, with my mouth open and nothing in it but my tongue and a bad taste on that.

I went out to the kitchen and shook the Scotch bottle, but it was empty. I opened some rye and swallowed a drink and it tasted sour. Something was bothering me. I had a feeling it was going to bother me a lot more before I was through.

They must have missed George by a whisker. I heard the elevator come up again almost as soon as it had stopped going down. Solid steps grew louder along the hallway. A fist hit the door. I went over and opened it.

One was in brown, one in blue, both large, hefty, and bored.

The one in brown pushed his hat back on his head with a freckled hand and said: 'You John Dalmas?'

'Me,' I said.

They rode me back into the room without seeming to. The one in blue shut the door. The one in brown palmed a shield and let me catch a glint of the gold and enamel.

'Finlayson, Detective-Lieutenant, working out of Central Homicide,' he said. 'This is Sebold, my partner. We're a couple of swell guys not to get funny with. We hear you're kind of sharp with a gun.'

Sebold took his hat off and dusted his salt-and-pepper hair back with the flat of his hand. He drifted noiselessly out to the kitchen.

Finlayson sat down on the edge of a chair and flicked his chin with a thumbnail as square as an ice cube and yellow as a mustard plaster. He was older than Sebold, but not so good-looking. He had the frowsy expression of a veteran cop who hadn't got very far.

I sat down. I said: 'How do you mean, sharp with a gun?'

'Shooting people is how I mean.'

I lit a cigarette. Sebold came out of the kitchen and went into the dressing-room behind the wall-bed.

'We understand you're a private-licence guy,' Finlayson said heavily.

'That's right.'

'Give.' He held his hand out. I gave him my wallet. He chewed it over and handed it back. 'Carry a gun?'

I nodded. He held out his hand for it. Sebold came out of the dressing-room. Finlayson sniffed at the Lüger, snapped the magazine out, cleared the breech and held the gun so that a little light shone up through the magazine opening into the breech end of the barrel. He looked down the muzzle, squinting. He handed the gun to Sebold. Sebold did the same thing.

'Don't think so,' Sebold said. 'Clean, but not that clean. Couldn't have been cleaned within the hour. A little dust.'

'Right.'

Finlayson picked the ejected shell off the carpet, pressed

it into the magazine and snapped the magazine back in place. He handed me the gun. I put it back under my arm.

'Been out anywhere to-night?' he asked tersely.

'Don't tell me the plot,' I said. 'I'm just a bit-player.'

'Smart guy,' Sebold said dispassionately. He dusted his hair again and opened a desk drawer. 'Funny stuff. Good for a column. I like 'em that way – with my blackjack.'

Finlayson sighed. 'Been out to-night, shamus?'

'Sure. In and out all the time. Why?'

He ignored the question. 'Where you been?'

'Out to dinner. Business call or two.'

'Where at?'

'I'm sorry, boys. Every business has its private files.'

'Had company, too,' Sebold said, picking up George's glass and sniffing it. 'Recent – within the hour.'

'You're not that good,' I told him sourly.

'Had a ride in a big Caddy?' Finlayson bored on, taking a deep breath. 'Over West L.A. direction?'

'Had a ride in a Chrysler – over Vine Street direction.'

'Maybe we better just take him down,' Sebold said, looking at his finger-nails.

'Maybe you better skip the gang-buster stuff and tell me what's stuck in your nose. I get long with cops – except when they act as if the law is only for citizens.'

Finlayson studied me. Nothing I had said made an impression on him. Nothing Sebold said made any impression on him. He had an idea and he was holding it like a sick baby.

'You know a little rat named Frisky Lavon?' he sighed. 'Used to be a dummy-chucker, then found out he could bug his way outa raps. Been doing that for say twelve years. Totes a gun and acts simple. But he quit acting to-night at seven-thirty about. Quit cold – with a slug in his head.'

'Never heard of him,' I said.

'You bumped anybody off to-night?'

'I'd have to look at my notebook.'

Sebold leaned forward politely. 'Would you care for a smack in the kisser?' he inquired.

Finlayson held his hand out sharply. 'Cut it, Ben. Cut it. Listen, Dalmas. Maybe we're going at this wrong. We're not talking about murder. Could have been legitimate. This Frisky Lavon got froze off to-night on Calvello Drive in Bel-Air. Out in the middle of the street. Nobody seen or heard anything. So we kind of want to know.'

'All right,' I growled. 'What makes it my business? and keep that piano tuner out of my hair. He has a nice suit and his nails are clean, but he bears down on his shield too hard.'

'Nuts to you,' Sebold said.

'We got a funny phone call,' Finlayson said. 'Which is where you come in. We ain't just throwing our weight around. And we want a forty-five. They ain't sure what kind yet.'

'He's smart. He threw it under the bar at Levy's,' Sebold sneered.

'I never had a forty-five,' I said, 'A guy who needs that much gun ought to use a pick.'

Finlayson scowled at me and counted his thumbs. Then he took a deep breath and suddenly went human on me. 'Sure, I'm just a dumb flatheel,' he said. 'Anybody could pull my ears off and I wouldn't even notice it. Let's all quit horsing around and talk sense.

'This Frisky was found dead after a no-name phone call to West L.A. police. Found dead outside a big house belonging to a man named Jeeter who owns a string of investment companies. He wouldn't use a guy like Frisky for a pen-wiper, so there's nothing in that. The servants there didn't hear nothing, nor the servants at any of the four houses on the block. Frisky is lying in the street and somebody run over his foot, but what killed him was a forty-five slug smack in his face.

'West L.A. ain't hardly started the routine when some guy calls up Central and says to tell Homicide if they want to know who got Frisky Lavon, ask a private eye named John Dalmas, complete with address and everything, then a quick hang-up.

'O.K. The guy on the board gives me the dope and I don't know Frisky from a hole in my sock, but I ask Identification and sure enough they have him and just about the time I'm looking it over, the flash comes from West L.A. and the description seems to check pretty close. So we get together and it's the same guy all right and the chief of detectives has us drop around here. So we drop around.'

'So here you are,' I said. 'Will you have a drink?'

'Can we search the joint, if we do?'

'Sure. It's good lead – that phone call, I mean – if you put in about six months on it.'

'We already got that idea,' Finlayson growled. 'A hundred guys could have chilled this little wart, and two-three of them maybe could have thought it was a smart rib to pin it on you. Them two-three is what interests us.'

I shook my head.

'No ideas at all, huh?'

'Just for wisecracks,' Sebold said.

Finlayson lumbered to his feet. 'Well, we gotta look around.'

'Maybe we had ought to have brought a search warrant,' Sebold said, tickling his upper lip with the end of his tongue.

'I don't *have* to fight this guy, do I?' I asked Finlayson. 'I mean, is it all right if I leave him his gag lines and just keep my temper?'

Finlayson looked at the ceiling and said drily: 'His wife left him day before yesterday. He's just trying to compensate, as the fellow says.'

Sebold turned white and twisted his knuckles savagely. Then he laughed shortly and got to his feet.

They went at it. Ten minutes of opening and shutting drawers and looking at the backs of shelves and under seat cushions and letting the bed down and peering into the electric refrigerator and the garbage pail fed them up.

They came back and sat down again. 'Just a nut,' Finlayson said. 'Some guy that picked your name outa the directory maybe. Could be anything.'

'Now I'll get that drink.'

'I don't drink,' Sebold snarled.

Finlayson crossed his hands on his stomach. 'That don't mean any liquor gets poured in the flower pot, son.'

I got three drinks and put two of them beside Finlayson. He drank half of one of them and looked at the ceiling, 'I got another killing, too,' he said thoughtfully. 'A guy in your racket, Dalmas. A fat guy on Sunset. Name of Arbogast. Ever hear of him?'

'I thought he was a handwriting expert,' I said.

'You're talking about police business,' Sebold told his partner coldly.

'Sure. Police business that's already in the morning paper. This Arbogast was shot three times with a twenty-two. Target gun. You know any crooks that pack that kind of heat?'

I held my glass tightly and took a long slow swallow. I hadn't thought Waxnose looked dangerous enough, but you never knew.

'I did,' I said slowly. 'A killer named Al Tessilore. But he's in Folsom. He used a Colt Woodsman.'

Finlayson finished the first drink, sued the second in about the same time, and stood up. Sebold stood up, still mad.

Finlayson opened the door. 'Come on, Ben.' They went out.

I heard their steps along the hall, the clang of the elevator once more. A car started just below in the street and growled off into the night.

'Clowns like that don't kill,' I said out loud. But it looked as if they did.

I waited fifteen minutes before I went out again. The phone rang while I was waiting, but I didn't answer it.

I drove towards the El Milano and circled around enough to make sure I wasn't followed.

6

The lobby hadn't changed any. The blue carpet still tickled my ankles when I ambled over to the desk, the same pale clerk was handing a key to a couple of horse-faced females in tweeds, and when he saw me he put his weight on his left foot again and the door at the end of the desk popped open and out popped the fat and erotic Hawkins, with what looked like the same cigar stub in his face.

He hustled over and gave me a big warm smile this time, took hold of my arm. 'Just the guy I was hoping to see,' he chuckled. 'Let us go upstairs a minute.'

'What's the matter?'

'Matter?' His smile became broad as the door to a two-car garage. 'Nothing ain't the matter. This way.'

He pushed me into the elevator and said 'Eight' in a fat cheerful voice and up we sailed and out we got and slid along the corridor. Hawkins had a hard hand and knew where to hold an arm. I was interested enough to let him get away with it. He pushed the buzzer beside Miss Huntress's door and Big Ben chimed inside and the door opened and I was looking at a deadpan in a derby hat and a dinner coat. He had his right hand in the side pocket of the coat, and under the derby a pair of scarred eyebrows and under the eyebrows a pair of eyes that had as much expression as the cap on a gas tank.

The mouth moved enough to say: 'Yeah?'

'Company for the boss,' Hawkins said expansively.

'What company?'

'Let me play too,' I said. 'Limited liability company. Gimme the apple.'

'Huh?' The eyebrows went this way and that and the jaw came out. 'Nobody ain't kiddin' nobody, I hope.'

'Now, now, gents – ' Hawkins began.

A voice behind the derby-hatted man interrupted him. 'What's the matter, Beef?'

'He's in a stew,' I said.

'Listen, mug –'

'Now, now, gents –' as before.

'Ain't nothing the matter,' Beef said, throwing his voice over his shoulder as if it were a coil of rope. 'The hotel dick got a guy up here and he says he's company.'

'Show the company in, Beef.' I liked this voice. It was smooth, quiet, and you could have cut your name in it with a thirty-pound sledge and a cold chisel.

'Lift the dogs,' Beef said, and stood to one side.

We went in. I went first, then Hawkins, then Beef wheeled neatly behind us like a door. We went in so close together that we must have looked like a three-decker sandwich.

Miss Huntress was not in the room. The log in the fireplace had almost stopped smouldering. There was still that smell of sandalwood on the air. With it cigarette smoke blended.

A man stood at the end of the davenport, both hands in the pockets of a blue camel's hair coat with the collar high to a black snapbrim hat. A loose scarf hung outside his coat. He stood motionless, the cigarette in his mouth lisping smoke. He was tall, black-haired, suave, dangerous. He said nothing.

Hawkins ambled over to him. 'This is the guy I was telling you about, Mr Estel,' the fat man burbled. 'Come in earlier to-day and said he was from you. Kinda fooled me.'

'Give him a ten, Beef.'

The derby hat took its left hand from somewhere and there was a bill in it. It pushed the bill at Hawkins. Hawkins took the bill, blushing.

'This ain't necessary, Mr Estel. Thanks a lot just the same.'

'Scram.'

'Huh?' Hawkins looked shocked.

'You heard him,' Beef said truculently. 'Want your fanny out the door first, huh?'

Hawkins drew himself up. 'I gotta protect the tenants. You gentlemen know how it is. A man in a job like this.'

'Yeah. Scram,' Estel said without moving his lips.

Hawkins turned and went out quickly, softly. The door clicked gently shut behind him. Beef looked back at it, then moved behind me.

'See if he's rodded, Beef.'

The derby hat saw if I was rodded. He took the Lüger and went away from me. Estel looked casually at the Lüger, back at me. His eyes held an expression of indifferent dislike.

'Name's John Dalmas, eh? A private dick.'

'So what?' I said.

'Somebody is goin' to get somebody's face pushed into somebody's floor,' Beef said coldly.

'Aw, keep that crap for the boiler-room,' I told him. 'I'm sick of hard guys for this evening. I said "so what," and "so what" is what I said.'

Marty Estel looked mildly amused. 'Hell, keep your skirt in. I've got to look after my friends, don't I? You know who I am. O.K., I know what you talked to Miss Huntress about. And I know something about you that you don't know I know.'

'All right,' I said. 'This fat slob Hawkins collected ten from me for letting me up here this afternoon – knowing perfectly well who I was – and he has just collected ten from your iron man for slipping me the nasty. Give me back my gun and tell me what makes my business your business.'

'Plenty. First off, Harriet's not home. We're waiting for her on account of a thing that happened. I can't wait any longer. Got to go to work at the club. So what did you come after this time?'

'Looking for the Jeeter boy. Somebody shot at his car to-night. From now on he needs somebody to walk behind him.'

'You think I play games like that?' Estel asked me coldly.

I walked over to a cabinet and opened it and found a bottle of Scotch. I twisted the cap off, lifted a glass from the tabouret and poured some out. I tasted it. It tasted all right.

I looked around for ice, but there wasn't any. It had all melted long since in the bucket.

'I asked you a question,' Estel said gravely.

'I heard it. I'm making my mind up. The answer is, I wouldn't have thought it – no. But it happened. I was there. I was in the car – instead of young Jeeter. His father had sent for me to come to the house to talk things over.'

'What things?'

I didn't bother to look surprised. 'You hold fifty grand of the boy's paper. That looks bad for you, if anything happens to him.'

'I don't figure it that way. Because the way I would lose my dough. The old man won't pay – granted. But I wait a couple of years and I collect from the kid. He gets his estate out of trust when he's twenty-eight. Right now he gets a grand a month and he can't even will anything, because it's still in trust. Savvy?'

'So you wouldn't knock him off,' I said, using my Scotch. 'But you might throw a scare into him.'

Estel frowned. He discarded his cigarette into a tray and watched it smoke a moment before he picked it up again and snubbed it out. He shook his head.

'If you're going to bodyguard him, it would almost pay me to stand part of your salary, wouldn't it? Almost. A man in my racket can't take care of everything. He's of age and it's his business who he runs around with. For instance, women. Any reason why a nice girl shouldn't cut herself a piece of five million bucks?'

I said: 'I think it's a swell idea. What was it you knew about me that I didn't know you knew?'

He smiled, faintly.

'What was it you were waiting to tell Miss Huntress – the thing that happened?'

He smiled faintly again. 'Listen, Dalmas, there are lots of ways to play any game. I play mine on the house percentage, because that's all I need to win. What makes me get tough?'

I rolled a fresh cigarette around in my fingers and tried to roll it around my glass with two fingers. 'Who said you were tough? I always heard the nicest things about you.'

Marty Estel nodded and looked faintly amused. 'I have sources of information,' he said quietly. 'When I have fifty grand invested in a guy, I'm apt to find out a little about him. Jeeter hired a man named Arbogast to do a little work. Arbogast was killed in his office to-day – with a twenty-two. That could have nothing to do with Jeeter's business. But there was a tail on you when you went there and you didn't give it to the law. Does that make you and me friends?'

I licked the edge of my glass, nodded. 'It seems it does.'

'From now on just forget about bothering Harriet, see?'

'O.K.'

'So we understand each other real good, now.'

'Yeah.'

'Well, I'll be going. Give the guy back his Lüger, Beef.'

The derby hat came over and smacked my gun into my hand hard enough to break a bone.

'Staying?' Estel asked, moving towards the door.

'I guess I'll wait a little while. Until Hawkins comes up to touch me for another ten.'

Estel grinned. Beef walked in front of him wooden-faced to the door and opened it. Estel went out. The door closed. The room was silent. I sniffed at the dying perfume of sandalwood and stood motionless, looking around.

Somebody was nuts. I was nuts. Everybody was nuts. None of it fitted together worth a nickel. Marty Estel, as he said, had no good motive for murdering anybody, because that would be the surest way to kill his chances to collect his money. Even if he had a motive for murdering anybody, Waxnose and Frisky didn't seem like the team he would select for the job. I was in bad with the police, I had spent ten dollars of my twenty expense money, and I didn't have enough leverage anywhere to lift a dime off a cigar counter.

I finished my drink, put the glass down, walked up and down the room, smoked a third cigarette, looked at my watch, shrugged and felt disgusted. The inner doors of the suite were closed. I went across to the one out of which young Jeeter must have sneaked that afternoon. Opening it I looked into a bedroom done in ivory and ashes of roses. There was a big double bed with no footboard, covered with figured brocade. Toilet articles glistened on a built-in dressing table with a panel-light. The light was lit. A small lamp on a table beside the door was lit also. A door near the dressing table showed the cool green of bathroom tiles.

I went over and looked in there. Chromium, a glass stall shower, monogrammed towels on a rack, a glass shelf for perfume and bath salts at the foot of the tub, everything nice and refined. Miss Huntress did herself well. I hoped she was paying her own rent. It didn't make any difference to me – I just liked it that way.

I went back towards the living room, stopped in the doorway to take another pleasant look around, and noticed something I ought to have noticed the instant I stepped into the room. I noticed the sharp tang of cordite on the air, almost, but not quite gone. And then I noticed something else.

The bed had been moved over until its head overlapped the edge of a closet door which was not quite closed. The weight of the bed was holding it from opening. I went over there to find out why it wanted to open. I went slowly and about half-way there I noticed that I was holding a gun in my hand.

I leaned against the closet door. It didn't move. I threw more weight against it. It still didn't move. Braced against it I pushed the bed away with my foot, gave ground slowly.

A weight pushed against me hard. I had gone back a foot

or so before anything else happened. Then it happened suddenly. He came out – sideways, in a sort of roll. I put some more weight back on the door and held him like that a moment, looking at him.

He was still big, still blond, still dressed in rough sporty material, with scarf and open-necked shirt. But his face wasn't red any more.

I gave ground again and he rolled down the back of the door, turning a little like a swimmer in the surf, thumped the floor and lay there, almost on his back, still looking at me. Light from the bedside lamp glittered on his head. There was a scorched and soggy stain on the rough coat – about where his heart would be. So he wouldn't get that five million after all. And nobody would get anything and Marty Estel wouldn't get his fifty grand. Because young Mister Gerald was dead.

I looked back into the closet where he had been. Its door hung wide open now. There were clothes on racks, feminine clothes, nice clothes. He had been backed in among them, probably with his hands in the air and a gun against his chest. And then he had been shot dead, and whoever did it hadn't been quite quick enough or quite strong enough to get the door shut. Or had been scared and had just yanked the bed over against the door and left it that way.

Something glittered down on the floor. I picked it up. A small automatic, .25 calibre, a woman's purse gun with a beautifully engraved butt inlaid with silver and ivory. I put the gun in my pocket. That seemed a funny thing to do, too.

I didn't touch him. He was as dead as John D. Arbogast and looked a whole lot deader. I left the door open and listened, walked quickly back across the room and into the living-room and shut the bedroom door, smearing the knob as I did it.

A lock was being tinkled at with a key. Hawkins was back again, to see what delayed me. He was letting himself in with his pass-key.

I was pouring a drink when he came in.

He came well into the room, stopped with his feet planted and surveyed me coldly.

'I seen Estel and his boy leave,' he said. 'I didn't see you leave. So I come up. I gotta –'

'You gotta protect the guests,' I said.

'Yeah. I gotta protect the guests. You can't stay up here, pal. Not without the lady of the house is home.'

'But Marty Estel and his hard boy can.'

He came a little closer to me. He had a mean look in his eye. He had always had it, probably, but I noticed it more now.

'You don't want to make nothing of that, do you?' he asked me.

'No. Every man to his own chisel. Have a drink.'

'That ain't your liquor.'

'Miss Huntress gave me a bottle. We're pals. Marty Estel and I are pals. Everybody is pals. Don't you want to be pals?'

'You ain't trying to kid me, are you?'

'Have a drink and forget it.'

I found a glass and poured him one. He took it.

'It's the job if anybody smells it on me,' he said.

'Uh-huh.'

He drank slowly, rolling it around on his tongue. 'Good Scotch.'

'Won't be the first time you tasted it, will it?'

He started to get hard again, then relaxed. 'Hell, I guess you're just a kidder.' He finished the drink, put the glass down, patted his lips with a large and very crumpled handkerchief and sighed.

'O.K.,' he said. 'But we'll have to leave now.'

'All set. I guess she won't be home for a while. You see them go out?'

'Her and the boy friend. Yeah, long time ago.'

I nodded. We went towards the door and Hawkins saw

me out. He saw me downstairs and off the premises. But he didn't see what was in Miss Huntress's bedroom. I wondered if he would go back up. If he did, the Scotch bottle would probably stop him.

I got into my car and drove off home – to talk to Anna Halsey on the phone. There wasn't any case any more – for us.

7

I parked close to the kerb this time. I wasn't feeling gay any more. I rode up in the elevator and unlocked my door and clicked the light on.

Waxnose sat in my best chair, an unlit hand-rolled brown cigarette between his fingers, his bony knees crossed, and his long Woodsman resting solidly on his leg. He was smiling. It wasn't the nicest smile I ever saw.

'Hi, pal,' he drawled. 'You still ain't had that door fixed. Kind of shut it, huh?' His voice, for all the drawl, was deadly.

I shut the door, stood looking across the room at him.

'So you killed my pal,' he said.

He stood up slowly, came across the room slowly and leaned the .22 against my throat. His smiling thin-lipped mouth seemed as expressionless, for all its smile, as his wax-white nose. He reached quietly under my coat and took the Lüger. I might as well leave it home from now on. Everybody in town seemed to be able to take it away from me.

He stepped back across the room and sat down again in the chair. 'Steady does it,' he said almost gently. 'Park the body, friend. No false moves. No moves at all. You and me are at the jumping-off place. The clock's tickin' and we're waiting to go.'

I sat down and stared at him. A curious bird. I moistened my dry lips. 'You told me his gun had no firing pin,' I said.

'Yeah. He fooled me on that, the little so-and-so. And I

told you to lay off the Jeeter kid. That's cold now. It's Frisky I'm thinking about. Crazy, ain't it? Me bothering about a dimwit like that packin' him around with me, and letting him get hisself bumped off.' He sighed and added simply, 'He was my kid brother.'

'I didn't kill him,' I said.

He smiled a little more. He had never stopped smiling. The corners of his mouth just tucked in a little deeper.

'Yeah?'

He slid the safety catch off the Lüger, laid it carefully on the arm of the chair at his right, and reached into his pocket. What he brought out made me as cold as an ice bucket.

It was a metal tube, dark and rough-looking, about four inches long and drilled with a lot of small holes. He held his Woodsman in his left hand and began to screw the tube casually on the end of it.

'Silencer,' he said. 'They're the bunk, I guess you smart guys think. This one ain't the bunk – not for three shots. I oughta know. I made it myself.'

I moistened my lips again. 'It'll work for one shot,' I said. 'Then it jams your action. That one looks like cast-iron. It will probably blow your hand off.'

He smiled his waxy smile, screwed it on, slowly, lovingly, gave it a last hard turn and sat back relaxed. 'Not this baby. She's packed with steel wool and that's good for three shots, like I said. Then you got to repack it. And there ain't enough back pressure to jam the action on this gun. You feel good? I'd like you to feel good.'

'I feel swell, you sadistic — — —,' I said.

'I'm having you lie down on the bed after a while. You won't feel nothing. I'm kind of fussy about my killings. Frisky didn't feel nothing, I guess. You got him neat.'

'You don't see good,' I sneered. 'The chauffeur got him with a Smith & Wesson forty-four. I didn't even fire.'

'Uh-huh.'

'O.K., you don't believe me,' I said. 'What did you kill

Arbogast for? There was nothing fussy about that killing. He was just shot at his desk, three times with a twenty-two and he fell down on the floor. What did he ever do to your filthy little brother?'

He jerked the gun up, but his smile held. 'You got guts,' he said. 'Who is this here Arbogast?'

I told him. I told him slowly and carefully, in detail. I told him a lot of things. And he began in some vague way to look worried. His eyes flickered at me, away, back again, restlessly, like a humming-bird.

'I don't know any party named Arbogast, pal,' he said slowly. 'Never heard of him. And I ain't shot any fat guys to-day.'

'You killed him,' I said. 'And you killed young Jeeter – in the girl's apartment at the El Milano. He's lying there dead right now. You're working for Marty Estel. He's going to be awfully damn sorry about that kill. Go ahead and make it three in a row.'

His face froze. The smile went away at last. His whole face looked waxy now. He opened his mouth and breathed through it, and his breath made a restless worrying sound. I could see the faint glitter of sweat on his forehead, and I could feel the cold from the evaporation of sweat on mine.

Waxnose said very gently: 'I ain't killed anybody at all, friend. Not anybody. I wasn't hired to kill people. Until Frisky stopped that slug I didn't have no such ideas. That's straight.'

I tried not to stare at the metal tube on the end of the Woodsman.

A flame flickered at the back of his eyes, a small, weak, smoky flame. It seemed to grow larger and clearer. He looked down at the floor between his feet. I looked around at the light-switch, but it was too far away. He looked up again. Very slowly he began to unscrew the silencer. He had it loose in his hand. He dropped it back into his pocket, stood up, holding the two guns, one in each hand. Then he had another idea. He sat down again, took all the shells out of the Lüger quickly and threw it on the floor after them.

He came towards me softly across the room. 'I guess this is your lucky day,' he said. 'I got to go a place and see a guy.'

'I knew all along it was my lucky day. I've been feeling so good.'

He moved delicately around me to the door and opened it a foot and started through the narrow opening, smiling again.

'I gotta see a guy,' he said very gently, and his tongue moved along his lips.

'Not yet,' I said, and jumped.

His gun-hand was at the edge of the door, almost beyond the edge. I hit the door hard and he couldn't bring it in quickly enough. He couldn't get out of the way. I pinned him in the doorway, and used all the strength I had. It was a crazy thing. He had given me a break and all I had to do was to stand still and let him go. But I had a guy to see too – and I wanted to see him first.

Waxnose leered at me. He grunted. He fought with his hand beyond the door edge. I shifted and hit his jaw with all I had. It was enough. He went limp. I hit him again. His head bounced against the wood. I heard a light thud beyond the door edge. I hit him a third time. I never hit anything any harder.

I took my weight back from the door then and he slid towards me, blank-eyed, rubber-kneed and I caught him and twisted his empty hands behind him and let him fall. I stood over him panting. I went to the door. His Woodsman lay almost on the sill. I picked it up, dropped it into my pocket – not the pocket that held Miss Huntress's gun. He hadn't even found that.

There he lay on the floor. He was thin, he had no weight, but I panted just the same. In a little while his eyes flickered open and looked up at me.

'Greedy guy,' he whispered wearily. 'Why did I ever leave Saint Looey?'

I snapped handcuffs on his wrists and pulled him by the shoulders into the dressing-room and tied his ankles with a piece of rope. I left him lying on his back, a little sideways, his nose as white as ever, his eyes empty now, his lips moving a little as if he were talking to himself. A funny lad, not all bad, but not so pure I had to weep over him either.

I put my Lüger together and left with my three guns. There was nobody outside the apartment house.

8

The Jeeter mansion was on a nine- or ten-acre knoll, a big colonial pile with fat white columns and dormer windows and magnolias and a four-car garage. There was a circular parking space at the tope of the driveway with two cars parked in it – one was the big dreadnought in which I'd ridden and the other a canary-yellow sports convertible I had seen before.

I rang a bell the size of a silver dollar. The door opened and a tall narrow cold-eyed bird in dark clothes looked out at me.

'Mr Jeeter home? Mr Jeeter, Senior?'

'May I arsk who is calling?' the accent was a little too thick, like cut Scotch.

'John Dalmas. I'm working for him. Maybe I had ought to of gone to the servant's entrance.'

He hitched a finger at a wing collar and looked at me without pleasure. 'Aw, possibly. You may step in. I shall inform Mr Jeeter. I believe he is engaged at the moment. Kindly wait 'ere in the 'all.'

'The act stinks,' I said. 'English butlers aren't dropping their h's this year.'

'Smart guy, huh?' he snarled, in a voice from not any farther across the Atlantic than Hoboken. 'Wait here.' He slid away.

I sat down in a carved chair and felt thirsty. After a while the butler came cat-footing back along the hall and jerked his chin at me unpleasantly.

We went along a mile of hallway. At the end it broadened without any doors into a huge sunroom. On the far side of the sunroom the butler opened a wide door and I stepped past him into an oval room with a black-and-silver oval rug, a black marble table in the middle of the rug, stiff high-backed carved chairs against the walls, a huge oval mirror with a rounded surface that made me look like a pygmy with water on the brain, and in the room three people.

By the door opposite where I came in, George the chauffeur stood stiffly in his neat dark uniform, with his peaked cap in his hand. In the least uncomfortable of the chairs sat Miss Harriet Huntress holding a glass in which there was half a drink. And around the silver margin of the oval rug, Mr Jeeter, Senior, was trying his legs out in a brisk canter, still under wraps, but mad inside. His face was red and the veins on his nose were distended. His hands were in the pockets of a velvet smoking jacket. He wore a pleated shirt with a black pearl in the bosom, a batwing black tie, and one of his patent leather Oxfords was unlaced.

He whirled and yelled at the butler behind me: 'Get out and keep those doors shut! And I'm not at home to anybody, understand? Nobody!'

The butler closed the doors. Presumably, he went away. I didn't hear him go.

George gave me a cool one-sided smile and Miss Huntress gave me a bland stare over her glass. 'You made a nice comeback,' she said demurely.

'You took a chance leaving me alone in your apartment,' I told her. 'I might have sneaked some of your perfume.'

'Well, what do you want?' Jeeter yelled at me. 'A nice

sort of detective you turned out to be. I put you on a confidential job and you walk right in on Miss Huntress and explain the whole thing to her.'

'It worked, didn't it?'

He stared. They all stared. 'How do you know that?' he barked.

'I know a nice girl when I see one. She's here telling you she had an idea she got not to like, and for you to quit worrying about it. Where's Mister Gerald?'

Old Man Jeeter stopped and gave me a hard level stare. 'I still regard you as incompetent,' he said. 'My son is missing.'

'I'm not working for you. I'm working for Anna Halsey. Any complaints you have to make should be addressed to her. Do I pour my own drink or do you have a flunkey in a purple suit to do it? And what do you mean, your son is missing?'

'Should I give him the heave, sir?' George asked quietly.

Jeeter waved his hand at a decanter and siphon and glasses on the black marble table and started around the rug again. 'Don't be silly,' he snapped at George.

George flushed a little, high on his cheekbones. His mouth looked tough.

I mixed myself a drink and sat down with it and tasted it and asked again: 'What do you mean your son is missing, Mr Jeeter?'

'I'm paying you good money,' he started to yell at me, still mad.

'When?'

He stopped dead in his canter and looked at me again. Miss Huntress laughed lightly. George scowled.

'What do you suppose I mean – my son is missing?' he snapped. 'I should have thought that would be clear enough even to you. Nobody knows where he is. Miss Huntress doesn't know. I don't know. No one at any of the places where he might be knows.'

'But I'm smarter than they are,' I said. '*I* know.'

Nobody moved for a long minute. Jeeter stared at me fish-eyed. George stared at me. The girl stared at me. She looked puzzled. The other two just stared.

I looked at her. 'Where did you go when you went out, if you're telling?'

Her dark blue eyes were water-clear. 'There's no secret about it. We went out together – in a taxi. Gerald had had his driving licence suspended for a month. Too many tickets. We went down towards the beach and I had a change of heart, as you guessed. I decided I was just being a chiseler after all. I didn't want Gerald's money really. What I wanted was revenge. On Mr Jeeter here for ruining my father. Done all legally of course, but done just the same. But I got myself in a spot where I couldn't have my revenge and not look like a cheap chiseler. So I told Gerald to find some other girl to play with. He was sore and we quarrelled. I stopped the taxi and got out in Beverly Hills. He went on. I don't know where. Later I went back to the El Milano and got my car out of the garage and came here. To tell Mr Jeeter to forget the whole thing and not bother to stick sleuths on to me.'

'You say you went with him in a taxi,' I said. 'Why wasn't George driving him, if he couldn't drive himself?'

I stared at her, but I wasn't talking to her. Jeeter answered me, frostily. 'George drove me home from the office, of course. At that time Gerald had already gone out. Is there anything important about that?'

I turned to him. 'Yeah. There's going to be. Mister Gerald is at the El Milano. Hawkins the house dick told me. He went back there to wait for Miss Huntress and Hawkins let him into her apartment. Hawkins will do you those little favours – for ten bucks. He may be there still and he may not.'

I kept on watching them. It was hard to watch all three of them. But they didn't move. They just looked at me.

'Well – I'm glad to hear it,' Old Man Jeeter said. 'I was afraid he was off somewhere getting drunk.'

'No. He's not off anywhere getting drunk,' I said. 'By the way, among these places you called to see if he was there, you didn't call the El Milano?'

George nodded. 'Yes, I did. They said he wasn't there. Looks like this house peeper tipped the phone girl off not to say anything.'

'He wouldn't have to do that. She'd just ring the apartment and he wouldn't answer – naturally.' I watched old man Jeeter hard then, with a lot of interest. It was going to be hard for him to take that up, but he was going to have to do it.

He did. He licked his lips first. 'Why – naturally, if I may ask?' he said coldly.

I put my glass down on the marble table and stood against the wall, with my hands hanging free. I still tried to watch them – all three of them.

'Let's go back over this thing a little,' I said. 'We're all wise to the situation. I know George is, although he shouldn't be, being just a servant. I know Miss Huntress is. And of course, *you* are, Mr Jeeter. So let's see what we have got. We have a lot of things that don't add up, but I'm smart. I'm going to add them up anyhow. First off a handful of photostats of notes from Marty Estel. Gerald denies having given these and Mr Jeeter won't pay them, but he has a handwriting man named Arbogast check the signatures, to see if they look genuine. They do. They are. This Arbogast may have done other things. I don't know. I couldn't ask him. When I went to see him, he was dead – shot three times – as I've since heard – with a twenty-two. No, I didn't tell the police, Mr Jeeter.'

The tall silver-haired man looked horribly shocked. His lean body shook like a bullrush. 'Dead?' he whispered. 'Murdered?'

I looked at George. George didn't move a muscle. I

looked at the girl. She sat quietly, waiting, tight-lipped.

I said, 'There's only one reason to suppose his killing had anything to do with Mr Jeeter's affairs. He was shot with a twenty-two – and there is a man in this case who wears a twenty-two.'

I still had their attention. And their silence.

'Why he was shot I haven't the faintest idea. He was not a dangerous man to Miss Huntress or Marty Estel. He was too fat to get around much. My guess is he was a little too smart. He got a simple case of signature identification and he went on from there to find out more than he should. And after he had found out more than he should – he guessed more than he ought – and maybe he even tried a little black-mail. And somebody rubbed him out this afternoon with a twenty-two. O.K., I can stand it. I never knew him.

'So I went over to see Miss Huntress and after a lot of finagling around with this itchy-handed house dick I got to see her and we had a chat, and then Mister Gerald stepped neatly out of hiding and bopped me a nice one on the chin and over I went and hit my head on a chair leg. And when I came out of that the joint was empty. So I went home.

'And home I found the man with the twenty-two and with him a dimwit called Frisky Lavon, with a bad breath and a very large gun, neither of which matters now as he was shot dead in front of your house to-night, Mr Jeeter – shot trying to stick up your car. The cops know about that one – they came to see me about it – because the other guy, the one that packs the twenty-two, is the little dimwit's brother and he thought I shot Dimwit and tried to pull the bee on me. But it didn't work. That's two killings.

'We now come to the third and most important. I went back to the El Milano because it no longer seemed a good idea for Mister Gerald to be running around casually. He seemed to have a few enemies. It even seemed that he was supposed to be in the car this evening when Frisky Lavon shot at it – but of course that was just a plant.'

Old Jeeter drew his white eyebrows together in an expression of puzzlement. George didn't look puzzled. He didn't look anything. He was as wooden-faced as a cigarstore Indian. The girl looked a little white now, a little tense. I ploughed on.

'Back at the El Milano I found that Hawkins had let Marty Estel and his bodyguard into Miss Huntress's apartment to wait for her. Marty had something to tell her – that Arbogast had been killed. That made it a good idea for her to lay off young Jeeter for a while – until the cops quieted down anyhow. A thoughtful guy, Marty. A much more thoughtful guy than you would suppose. For instance, he knew about Arbogast and he knew Mr Jeeter went to Anna Halsey's office this morning and he knew somehow – Anna might have told him herself, I wouldn't put it past her – that I was working on the case now. So he had me tailed to Arbogast's place and away, and he found out later from his cop friends that Arbogast had been murdered, and he knew I hadn't given it out. So he had me there and that made us pals. He went away after telling me this and once more I was left alone in Miss Huntress's apartment. But this time for no reason at all I poked around. And I found young Mister Gerald, in the bedroom, in a closet.'

I stepped quickly over to the girl and reached into my pocket and took out the small fancy .25 automatic and laid it down on her knee.

'Ever see this before?'

Her voice had a curious tight sound, but her dark blue eyes looked at me levelly.

'Yes. It's mine.'

'You kept it where?'

'In the drawer of a small table beside the bed.'

'Sure about that?'

She thought. Neither of the two men stirred.

George began to twitch the corner of his mouth. She shook her head suddenly, sideways.

'No. I have an idea I took it out to show somebody –
because I don't know much about guns – and left it lying on
the mantel in the living-room. In fact, I'm almost sure I did.
It was Gerald I showed it to.'

'So he might have reached for it there, if anybody tried to
make a wrong play at him?'

She nodded, troubled. 'What do you mean – he's in the
closet?' she asked in a small quick voice.

'You know. Everybody in this room knows what I mean.
They know that I showed you that gun for a purpose.' I
stepped away from her and faced George and his boss. 'He's
dead, of course. Shot through the heart – probably with this
gun. It was left there with him. That's why it would be left.'

The old man took a step and stopped and braced himself
against the table. I wasn't sure whether he had turned
white or whether he had been white already. He stared
stonily at the girl. He said very slowly, between his teeth:
'You damned murderess!'

'Couldn't it have been suicide?' I sneered.

He turned his head enough to look at me. I could see that
the idea interested him. He half nodded.

'No,' I said, 'It couldn't have been suicide.'

He didn't like that so well. His face congested with blood
and the veins on his nose thickened. The girl touched the
gun lying on her knee, then put her hand loosely around the
butt. I saw her thumb slide very gently towards the safety
catch. She didn't know much about guns, but she knew that
much.

'It couldn't be suicide.' I said again, very slowly. 'As an
isolated event – maybe. But not with all the other stuff that's
been happening. Arbogast, the stick-up down on Calvello
Drive outside this house, the thugs planted in my apartment,
the job with the twenty-two.'

I reached into my pocket again and pulled out Waxnose's
Woodsman. I held it carelessly on the flat of my left hand.
'And curiously enough, I don't think it was *this* twenty-two

– although this happens to be the gunman's twenty-two. Yeah, I have the gunman too. He's tied up in my apartment. He came back to knock me off, but I talked him out of it. I'm a swell talker.'

'Except that you overdo it,' the girl said coolly, and lifted the gun a little.

'It's obvious who killed him, Miss Huntress,' I said. 'It's simply a matter of motive and opportunity. Marty Estel didn't, and didn't have it done. That would spoil his chances to get his fifty grand. Frisky Lavon's pal didn't, regardless of who he was working for, and I don't think he was working for Marty Estel. He couldn't have got into the El Milano to do the job, and certainly not into Miss Huntress's apartment. Whoever did it had something to gain by it and an opportunity to get to the place where it was done. Well, who has something to gain? Gerald had five million coming to him in two years out of a trust. He couldn't will it until he got it. So if he died, his natural heir got it. Who's his natural heir? You'd be surprised. Did you know that in the state of California and some others, but not in all, a man can by his own act become a natural heir? Just by adopting somebody who has money and no heirs!'

George moved then. His movement was once more as smooth as a ripple of water. The Smith & Wesson gleamed dully in his hand, but he didn't fire it. The small automatic in the girl's hand cracked. Blood spurted from George's brown hard hand. The Smith & Wesson dropped to the floor. He cursed. She didn't know much about guns – not very much.

'Of course!' she said grimly. 'George could get into the apartment without any trouble, if Gerald was there. He would go in through the garage, a chauffeur in uniform, ride up in the elevator and knock at the door. And when Gerald opened it, George would back him in with that Smith & Wesson. But how did he know Gerald was there?'

I said: 'He must have followed your taxi. We don't know

where he has been all evening since he left me. He had a car with him. The cops will find out. How much was in it for you, George?'

George held his right wrist with his left hand, held it tightly, and his face was twisted, savage. He said nothing.

'George would back him in with the Smith & Wesson,' the girl said wearily. 'Then he would see my gun on the mantelpiece. That would be better. He would use that. He would back Gerald into the bedroom, away from the corridor, into the closet, and there, quietly, calmly, he would kill him and drop the gun on the floor.'

'Nice people these college boys. Was it Dartmouth or Dannemora, George? George killed Arbogast, too. He killed him with a twenty-two because he knew that Frisky Lavon's brother had a twenty-two, and he knew that because he had hired Frisky and his brother to put over a big scare on Gerald – so that when he was murdered it would look as if Marty Estel had had it done. That was why I was brought out here to-night in the Jeeter car – so that the two thugs who had been warned and planted could pull their act and maybe knock me off, if I got tough. Only George likes to kill people. He made a neat shot at Frisky. He hit him in the face. It was so good a shot I think he meant it to be a miss. How about it, George?'

Silence.

I looked at old Jeeter at last. I had been expecting him to pull a gun himself, but he hadn't. He just stood there, open-mouthed, appalled, leaning against the black marble table, shaking.

'My God!' he whispered. 'My God!'

'You don't have one – except money. You –'

A door squeaked behind me. I whirled, but I needn't have bothered. A hard voice, about as English as Amos and Andy, said: 'Put 'em up bud.'

The butler, the very English butler, stood there in the doorway, a gun in his hand, tight-lipped. The girl turned her wrist and shot him just kind of casually, in the shoulder or something. He squealed like a stuck pig.

'Go away, you're intruding,' she said coldly.

He ran. We heard his steps running.

'He's going to fall,' she said.

I was wearing my Lüger in my right hand now, a little late in the season, as usual. I came around with it. Old Man Jeeter was holding on to the table, his face grey as a paving block. His knees were giving. George stood cynically, holding a handkerchief around his bleeding wrist, watching him.

'Let him fall,' I said. 'Down is where he belongs.'

He fell. His head twisted. His mouth went slack. He hit the carpet on his side and rolled a little and his knees came up. His mouth drooled a little. His skin turned violet.

'Go call the law, angel,' I said. 'I'll watch them now.'

'All right,' she said standing up. 'But you certainly need a lot of help in your private-detective business, Mr Dalmas.'

9

A shiny black bug with a pink head crawled slowly along the top of the old scarred desk. It wobbled as it crawled, like an old lady with too many parcels. At the edge it marched straight off into the air, fell on its back on the dirty brown linoleum, waved a few thin worn legs in the air and then played dead. A minute of that and it put the legs out again, struggled over on its face and trundled off, wobbling towards the corner of the room.

I had been in there for a solid hour, alone. There was the scarred desk in the middle, another against the wall, a brass spittoon on a mat, a police loudspeaker box on the wall, three squashed flies, a smell of cold cigars and old clothes. There were two hard armchairs with felt pads and two hard straight chairs without pads. The electric light fixture had been dusted about Coolidge's first term.

The door opened with a jerk and Finlayson and Sebold came in. Sebold looked as spruce and nasty as ever, but Finlayson looked older, more worn, mousier. He held a sheaf of papers in his hand. He sat down across the desk from me and gave me a hard bleak stare.

The loudspeaker on the wall put out a bulletin about a middle-aged Negro running south on San Pedro from 11th after a holdup. He was wearing a grey suit and felt hat. 'Approach carefully. This suspect is armed with a thirty-two calibre revolver. That is all.' (When they caught him he had an ammonia gun, brown pants, a torn blue sweater, no hat, was sixteen years old, had thirty-five cents in his pocket, and was a Mexican.)

'Guys like you get in a lot of trouble,' Finlayson said sourly. Sebold sat down against the wall and tilted his hat over his eyes and yawned and looked at his new stainless-steel wrist watch.

'Trouble is my business,' I said. 'How else would I make a nickel?'

'We oughta throw you in the can for all this cover-up stuff. How much you making on this one?'

'I was working for Anna Halsey who was working for old man Jeeter. I guess I made a bad debt.'

Sebold smiled his blackjack smile on me. Finlayson lit a cigar and licked at a tear on the side of it and pasted it down, but it leaked smoke just the same when he drew on it. He pushed papers across the desk at me.

'Sign three copies.'

I signed three copies.

He took them back, yawned and rumpled his old grey head. 'The old man's had a stroke,' he said. 'No dice there. Probably won't know what time it is when he comes out. This George Hasterman, this chauffeur guy, he just laughs at us. Too bad he got pinked. I'd like to wrastle him a bit.'

'He's tough,' I said.

'Yeah. O.K., you can beat it for now.'

I got up and nodded to them and went to the door. 'Well, good-night boys.'

Neither of them spoke to me.

I went out, along the corridor and down in the night elevator to the City Hall lobby. I went out the Spring Street side and down the long flight of empty steps and the wind blew cold. I lit a cigarette at the bottom. My car was still out at the Jeeter place. I lifted a foot to start walking to a taxi half a block down across the street. A voice spoke sharply from a parked car.

'Come here a minute.'

It was a man's voice, tight, hard. It was Marty Estel's voice. It came from a big sedan with two men in the front seat. I went over there. The rear window was down and Marty Estel leaned a gloved hand on it.

'Get in.' He pushed the door open. I got in. I was too tired to argue. 'Take it away, Skin.'

The car drove west through dark, almost quiet streets, almost clean streets. The night air was not pure but it was cool. We went up over a hill and began to pick up speed.

'What they get?' Estel asked coolly.

'They didn't tell me. They didn't break the chauffeur yet.'

'You can't convict a couple million bucks of murder in this man's town.' The driver called Skin laughed without turning his head. 'Maybe I don't even touch my fifty grand now . . . She likes you.'

'Uh-huh. So what?'

'Lay off her.'

'What will it get me?'

'It's what it'll get you if you don't.'

'Yeah, sure,' I said, 'Go to hell, will you please. I'm tired.'

I shut my eyes and leaned in the corner of the car and just like that went to sleep. I can do that sometimes, after a strain.

A hand shaking my shoulder woke me. The car had stopped. I looked out at the front of my apartment house.

'Home,' Marty Estel said, 'And remember. Lay off her.'

'Why the ride home? Just to tell me that?'

'She asked me to look out for you. That's why you're loose. She likes you. I like her. See? You don't want any more trouble.'

'Trouble –' I started to say, and stopped. I was tired of that gag for that night. 'Thanks for the ride, and apart from that, nuts to you.' I turned away and went into the apartment house and up.

The doorlock was still loose but nobody waited for me this time. They had taken Waxnose away long since. I left the door open and threw the windows up and I was still sniffing at policeman's cigar butts when the phone rang. It was her voice, cool, a little hard, not touched by anything, almost amused. Well, she'd been through enough to make her that way, probably.

'Hello, brown-eyes. Make it home all right?'

'Your pal Marty brought me home. He told me to lay off you. Thanks with all my heart, if I have any, but don't call me up any more.'

'A little scared, Mr Dalmas?'

'No. Wait for me to call you,' I said. 'Good-night, angel.'

'Good-night, brown-eyes.'

The phone clicked. I put it away and shut the door and pulled the bed down. I undressed and lay on it for a while in the cold air.

Then I got up and had a drink and a shower and went to sleep.

They broke George at last, but not enough. He said there had been a fight over the girl and young Jeeter had grabbed the gun off the mantel and George had fought with him and it had gone off. All of which, of course, looked possible – in the papers. They never pinned the Arbogast killing on him or on anybody. They never found the gun that did it, but it was not Waxnose's gun. Waxnose disappeared – I never heard where. They didn't touch old man Jeeter, because he never came out of his stroke, except to lie on his back and have nurses and tell people how he hadn't lost a nickel in the depression.

Marty Estel called me up four times to tell me to lay off Harriet Huntress. I felt kind of sorry for the poor guy. He had it bad. I went out with her twice and sat with her twice more at home, drinking her Scotch. It was nice, but I didn't have the money, the clothes, the time, or the manners. Then she stopped being at the El Milano and I heard she had gone to New York.

I was glad when she left – even though she didn't bother to tell me good-bye.

II

Red Wind

I

THERE was a desert wind blowing that night. It was one of those hot dry Santa Anas that come down through the mountain passes and curl your hair and make your nerves jump and your skin itch. On nights like that every booze party ends in a fight. Meek little wives feel the edge of the carving knife and study their husbands' necks. Anything can happen. You can even get a full glass of beer at a cocktail lounge.

I was getting one in a flossy new place across the street from the apartment house where I lived. It had been open about a week and it wasn't doing any business. The kid behind the bar was in his early twenties and looked as if he had never had a drink in his life.

There was only one other customer, a souse on a bar stool with his back to the door. He had a pile of dimes stacked neatly in front of him, about two dollars' worth. He was drinking straight rye in small glasses and he was all by himself in a world of his own.

I sat further along the bar and got my glass of beer and said: 'You sure cut the clouds off them, buddy. I will say that for you.'

'We just opened up,' the kid said. 'We got to build up trade. Been in before, haven't you, mister?'

'Uh-huh.'

'Live around here?'

'In the Berglund Apartments across the street,' I said. 'And the name is John Dalmas.'

'Thanks, mister. Mine's Lew Petrolle.' He leaned close to me across the polished dark bar. 'Know that guy?'

'No.'

'He ought to go home, kind of. I ought to call a taxi and send him home. He's doing his next week's drinking too soon.'

'A night like this,' I said. 'Let him alone.'

'It's not good for him,' the kid said, scowling at me.

'Rye!' the drunk croaked, without looking up. He snapped his fingers so as not to disturb his piles of dimes by banging on the bar.

The kid looked at me and shrugged. 'Should I?'

'Whose stomach is it? Not mine.'

The kid poured him another straight rye and I think he doctored it with water down behind the bar because when he came up with it he looked as guilty as if he'd kicked his grandmother. The drunk paid no attention. He lifted two dimes off his pile with the exact care of a crack surgeon operating on a brain tumour.

The kid came back and put more beer in my glass. Outside the wind howled. Every once in a while it blew the stained-glass swing-door open a few inches. It was a heavy door.

The kid said: 'I don't like drunks in the first place and in the second place I don't like them getting drunk in here, and in the third place I don't like them in the first place.'

'Warner Brothers could use that,' I said.

'They did.'

Just then we had another customer. A car squeaked to a stop outside and the swinging door came open. A fellow came in who looked a little in a hurry. He held the door and ranged the place quickly with flat, shiny, dark eyes. He was well set up, dark, good-looking in a narrow-faced, tight-lipped way. His clothes were dark and a white handkerchief peeped coyly from his pocket and he looked cool as well as under a tension of some sort. I guessed it was the hot wind. I felt a bit the same myself only not cool.

He looked at the drunk's back. The drunk was playing checkers with his empty glasses. The new customer looked at me, then he looked along the line of half-booths at the other side of the place. They were all empty. He came on in – down past where the drunk sat swaying and muttering to himself – and spoke to the bar kid.

'Seen a lady in here, buddy? Tall, pretty, brown hair, in a print bolero jacket over a blue crepe silk dress. Wearing a wide-brimmed straw hat with a velvet band.' He had a tight voice I didn't like.

'No, sir. Nobody like that's been in,' the bar kid said.

'Thanks. Straight Scotch. Make it fast, will you?'

The kid gave it to him and the fellow paid and put the drink down in a gulp and started to go out. He took three or four steps and stopped, facing the drunk. The drunk was grinning. He swept a gun from somewhere so fast that it was just a blur coming out. He held it steady and he didn't look any drunker than I was. The tall dark guy stood quite still and then his head jerked back a little and then he was still again.

A car tore by outside. The drunk's gun was a .22 target automatic, with a large front sight. It made a couple of hard snaps and a little smoke curled – very little.

'So long, Waldo,' the drunk said.

Then he put the gun on the barman and me.

The dark guy took a week to fall down. He stumbled, caught himself, waved one arm, stumbled again. His hat fell off, and then he hit the floor with his face. After he hit it he might have been poured concrete for all the fuss he made.

The drunk slid down off the stool and scooped his dimes into a pocket and slid towards the door. He turned sideways, holding the gun across his body. I didn't have a gun. I hadn't thought I needed one to buy a glass of beer. The kid behind the bar didn't move or make the slightest sound.

The drunk felt the door lightly with his shoulder, keeping his eye on us, then pushed through it backwards. When it was wide a hard gust of air slammed in and lifted the hair of the man on the floor. The drunk said: 'Poor Waldo. I bet I made his nose bleed.'

The door swung shut. I started to rush it – from long practice in doing the wrong thing. In this case it didn't matter. The car outside let out a roar and when I got onto the sidewalk it was flicking a red smear of tail-light around the nearby corner. I got its licence number the way I got my first million.

There were people and cars up and down the block as usual. Nobody acted as if a gun had gone off. The wind was making enough noise to make the hard quick rap of .22 ammunition sound like a slammed door, even if anyone heard it. I went back into the cocktail bar.

The kid hadn't moved, even yet. He just stood with his hands flat on the bar, leaning over a little and looking down at the dark guy's back. The dark guy hadn't moved either. I bent down and felt his neck artery. He wouldn't move – ever.

The kid's face had as much expression as a cut of round steak and was about the same colour. His eyes were more angry than shocked.

I lit a cigarette and blew smoke at the ceiling and said shortly: 'Get on the phone.'

'Maybe he's not dead,' the kid said.

'When they use a .22 that means they don't make mistakes. Where's the phone?'

'I don't have one. I got enough expenses without that. Boy, can I kick eight hundred bucks in the face!'

'You own this place?'

'I did till this happened.'

He pulled his white coat off and his apron and came around the inner end of the bar. 'I'm locking the door,' he said, taking keys out.

He went out, swung the door to and jiggled the lock from the outside until the bolt clicked into place. I bent down rolled Waldo over. At first I couldn't even see where the shots went in. Then I could. A couple of tiny holes in his coat, over his heart. There was a little blood on his shirt.

The drunk was everything you could ask – as a killer.

The prowl-car boys came in about eight minutes. The kid, Lew Petrolle, was back behind the bar by then. He had his white coat on again and he was counting the money in the register and putting it in his pocket and making notes in a little book.

I sat at the edge of one of the half-booths and smoked cigarettes and watched Waldo's face get deader and deader. I wondered who the girl in the print coat was, why Waldo had left the engine of his car running outside, why he was in a hurry, whether the drunk had been waiting for him or just happened to be there.

The prowl-car boys came in perspiring. They were the usual large size and one of them had a flower stuck under his cap and his cap on a bit crooked. When he saw the dead man he got rid of the flower and leaned down to feel Waldo's pulse.

'Seems to be dead,' he said, and rolled him around a little more. 'Oh yeah, I see where they went in. Nice clean work. You two see him get it?'

I said yes. The kid behind the bar said nothing. I told them about it, that the killer seemed to have left in Waldo's car.

The cop yanked Waldo's wallet out, went through it rapidly and whistled. 'Plenty jack and no driver's licence.' He put the wallet away. 'O.K., we didn't touch him, see? Just a chance we could find did he have a car and put it on the air.'

'The hell you didn't touch him,' Lew Petrolle said.

The cop gave him one of those looks. 'O.K.,' pal, he said softly. 'We touched him.'

The kid picked up a clean highball glass and began to polish it. He polished it all the rest of the time we were there.

In another minute a homicide fast-wagon sirened up and screeched to a stop outside the door and four men came in, two dicks, a photographer, and a laboratory man. I didn't know either of the dicks. You can be in the detecting business a long time and not know all the men on a big city force.

One of them was a short, smooth, dark, quiet, smiling man, with curly black hair and soft intelligent eyes. The other was big, raw-boned, long-jawed, with a veined nose and glassy eyes. He looked like a heavy drinker. He looked tough, but he looked as if he thought he was a little tougher than he was. He shooed me into the last booth against the wall and his partner got the kid up in front and bluecoats went out. The fingerprint man and photographer set about their work.

A medical examiner came, stayed just long enough to get sore because there was no phone for him to call the morgue wagon.

The short dick emptied Waldo's pockets and then emptied his wallet and dumped everything into a large handkerchief on a booth table. I saw a lot of currency, keys, cigarettes, another handkerchief, very little else.

The big dick pushed me back into the end of the half-booth. 'Give,' he said. 'I'm Copernik, Detective-Lieutenant.'

I put my wallet in front of him. He looked at it, went through it, tossed it back, made a note in a book.

'John Dalmas, huh? A shamus. You here on business?'

'Drinking business,' I said. 'I live just across the street in the Berglund.'

'Know this kid up front?'

'I've been in here once since he opened up.'

'See anything funny about him now?'

'No.'

'Takes it too light for a young fellow, don't he? Never mind answering. Just tell the story.'

I told it – three times. Once for him to get the outline, once for him to get the details, and once for him to see if I had it too pat. At the end he said: 'This dame interests me. And the killer called the guy Waldo, yet didn't seem to be anyways sure he would be in. I mean, if Waldo wasn't sure the dame would be here, nobody could be sure Waldo would be here.'

'That's pretty deep,' I said.

He studied me. I wasn't smiling. 'Sounds like a grudge job, don't it? Don't sound planned. No getaway except by accident. A guy don't leave his car unlocked much in this town. And the killer works in front of two good witnesses. I don't like that.'

'I don't like being a witness,' I said. 'The pay's too low.'

He grinned. His teeth had a freckled look. 'Was the killer drunk really?'

'With that shooting? No.'

'Me too. Well, it's a simple job. The guy will have a record and he's left plenty prints. Even if we don't have his mug here we'll make him in hours. He had something on Waldo, but he wasn't meeting Waldo to-night. Waldo just cropped in to ask about a dame he had a date with and had missed connexions on. It's a hot night and this wind would kill a girl's face. She'd be apt to drop in somewhere to wait. So the killer feeds Waldo two in the right place and scrams and don't worry about you boys at all. It's that simple.'

'Yeah,' I said.

'It's so simple it stinks,' Copernik said.

He took his felt hat off and tousled up his ratty blond hair and leaned his head on his hands. He had a long mean horse face. He got a handkerchief out and mopped it, and the back of his neck and the back of his hands. He got a comb out and combed his hair – he looked worse with it combed – and put his hat back on.

'I was just thinking,' I said.

'Yeah? What?'

'This Waldo knew just how the girl was dressed. So he must already have been with her to-night.'

'So what? Maybe he had to go to the can. And when he came back she'd gone. Maybe she changed her mind about him.'

'That's right,' I said.

But that wasn't what I was thinking at all. I was thinking that Waldo had described the girl's clothes in a way the ordinary man wouldn't know how to describe them. Printed bolero jacket over blue crepe silk dress. I didn't even know what a bolero jacket was. And I might have said blue dress or even blue silk dress, but never blue crepe silk dress.

After a while two men came with a basket. Lew Petrolle was still polishing his glass and talking to the short dark dick.

We all went down to headquarters.

Lew Petrolle was all right when they checked on him. His father had a grape ranch near Antioch in Contra Costa County. He had given Lew a thousand dollars to go into business and Lew had opened the cocktail bar, neon sign and all, on eight hundred flat.

They let him go and told him to keep the bar closed until they were sure they didn't want to do any more printing. He shook hands all around and grinned and said he guessed the killing would be good for business after all, because nobody believed a newspaper account of anything and people would come to him for the story and buy drinks while he was telling it.

'There's a guy won't ever do any worrying,' Copernik said, when he was gone. 'Over anybody else.'

'Poor Waldo,' I said. 'The prints any good?'

'Kind of smudged,' Copernik said sourly. 'But we'll get a classification and teletype it to Washington some time to-night. If it don't click, you'll be in for a day on the steel picture-racks downstairs.'

I shook hands with him and his partner, whose name was Ybarra, and left. They didn't know who Waldo was yet either. Nothing in his pockets told.

2

I got back to my street about 9 p.m. I looked up and down the block before I went into the Berglund. The cocktail bar was further down on the other side, dark, with a nose or two against the glass, but no real crowd. People had seen the law and the morgue wagon, but they didn't know what had happened. Except the boys playing pinball games in the drugstore on the corner. They know everything, except how to hold a job.

The wind was still blowing, oven-hot, swirling dust and torn paper up against the walls.

I went into the lobby of the apartment house and rode the automatic elevator up to the fourth floor. I unwound the doors and stepped out and there was a tall girl standing there waiting for the car.

She had brown wavy hair under a wide-brimmed straw hat with a velvet band and loose bow. She had wide blue eyes and eyelashes that didn't quite reach her chin. She wore a blue dress that might have been crepe silk, simple in lines but not missing any cues. Over it she wore what might have been a print bolero jacket.

I said: 'Is that a bolero jacket?'

She gave me a distant glance and made a motion as if to brush a cobweb out of the way.

'Yes. Would you mind – I'm rather in a hurry. I'd like – '

I didn't move. I blocked her off from the elevator. We stared at each other and she flushed very slowly.

'Better not go out on the street in those clothes,' I said.

'Why, how dare you – '

The elevator clanked and started down again. I didn't know what she was going to say. Her voice lacked the edgy twang of a beer-parlour frill. It had a soft light sound, like spring rain.

'It's not a make,' I said. 'You're in trouble. If they come

to this floor in the elevator, you have just that much time to get off the hall. First take off the hat and jacket – and snap it up!'

She didn't move. Her face seemed to whiten a little behind the not-too-heavy make-up.

'Cops,' I said, 'are looking for you. In those clothes. Give me the chance and I'll tell you why.'

She turned her head swiftly and looked back along the corridor. With her looks I didn't blame her for trying one more bluff.

'You're impertinent, whoever you are. I'm Mrs Leroy in Apartment Thirty-one. I can assure you – '

'That you're on the wrong floor,' I said. 'This is the fourth.' The elevator had stopped down below. The sound of doors being wrenched open came up the shaft.

'Off!' I rapped. 'Now!'

She switched her hat off and slipped out of the bolero jacket, fast. I grabbed them and wadded them into a mess under my arm. I took her elbow and turned her and we were going down the hall.

'I live in Forty-two. The front one across from yours, just a floor up. Take your choice. Once again – I'm not on the make.'

She smoothed her hair with that quick gesture, like a bird preening itself. Ten thousand years of practice behind it.

'Mine,' she said, and tucked her bag under her arm and strode down the hall fast. The elevator stopped at the floor below. She stopped when it stopped. She turned and faced me.

'The stairs are back by the elevator shaft,' I said gently.

'I don't have an apartment,' she said.

'I didn't think you had.'

'Are they searching for me?'

'Yes, but they won't start gouging the block stone by stone before to-morrow. And then only if they don't make Waldo.'

She stared at me. 'Waldo?'

'Oh, you don't know Waldo,' I said.

She shook her head slowly. The elevator started down in the shaft again. Panic flicked in her blue eyes like a ripple on water.

'No,' she said breathlessly, 'but take me out of this hall.'

We were almost at my door. I jammed the key in and shook the lock around and heaved the door inward. I reached in far enough to switch lights on. She went in past me like a wave. Sandalwood floated on the air, very faint.

I shut the door, threw my hat into a chair and watched her stroll over to a card table on which I had a chess problem set out that I couldn't solve. Once inside, with the door locked, her panic had left her.

'So you're a chess-player,' she said, in that guarded tone, as if she had come to look at my etchings. I wished she had.

We both stood still then and listened to the distant clang of elevator doors and then steps – going the other way.

I grinned, but with strain, not pleasure, went out into the kitchenette and started to fumble with a couple of glasses and then realized I still had her hat and bolero jacket under my arm, went into the dressing-room behind the wall bed and stuffed them into a drawer, went back out to the kitchenette, dug out some extra fine Scotch and made a couple of highballs.

When I went in with the drinks she had a gun in her hand. It was a small automatic with a pearl grip. It jumped up at me and her eyes were full of horror.

I stopped, with a glass in each hand, and said: 'Maybe this hot wind has got you crazy too. I'm a private detective. I'll prove it if you let me.'

She nodded slightly and her face was white. I went over slowly and put a glass down beside her, and went back and set mine down and got a card out that had no bent corners. She was sitting down, smoothing one blue knee with her left hand, and holding the gun on the other. I put the card down beside her drink and sat with mine.

'Never let a guy get that close to you,' I said. 'Not if you mean business. And your safety catch is on.'

She flashed her eyes down, shivered, and put the gun back in her bag. She drank half the drink without stopping, put the glass down hard and picked the card up.

'I don't give many people that liquor,' I said. 'I can't afford to.'

Her lips curled. 'I suppose you would want money.'

'Huh?'

She didn't say anything. Her hand was close to her bag again.

'Don't forget the safety catch,' I said. Her hand stopped. I went on: 'This fellow I called Waldo is quite tall, say five-eleven, slim, dark, brown eyes with a lot of glitter. Nose and mouth too thin. Dark suit, white handkerchief showing, and in a hurry to find you. Am I getting anywhere?'

She took her glass again. 'So that's Waldo,' she said. 'Well, what about him?' Her voice seemed to have a slight liquor edge now.

'Well, a funny thing. There's a cocktail bar across the street . . . Say, where have you been all evening?'

'Sitting in my car,' she said coldly, 'most of the time.'

'Didn't you see a fuss across the street up the block?'

Her eyes tried to say no and missed. Her lips said: 'I knew there was some kind of disturbance. I saw policemen and red searchlights. I supposed someone had been hurt.'

'Someone was. And this Waldo was looking for you before that. In the cocktail bar. He described you and your clothes.'

Her eyes were set like rivets now and had the same amount of expression. Her mouth began to tremble and kept on trembling.

'I was in there,' I said, 'talking to the kid that runs it. There was nobody in there but a drunk on a stool and the kid and myself. The drunk wasn't paying any attention to anything. Then Waldo came in and asked about you and we said no, we hadn't seen you and he started to leave.'

I sipped my drink. I like an effect as well as the next fellow. Her eyes ate me.

'Just started to leave. Then this drunk that wasn't paying any attention to anyone called him Waldo and took a gun out. He shot him twice – ' I snapped my fingers twice – 'like that. Dead.'

She fooled me. She laughed in my face. 'So my husband hired you to spy on me,' she said. 'I might have known the whole thing was an act. You and your Waldo.'

I gawked at her.

'I never thought of him as jealous,' she snapped. 'Not of a man who had been our chauffeur anyhow. A little about Stan, of course – that's natural. But Joseph Choate – '

I made motions in the air. 'Lady, one of us has this book open at the wrong page,' I grunted. 'I don't know anybody named Stan or Joseph Choate. So help me, I didn't even know you had a chauffeur. People around here don't run to them. As for husbands – yeah, we do have a husband once in a while. Not often enough.'

She shook her head slowly and her hand stayed near her bag and her blue eyes had glitters in them.

'Not good enough. Mr Dalmas. No, not nearly good enough. I know you private detectives. You're all rotten. You tricked me into your apartment, if it is your apartment. More likely it's the apartment of some horrible man who will swear anything for a few dollars. Now you're trying to scare me. So you can blackmail me – as well as get money from my husband. All right,' she said breathlessly, 'how much do I have to pay?'

I put my empty glass aside and leaned back. 'Pardon me if I light a cigarette,' I said. 'My nerves are frayed.'

I lit it while she watched me grimly, no fear – or not enough fear for any real guilt to be under it. 'So Joseph Choate is his name,' I said. 'The guy that killed him in the cocktail bar called him Waldo.'

She smiled a bit disgustedly, but almost tolerantly. 'Don't stall. How much?'

'Why were you trying to meet this Joseph Choate?'

'I was going to buy something he stole from me, of course. Something that's valuable in the ordinary way too. Almost fifteen thousand dollars. The man I loved gave it to me. He's dead. There! He's dead! He died in a burning plane. Now, go back and tell my husband that, you slimy little rat!'

'Hey, I weigh a hundred and ninety stripped,' I yelled.

'You're still slimy,' she yelled back. 'And don't bother about telling my husband. I'll tell him myself. He probably knows anyway.'

I grinned. 'That's smart. Just what was I supposed to find out?'

She grabbed her glass and finished what was left of her drink. 'So he thinks I'm meeting Joseph,' she sneered. 'Well, I was. But not to make love. Not with a chauffeur. Not with a bum I picked off the front step and gave a job to. I don't have to dig down that far, if I want to play around.'

'Lady,' I said, 'you don't indeed.'

'Now I'm going,' she said. 'You just try and stop me.' She snatched the pearl-handled gun out of her bag.

I grinned and kept on grinning. I didn't move.

'Why you nasty little string of nothing,' she stormed. 'How do I know you're a private detective at all? You might be a crook. This card you gave me doesn't mean anything. Anybody can have cards printed.'

'Sure,' I said. 'And I suppose I'm smart enough to live here two years because you were going to move in to-day so I could blackmail you for not meeting a man named Joseph Choate who was bumped off across the street under the name of Waldo. Have you got the money to buy this something that cost fifteen grand?'

'Oh! You think you'll hold me up, I suppose!'

'Oh!' I mimicked her, 'I'm a stick-up artist now, am I? Lady, will you please either put that gun away or take the safety catch off? It hurts my professional feelings to see a nice gun made a monkey of that way.'

'You're a full portion of what I don't like,' she said. 'Get out of my way.'

I didn't move. She didn't move. We were both sitting down – and not even close to each other.

'Let me in on one secret before you go,' I pleaded. 'What in hell did you take the apartment down on the floor below for? Just to meet a guy down on the street?'

'Stop being silly,' she snapped. 'I didn't. I lied. It's his apartment.'

'Joseph Choate's?'

She nodded sharply.

'Does my description of Waldo sound like Joseph Choate?'

She nodded sharply again.

'All right. That's one fact learned at last. Don't you realize Waldo described your clothes before he was shot – when he was looking for you – that the description was passed on to the police – that the police don't know who Waldo is – and are looking for somebody in those clothes to help tell them? Don't you get that much?'

The gun suddenly started to shake in her hand. She looked down at it, sort of vacantly, slowly put it back in her bag.

'I'm a fool,' she whispered, 'to be even talking to you.' She stared at me for a long time, then pulled in a deep breath. 'He told me where he was staying. He didn't seem afraid. I guess blackmailers are like that. He was to meet me on the street, but I was late. It was full of police when I got here. So I went back and sat in my car for a while. Then I came up to Joseph's apartment and knocked. Then I went back to my car and waited again. I came up here three times in all. The last time I walked up a flight to take the elevator. I had already been seen twice on the third floor. I met you. That's all.'

'You said something about a husband,' I grunted. 'Where is he?'

'He's at a meeting.'

'Oh, a meeting,' I said nastily.

'My husband's a very important man. He has lots of meetings. He's a hydro-electric engineer. He's been all over the world. I'd have you know – '

'Skip it,' I said. 'I'll take him to lunch some day and have him tell me himself. Whatever Joseph had on you is dead stock now. Like Joseph.'

She believed it at last. I hadn't thought she ever would somehow. 'He's really dead?' she whispered. 'Really?'

'He's dead,' I said. 'Dead, dead, dead. Lady, he's dead.'

Her face fell apart like a bride's piecrust. Her mouth wasn't large, but I could have got my fist into it at that moment. In the silence the elevator stopped at my floor.

'Scream,' I rapped, 'and I'll give you two black eyes.'

It didn't sound nice, but it worked. It jarred her out of it. Her mouth shut like a trap.

I heard steps coming down the hall. We all have hunches. I put my finger to my lips. She didn't move now. Her face had a frozen look. Her big blue eyes were as black as the shadows below them. The hot wind boomed against the shut windows. Windows have to be shut when a Santa Ana blows, heat or no heat.

The steps that came down the hall were the casual ordinary steps of one man. But they stopped outside my door, and somebody knocked.

I pointed to the dressing-room behind the wall-bed. She stood up without a sound, her bag clenched against her side. I pointed again, to her glass. She lifted it swiftly, slid across the carpet, through the door, drew the door quietly shut after her.

I didn't know just what I was going to all this trouble for.

The knocking sounded again. The backs of my hands were wet. I creaked my chair and stood up and made a loud yawning sound. Then I went over and opened the door – without a gun. That was a mistake.

3

I didn't know him at first. Perhaps for the opposite reason Waldo hadn't seemed to know him. He'd had a hat on all the time over at the cocktail bar and he didn't have one on now. His hair ended completely and exactly where his hat would start. Above that line was hard white sweatless skin almost as glaring as scar tissue. He wasn't just twenty years older. He was a different man.

But I knew the gun he was holding, the .22 target automatic with the big front sight. And I knew his eyes. Bright, brittle, shallow eyes like the eyes of a lizard.

He was alone. He put the gun against my face very lightly and said between his teeth: 'Yeah, me. Let's go on in.'

I backed in just far enough and stopped. Just the way he would want me to, so he could shut the door without moving much. I knew from his eyes that he would want me to do just that.

I wasn't scared. I was paralysed.

When he had the door shut he backed me some more, slowly, until there was something against the back of my legs. His eyes looked into mine.

'That's a card table,' he said. 'Some goon here plays chess. You?'

I swallowed. 'I don't exactly play it. I just fool around.'

'That means two,' he said with a kind of hoarse softness, as if some cop had hit him across the windpipe with a black-jack once, in a third-degree session.

'It's a problem,' I said. 'Not a game. Look at the pieces.'

'I wouldn't know.'

'Well, I'm alone,' I said, and my voice shook just enough.

'It don't make any difference,' he said. 'I'm washed up anyway. Some nose puts the but on me to-morrow, next week, what the hell? I just didn't like your map, pal. And that smug-faced pansy in the barcoat that played left tackle for Fordham or something. To hell with guys like you guys.'

I didn't speak or move. The big front sight raked my cheek lightly, almost caressingly. The man smiled.

'It's kind of good business too,' he said. 'Just in case. An old con like me don't make good prints – not even when he's lit. And if I don't make good prints all I got against me is two witnesses. The hell with it. You're slammin' off, pal. I guess you know that.'

'What did Waldo do to you?' I tried to make it sound as if I wanted to know, instead of just not wanting to shake too hard.

'Stooled on a bank job in Michigan and got me four years. Got himself a nolle prosse. Four years in Michigan ain't no summer cruise. They make you be good in them lifer states.'

'How'd you know he'd come in there?' I croaked.

'I didn't. Oh yeah, I was lookin' for him. I was wanting to see him all right. I got a flash of him on the street night before last but I lost him. Up to then I wasn't lookin' for him. Then I was. A cute guy, Waldo. How is he?'

'Dead,' I said.

'I'm still good,' he chuckled. 'Drunk or sober. Well, that don't make no doughnuts for me now. They make me downtown yet?'

I didn't answer him quick enough. He jabbed the gun into my throat and I choked and almost grabbed for it by instinct.

'Naw,' he cautioned me softly. 'Naw. You ain't that dumb.'

I put my hands back, down at my sides, open, the palms towards him. He would want them that way. He hadn't touched me, except with the gun. He didn't seem to care whether I might have one too. He wouldn't – if he just meant the one thing.

He didn't seem to care very much about anything, coming back on that block. Perhaps the hot wind did something to him. It was booming against my shut windows like the surf under a pier.

'They got prints,' I said. 'I don't know how good.'

'They'll be good enough – but not for teletype work. Take 'em airmail time to Washington and back to check 'em right. Tell me why I come here, pal.'

'You heard the kid and me talking in the bar. I told him my name, where I lived.'

'That's how, pal. I said why.' He smiled at me. It was a lousy smile to be the last one you might see.

'Skip it,' I said. 'The hangman won't ask you to guess why he's there.'

'Say, you're tough at that. After you, I visit that kid. I trailed him home from headquarters, but I figure you're the guy to put the bee on first. I trail him home from the city hall, in the rent car Waldo had. From headquarters, pal. Them funny dicks. You can sit in their laps and they don't know you. Start runnin' for a street car and they open up with machine guns and bump two pedestrians, a hacker asleep in his cab, and an old scrubwoman on the second floor workin' a mop. And they miss the guy they're after. Them funny lousy dicks.'

He twisted the gun muzzle in my neck. His eyes looked madder than before.

'I got time,' he said. 'Waldo's rent car don't get a report right away. And they don't make Waldo very soon. I know Waldo. Smart he was. A smooth boy, Waldo.'

'I'm going to vomit,' I said, 'if you don't take that gun out of my throat.'

He smiled and moved the gun down to my heart. 'This about right? Say when.'

I must have spoken louder than I meant to. The door of the dressing-room by the wall-bed showed a crack of darkness. Then an inch. Then four inches. I saw eyes, but I didn't look at them. I stared hard into the baldheaded man's eyes. Very hard. I didn't want him to take his eyes off mine.

'Scared?' he asked softly.

I leaned against his gun and began to shake. I thought he would enjoy seeing me shake. The girl came out through the door. She had her gun in her hand again. I was sorry as hell for her. She'd try to make the door – or scream. Either way it would be curtains – for both of us.

'Well, don't take all night about it,' I bleated. My voice sounded far away, like a voice on a radio on the other side of a street.

'I like this, pal,' he smiled. 'I'm like that.'

The girl floated in the air, somewhere behind him. Nothing was ever more soundless than the way she moved. It wouldn't do any good, though. He wouldn't fool around with her at all. I had known him all my life but I had been looking into his eyes for only five minutes.

'Suppose I yell,' I said.

'Yeah. Suppose you yell. Go ahead and yell,' he said, with his killer's smile.

She didn't go near the door. She was right behind him.

'Well – here's where I yell,' I said.

As if that was the cue she jabbed the little gun hard into his short ribs, without a single sound.

He had to react. It was like a knee reflex. His mouth snapped open and both his arms jumped out from his sides and he arched his back just a little. The gun was pointing at my right eye.

I sank and kneed him with all my strength, in the groin.

His chin came down and I hit it. I hit it as if I was driving the last spike on the first transcontinental railroad. I can still feel it when I flex my knuckles.

His gun raked the side of my face but it didn't go off. He was already limp. He writhed down, gasping, his left side against the floor. I kicked his right shoulder – hard. The gun jumped away from him, skidded on the carpet, under a chair. I heard the chessmen tinkling on the floor behind me somewhere.

The girl stood over him, looking down. Then her wide dark horrified eyes came up and fastened on mine.

'That buys me,' I said. 'Anything I have is yours – now and forever.'

She didn't hear me. Her eyes were strained open so hard that the whites showed under the vivid blue iris. She backed quickly to the door with her little gun up, felt behind her for the knob and twisted it. She pulled the door open and slipped out.

The door shut.

She was bareheaded and without her bolero jacket.

She had only the gun, and the safety catch on that was still set so that she couldn't fire it.

It was silent in the room then, in spite of the wind. Then I heard him gasping on the floor. His face had a greenish pallor. I moved behind him and pawed him for more guns, and didn't find any. I got a pair of store cuffs out of my desk and pulled his arms in front of him and snapped then on his wrists. They would hold if he didn't shake them too hard.

His eyes measured me for a coffin, in spite of their suffering. He lay in the middle of the floor, still on his left side, a twisted, wizened, bald-headed little guy with drawn-back lips and teeth spotted with cheap silver fillings. His mouth looked like a black pit and his breath came in little waves, choked, stopped, came on again, limping.

'I'm sorry, guy,' I grunted. 'What could I do?'

That – to this sort of killer.

I went into the dressing-room and opened the drawer of the chest. Her hat and jacket lay there on my shirts. I put them underneath, at the back, and smoothed the shirts over them. Then I went out to the kitchenette and poured a stiff jolt of whisky and put it down and stood a moment listening to the hot wind howl against the window glass. A garage door banged, and a power-line wire with too much play between the insulators thumped the side of the building with a sound like somebody beating a carpet.

The drink worked on me. I went back in the living-room and opened a window. The guy on the floor hadn't smelled her sandalwood, but somebody else might.

I shut the window again, wiped the palms of my hands and used the phone to dial headquarters.

Copernik was still there. His smart-aleck voice said: 'Yeah? Dalmas? Don't tell me. I bet you got an idea.'

'Make that killer yet?'

'We're not saying, Dalmas. Sorry as all hell and so on. You know how it is.'

'O.K. I don't care who he is. Just come and get him off the floor of my apartment.'

'Holy –' Then his voice hushed and went down low. 'Wait a minute, now. Wait a minute.' A long way off I seemed to hear a door shut. Then his voice again. 'Shoot,' he said softly.

'Handcuffed,' I said. 'All yours. I had to knee him, but he'll be all right. He came here to eliminate a witness.'

Another pause. The voice was full of honey. 'Now listen, boy, who else is in this with you?'

'Who else? Nobody. Just me.'

'Keep it that way, boy. All quiet. O.K.?'

'Think I want all the bums in the neighbourhood in here sightseeing?'

'Take it easy, boy. Easy. Just sit tight and sit still. I'm practically there. No touch nothing. Get me?'

'Yeah.' I gave him the address and apartment number again to save him time.

I could see his big bony face glisten. I got the .22 target gun from under the chair and sat holding it until feet hit the hallway outside my door and knuckles did a quiet tattoo on the panel door.

Copernik was alone. He filled the doorway quickly, pushed me back into the room with a tight grin and shut the door. He stood with his back to it, his hand under the left side of his coat. A big hard bony man with flat cruel eyes.

He lowered them slowly and looked at the man on the floor. The lad's neck was twitching a little. His eyes moved in short stabs – sick eyes.

'Sure it's the guy?' Copernik's voice was hoarse.

'Positive. Where's Ybarra?'

'Oh, he was busy.' He didn't look at me when he said that. 'Those your cuffs?'

'Yeah.'

'Key.'

I tossed it to him. He went down swiftly on one knee beside the killer and took my cuffs off his wrists, tossed them to one side. He got his own off his hip, twisted the bald man's hands behind him and snapped the cuffs on.

'All right, you – ' the killer said tonelessly.

Copernik grinned and balled his fist and hit the hand-cuffed man in the mouth a terrific blow. His head snapped back almost enough to break his neck. Blood dribbled from the lower corner of his mouth.

'Get a towel,' Copernik ordered.

I got a hand towel and gave it to him. He stuffed it between the handcuffed man's teeth, viciously, stood up and rubbed his bony fingers through his ratty blond hair.

'All right. Tell it.'

I told it – leaving the girl out completely. It sounded a little funny. Copernik watched me, said nothing. He rubbed the side of his veined nose. Then he got his comb out and worked on his hair just as he had done earlier in the evening, in the cocktail bar.

I went over and gave him the gun. He looked at it casually, dropped it into his side pocket. His eyes had something in them and his face moved in a hard bright grin.

I bent down and began picking up my chessmen and dropping them into the box. I put the box on the mantel, straightened out a leg of the card table, played around for a while. All the time Copernik watched me. I wanted him to think something out.

At last he came out with it. 'This guy uses a twenty-two,' he said. 'He uses it because he's good enough to get by with that much gun. That means he's good. He knocks at your door, pokes that gat in your belly, walks you back into the room, says he's here to close your mouth for keeps – and yet you take him. You not having any gun. You take him alone. You're kind of good yourself, pal.'

'Listen,' I said, and looked at the floor. I picked up another chessman and twisted it between my fingers. 'I was doing a chess problem,' I said. 'Trying to forget things.'

'You got something on your mind, pal,' Copernik said softly. 'You wouldn't try to fool an old copper, would you, boy?'

'It's a swell pinch and I'm giving it to you,' I said. 'What the hell more do you want?'

The man on the floor made a vague sound behind the towel. His bald head glistened with sweat.

'What's the matter, pal? You been up to something?' Copernik almost whispered.

I looked at him quickly, looked away again. 'All right,' I said. 'You know damn well I couldn't take him alone. He had the gun on me and he shoots where he looks.'

Copernik closed one eye and squinted at me amiably with the other. 'Go on, pal. I kind of thought of that too.'

I shuffled around a little more, to make it look good. I said slowly: 'There was a kid here who pulled a job over in Boyle Heights, a heist job, and didn't take. A two-bit service station stickup. I know his family. He's not really bad. He was here trying to beg train money off me. When the knock came he sneaked in – there.'

I pointed at the wall-bed and the door beside. Copernik's head swivelled slowly, swivelled back. His eyes winked again. 'And this kid had a gun,' he said.

I nodded. 'And he got behind them. That takes guts, Copernik. You've got to give the kid a break. You've got to let him stay out of it.'

'Tag out for this kid?' Copernik asked softly.

'Not yet, he says. He's scared there will be.'

Copernik smiled. 'I'm a homicide man,' he said. 'What have you done, pal?'

I pointed down at the gagged and handcuffed man on the floor. 'You took him, didn't you?' I said gently.

Copernik kept on smiling. A big whitish tongue came out and massaged his thick lower lip. 'How'd I do it?' he whispered.

'Get the slugs out of Waldo?'

'Sure. Long twenty-twos. One smashed on a rib, one good.'

'You're a careful guy. You don't miss any angles. You don't know anything about me. You dropped in on me to see what guns I had.'

Copernik got up and went down on one knee again beside the killer. 'Can you hear me, guy?' he asked with his face close to the face of the man on the floor.

The man made some vague sound. Copernik stood up and yawned. 'Who the hell cares what he says? Go on, pal.'

'You wouldn't expect to find I had anything, but you wanted to look around my place. And while you were mousing around in there' – I pointed to the dressing-room – 'and me not saying anything, being a little sore, maybe, a knock came on the door. So he came in. So after a while you sneaked out and took him.'

'Ah.' Copernik grinned widely, with as many teeth as a horse. 'You're on, pal. I socked him and I kneed him and I took him. You didn't have no gun and the guy swivelled on me pretty sharp and I left-hooked him down the backstairs. O.K.?'

'O.K.,' I said.

'You'll tell it like that downtown?'

'Yeah,' I said.

'I'll protect you, pal. Treat me right and I'll always play ball. Forget about that kid. Let me know if he needs a break.'

He came over and held out his hand. I shook it. It was as clammy as a dead fish. Clammy hands and the people who own them make me sick.

'There's just one thing,' I said. 'This partner of yours – Ybarra. Won't he be a bit sore you didn't bring him along on this?'

Copernik tousled his hair and wiped his hatband with a large yellowish silk handkerchief.

'That guinea?' he sneered. 'To hell with him!' He came close to me and breathed in my face. 'No mistakes, pal – about that story of ours.'

His breath was bad. It would be.

4

There were just five of us in the chief-of-detectives' office when Copernik laid it before them. A stenographer, the chief, Copernik, myself, Ybarra. Ybarra sat on a chair tilted against the side wall. His hat was down over his eyes but their softness loomed underneath, and the small still smile hung at the corners of the cleancut Latin lips. He didn't look directly at Copernik. Copernik didn't look at him at all.

Outside in the corridor there had been photos of Copernik shaking hands with me, Copernik with his hat on straight and his gun in his hand and a stern, purposeful look on his face.

They said they knew who Waldo was, but they wouldn't tell me. I didn't believe they knew, because the chief-of-detectives had a morgue photo of Waldo on his desk. A beautiful job, his hair combed, his tie straight, the light hitting his eyes just right to make them glisten. Nobody would have known it was a photo of a dead man with two bullet holes in his heart. He looked like a dance-hall sheik making up his mind whether to take the blonde or the redhead.

It was about midnight when I got home. The apartment-door was locked and while I was fumbling for my keys a low voice spoke to me out of the darkness.

All it said was: 'Please!' but I knew it. I turned and looked at a dark Cadillac coupé parked just off the loading zone. It had no lights. Light from the street touched the brightness of a woman's eyes.

I went over there. 'You're a darn fool,' I said.

She said: 'Get in.'

I climbed in and she started the car and drove it a block and a half along Franklin and turned down Kingsley Drive. The hot wind still burned and blustered. A radio lilted from an open, sheltered, side window of an apartment house. There were a lot of parked cars but she found a vacant space behind a small brand-new Packard cabriolet that had the dealer's sticker on the windshield glass. After she'd jockeyed us up to the kerb she leaned back in the corner with her gloved hands on the wheel.

She was all in black now, or dark brown, with a small foolish hat. I smelled the sandalwood in her perfume.

'I wasn't very nice to you, was I?' she said.

'All you did was save my life.'

'What happened?'

'I called the law and fed a few lies to a cop I don't like and gave him all the credit for the pinch and that was that. That guy you took away from me was the man who killed Waldo.'

'You mean – you didn't tell them about me?'

'Lady,' I said again, 'all you did was save my life. What else do you want done? I'm ready, willing, and I'll try to be able.'

She didn't say anything, or move.

'Nobody learned who you are from me,' I said. 'Incidentally, I don't know myself.'

'I'm Mrs Frank C. Barsaly, Two-twelve Fremont Place,

Olympia. Two-four-five-nine-six. Is that what you wanted?'

'Thanks,' I mumbled, and rolled a dry unlit cigarette around in my fingers. 'Why did you come back?' Then I snapped the fingers of my left hand. 'The hat and jacket,' I said, 'I'll go up and get them.'

'It's more than that,' she said. 'I want my pearls.'

I might have jumped a little. It seemed as if there had been enough without pearls.

A car tore by down the street going twice as fast as it should. A thin bitter cloud of dust lifted in the street lights and whirled and vanished. The girl ran the window up quickly against it.

'All right,' I said. 'Tell me about the pearls. We have had a murder and a mystery woman and a mad killer and a heroic rescue and a police detective framed into making a false report. Now we will have pearls. All right – feed it to me.'

'I was to buy them for five thousand dollars. From the man you call Waldo and I call Joseph Choate. He should have had them.'

'No pearls,' I said. 'I saw what came out of his pockets. A lot of money but no pearls.'

'Could they be hidden in his apartment?'

'Yes,' I said. 'So far as I know he could have had them hidden anywhere in California except in his pockets. How's Mr Barsaly this hot night?'

'He's still downtown at his meeting. Otherwise I couldn't have come.'

'Well, you could have brought him,' I said. 'He could have sat in the rumble seat.'

'Oh, I don't know,' she said. 'Frank weighs two hundred pounds and he's pretty solid. I don't think he would like to sit in the rumble seat, Mr Dalmas.'

'What the hell are we talking about, anyway?'

She didn't answer. Her gloved hands tapped lightly, provokingly on the rim of the slender wheel. I threw the unlit cigarette out of the window, turned a little and took hold of her.

I was shaking when I let go of her. She pulled as far away from me as she could against the side of the car and rubbed the back of her glove against her mouth. I sat quite still.

We didn't speak for some time. Then she said very slowly: 'I meant you to do that. But I wasn't always that way. It's only been since Stan Phillips was killed in his plane. If it hadn't been for that, I'd be Mrs Phillips now. Stan gave me the pearls. They cost fifteen thousand dollars, he said, once. White pearls, forty-one of them, the largest about a third of an inch across. I don't know how many grains. I never had them appraised or showed them to a jeweller, so I don't know those things. But I loved them on Stan's account. I loved Stan. The way you do just the one time. Can you understand?'

'What's your first name?' I asked.

'Lola.'

'Go on talking, Lola.' I got another dry cigarette out of my pocket and fumbled it between my fingers just to give them something to do.

'They had a simple silver clasp in the shape of a two-bladed propeller. There was one small diamond where the boss would be. That was because I told Frank they were store pearls I had bought myself. He didn't know the difference. It's not so easy to tell, I dare say. You see – Frank is pretty jealous.'

In the darkness she came closer to me and her side touched my side. But I didn't move this time. The wind howled and the trees shook. I kept on rolling the cigarette around in my fingers.

'I suppose you've read that story,' she said. 'About the wife and the real pearls and her telling her husband – '

'I've read it,' I said.

'I hired Joseph. My husband was in Argentina at the time. I was pretty lonely.'

'*You* should be lonely,' I said.

'Joseph and I went driving a good deal. Sometimes we had a drink or two together. But that's all. I don't go around –'

'You told him about the pearls,' I snarled. 'And when your two hundred pounds of beef came back from Argentina and kicked him out – he took the pearls, because he knew they were real. And then offered them back to you for five grand.'

'Yes,' she said simply. 'Of course I didn't want to go to the police. And of course in the circumstances Joseph wasn't afraid of my knowing where he lived.'

'Poor Waldo,' I said. 'I feel kind of sorry for him. It was a hell of a time to run into an old friend that had a down on you.'

I struck a match on my shoe sole and lit the cigarette. The tobacco was so dry from the hot wind that it burned like grass. The girl sat quietly beside me, her hands on the wheel again.

'Hell with women – these fliers,' I said. 'And you're still in love with him, or think you are. Where did you keep the pearls?'

'In a Russian malachite jewellery box on my dressing-table. With some other costume jewellery. I had to, if I ever wanted to wear them.'

'And they were worth fifteen grand. And you think Joseph might have hidden them in his apartment. Thirty-one, wasn't it?'

'Yes,' she said. 'I guess it's a lot to ask.'

I opened the door and got out of the car. 'I've been paid,' I said. 'I'll go look. The doors in my apartment house are not very obstinate. The cops will find out where Waldo lived when they publish his photo, but not to-night, I guess.'

'It's awfully sweet of you,' she said. 'Shall I wait here?'

I stood with a foot on the running-board, leaning in, looking at her. I didn't answer her question. I just stood there looking in at the shine of her eyes. Then I shut the car door and walked up the street towards Franklin.

Even with the wind shrivelling my face I could still smell the sandalwood in her hair. And feel her lips.

I unlocked the Berglund door, walked through the silent lobby to the elevator, and rode up to 3. Then I soft-footed along the silent corridor and peered down at the sill of Apartment 31. No light. I rapped – the old light, confidential tatto of the bootlegger with the big smile and the extra-deep hip pockets. No answer. I took the piece of thick hard celluloid that pretended to be a window over the driver's licence in my wallet, and eased it between the lock and the jamb, leaning hard on the knob, pushing it towards the hinges. The edge of the celluloid caught the slope of the spring lock and snapped it back with a small brittle sound, like an icicle breaking. The door yielded and I went into near darkness. Street light filtered in and touched a high spot here and there.

I shut the door and snapped the light on and just stood. There was a queer smell in the air. I made it in a moment, – the smell of dark-cured tobacco. I prowled over to a smoking-stand by the window and looked down at four brown butts – Mexican or South American cigarettes.

Upstairs, on my floor, feet hit the carpet and somebody went into a bathroom. I heard the toilet flush. I went into the bathroom of Apartment 31. A little rubbish, nothing, no place to hide anything. The kitchenette was a longer job but I only half searched. I knew there were no pearls in that apartment. I knew Waldo had been on his way out and that he was in a hurry and that something was riding him when he turned and took two bullets from an old friend.

I went back to the living-room and swung the wall-bed and looked past its mirror side into the dressing-room for signs of still current occupancy. Swinging the bed farther I was no longer looking for pearls. I was looking at a man.

He was small, middle-aged, iron-grey at the temples, with

a very dark skin, dressed in a fawn-coloured suit with a wine-coloured tie. His neat little brown hands hung limply by his sides. His small feet, in pointed polished shoes, pointed almost at the floor.

He was hanging by a belt around his neck from the metal top of the bed. His tongue stuck out further than I thought it possible for a tongue to stick out.

He swung a little and I didn't like that, so I pulled the bed down and he nestled quietly between the two clamped pillows. I didn't touch him yet. I didn't have to touch him to know that he would be cold as ice.

I went around him into the dressing-room and used my handkerchief on drawer-knobs. The place was stripped clean except for the light litter of a man living alone.

I came out of there and began on the man. No wallet. Waldo would have taken that and ditched it. A flat box of cigarettes, half full, stamped in gold: 'Louis Tapia y Cia, Calle de Paysand, 19, Montevideo.' Matches from the Spezzia Club. An under-arm holster of dark grained leather and in it a 9 millimetre Mauser.

The Mauser made him a professional, so I didn't feel so badly. But not a very good professional, or bare hands would not have finished him, with the Mauser – a gun you can blast through a wall with – undrawn in his shoulder holster.

I made a little sense of it, not much. Four of the brown cigarettes had been smoked, so there had been either waiting or discussion. Somewhere along the line Waldo had got the little man by the throat and held him in just the right way to make him pass out in a matter of seconds. The Mauser had been less useful to him than a toothpick. Then Waldo had hung him up by the strap, probably dead already. That would account for haste, for cleaning out the apartment, for Waldo's anxiety about the girl. It would account for the car left unlocked outside the cocktail bar.

That is, it would account for these things if Waldo had

killed him, if this was really Waldo's apartment – if I wasn't just being kidded.

I examined some more pockets. In the left trouser one I found a gold penknife, some silver. In the left hip pocket a handkerchief, folded, scented. On the right hip another, unfolded but clean. In the right leg pocket four or five tissue handkerchiefs. A clean little guy. He didn't like to blow his nose on his handkerchief. Under these there was a small new keytainer holding four new keys – car keys. Stamped in gold on the keytainer was: Compliments of R. H. Vogelsang, Inc. 'The Packard House'.

I put everything as I had found it, swung the bed back, used my handkershief on knobs and other projections, and flat surfaces, killed the light and poked my nose out the door. The hall was empty. I went down to the street and around the corner to Kingsley Drive. The Cadillac hadn't moved.

I opened the car door and leaned on it. She didn't seem to have moved, either. It was hard to see any expression on her face. Hard to see anything but her eyes and chin, but not hard to smell the sandalwood.

'That perfume,' I said, 'would drive a deacon nuts. . . no pearls.'

'Well – thanks for trying,' she said in a low, soft, vibrant voice. 'I guess I can stand it. Shall I . . . Do we . . . Or . . .?'

'You go on home now,' I said. 'And whatever happens you never saw me before. Whatever happens. Just as you may never see me again.'

'I'd hate –'

'Good luck, Lola.' I shut the car door and stepped back.

The lights blazed on, the motor turned over. Against the wind at the corner the big coupé made a slow contemptuous turn and was gone. I stood there by the vacant space at the kerb where it had been.

It was quite dark there now. Windows had become blanks in the apartment where the radio sounded. I stood looking at the back of a Packard cabriolet which seemed to be brand new. I had seen it before – before I went upstairs, in the same place, in front of Lola's car. Parked, dark, silent, with a blue sticker pasted to the right-hand corner of the shiny windshield.

And in my mind I was looking at something else, a set of brand-new car keys in a keytainer stamped, 'The Packard House', upstairs, in a dead man's pocket.

I went up to the front of the cabriolet and put a small pocket flash on the blue slip. It was the same dealer all right. Written in ink below his name and slogan was a name and address – Eugenie Kolchenko, 5315 Arvieda Street, West Los Angeles.

It was crazy. I went back up to Apartment 31, jimmied the door as I had done before, stepped in behind the wall-bed and took the keytainer from the trousers pocket of the neat brown dangling corpse. I was back down on the street beside the cabriolet in five minutes. The keys fitted.

5

It was a small house, near a canyon rim out beyond Saw-telle, with a circle of writhing eucalyptus trees in front of it. Beyond that, on the other side of the street, one of those parties was going on where they come out and smash bottles on the sidewalk with a whoop like Yale making a touchdown against Princeton.

There was a wire fence at my number and some rose-trees, and a flagged walk and a garage that was wide open and had no car in it. There was no car in front of the house either. I rang the bell. There was a long wait, then the door opened rather suddenly.

I wasn't the man she had been expecting. I could see it in her glittering kohl-rimmed eyes. Then I couldn't see anything in them. She just stood and looked at me, a long, lean, hungry brunette, with rouged cheekbones, thick black hair parted in the middle, a mouth made for three-decker sandwiches, coral-and-gold pyjamas, sandals – and gilded toenails. Under her ear lobes a couple of miniature temple bells gonged lightly in the breeze. She made a slow disdainful motion with a cigarette in a holder as long as a baseball bat.

'We-el, what ees it, little man? You want sometheeng? You are lost from the bee-ootiful party across the street, hein?'

'Ha, ha,' I said, 'Quite a party, isn't it? No. I just brought your car home. Lost it, didn't you?'

Across the street somebody had delirium tremens in the front yard and a mixed quartet tore what was left of the night into small strips and did what they could to make the strips miserable. While this was going on the exotic brunette didn't move more than one eyelash.

She wasn't beautiful, she wasn't even pretty, but she looked as if things would happen where she was.

'You have said what?' she got out, at last, in a voice as silky as a burnt crust of toast.

'Your car.' I pointed over my shoulder and kept my eyes on her. She was the type that uses a knife.

The long cigarette holder dropped very slowly to her side and the cigarette fell out of it. I stamped it out, and that put me in the hall. She backed away from me and I shut the door.

The hall was like the long hall of a railroad flat. Lamps glowed pinkly in iron brackets. There was a bead curtain at the end, a tiger skin on the floor. The place went with her.

'You're Miss Kolchenko?' I asked, not getting any more action.

'Ye-es. I am Mees Kolchenko. What the 'ell you want?'

She was looking at me now as if I had come to wash the windows, but at an inconvenient time.

I got a card out with my left hand, held it out to her. She

read it in my hand, moving her head just enough. 'A detective?' she breathed.

'Yeah.'

She said something in a spitting language. Then in English: 'Come in! Thees damn wind dry up my skeen like so much teesue paper.'

'We're in,' I said. 'I just shut the door. Snap out of it, Nazimova. Who was he? The little guy?'

Beyond the bead curtain a man coughed. She jumped as if she had been stuck with an oyster fork. Then she tried to smile. It wasn't very successful.

'A reward,' she said softly. 'You weel wait 'ere? Ten dollars it is fair to pay, no?'

'No,' I said.

I reached a finger towards her slowly and added: 'He's dead.'

She jumped about three feet and let out a yell.

A chair creaked harshly. Feet pounded beyond the bead curtain, a large hand plunged into view and snatched it aside, and a big hard-looking blond man was with us. He had a purple robe over his pyjamas. His right hand held something in his robe pocket. He stood quite still as soon as he was through the curtain, his feet planted solidly, his jaw out, his colourless eyes like grey ice. He looked like a man who would be hard to take out on an off-tackle play.

'What's the matter, honey?' He had a solid, blurring voice, with just the right sappy tone to belong to a guy who would go for a woman with gilded toenails.

'I came about Miss Kolchenko's car,' I said.

'Well, you could take your hat off,' he said. 'Just for a light workout.'

I took it off and apologized.

'O.K.,' he said, and kept his right hand shoved down hard to the purple pocket. 'So you came about Miss Kolchenko's car. Take it from there.'

I pushed past the woman and went closer to him. She

shrank back against the wall and flattened her palms against it. Camille in a high-school play. The long holder lay empty at her toes.

When I was six feet from the big man he said easily: 'I can hear you from there. Just take it easy. I've got a gun in this pocket and I've had to learn to use one. Now about the car?'

'The man who borrowed it couldn't bring it,' I said, and pushed the card I was still holding towards his face. He barely glanced at it. He looked back at me.

'So what?' he said.

'Are you always this tough?' I asked, 'or only when you have your pyjamas on?'

'So why couldn't he bring it himself?' he asked. 'And skip the mushy talk.'

The dark woman made a stuffed sound at my elbow.

'It's all right, honeybunch,' the man said. 'I'll handle this. Go on in.'

She slid past both of us and flicked through the bead curtain.

I waited a little while. The big man didn't move a muscle. He didn't look any more bothered than a toad in the sun.

'He couldn't bring it because somebody bumped him off,' I said. 'Let's see you handle that.'

'Yeah?' he said. 'Did you bring him with you to prove it?'

'No,' I said. 'But if you put your tie and crush hat on, I'll take you down and show you.'

'Who the hell did you say you were, now?'

'I didn't say. I thought maybe you could read.' I held the card at him some more.

'Oh, that's right,' he said. 'John Dalmas, Private Investigator. Well, well. So I should go with you to look at who, why?'

'Maybe he stole the car,' I said.

The big man nodded. 'That's a thought. Maybe he did. Who?'

'The little brown guy who had the keys to it in his pocket, and had it parked around the corner from the Berglund Apartments.'

He thought that over, without any apparent embarrassment. 'You've got something there,' he said. 'Not much. But a little. I guess this must be the night of the Police Smoker. So you're doing all their work for them.'

'Huh?'

'The card says private detective to me,' he said. 'Have you got some cops outside that were too shy to come in?'

'No, I'm alone.'

He grinned. The grin showed white ridges in his tanned skin. 'So you find somebody dead and take some keys and find a car and come riding out here – all alone. No cops. Am I right?'

'Correct.'

He sighed. 'Let's go inside,' he said. He yanked the bead curtain aside and made an opening for me to go through. 'It might be you have an idea I ought to hear.'

I went past him and he turned, keeping his heavy pocket towards me. I hadn't noticed until I got quite close that there were beads of sweat on his face. It might have been the hot wind, but I don't think so.

We were in the living-room of the house.

We sat down and looked at each other across a dark floor, on which a few Navajo rugs and a few dark Turkish rugs made a decorating combination with some well-used over-stuffed furniture. There was a fireplace, a small baby grand, a Chinese screen, a tall Chinese lantern on a teakwood pedestal, and gold net curtains against lattice windows. The windows to the south were open. A fruit tree with a white-washed trunk whipped about outside the screen, adding its bit to the noise from across the street.

The big man eased back into a brocaded chair and put his slippered feet on a footstool. He kept his right hand where it had been since I met him – on his gun.

The brunette hung around in the shadows and a bottle gurgled and her temple bells gonged in her ears.

'It's all right, honeybunch,' the man said. 'It's all under control. Somebody bumped somebody off and this lad thinks we're interested. Just sit down and relax.'

The girl tilted her head and poured half a tumbler of whisky down her throat. She sighed, said, 'Goddam' in a casual voice, and curled up on a davenport. It took all of the davenport. She had plenty of legs. Her gilded toenails winked at me from the shadowy corner where she kept herself quiet from then on.

I got a cigarette out without being shot at, lit it and went into my story. It wasn't all true, but some of it was. I told them about the Berglund Apartments and that I had lived there and that Waldo was living there in Apartment 31 on the floor below mine and that I had been keeping an eye on him for business reasons.

'Waldo what?' the blond man put in. 'And what business reasons?'

'Mister,' I said, 'have you no secrets?' He reddened slightly.

I told him about the cocktail lounge across the street from the Berglund and what had happened there. I didn't tell him about the printed bolero jacket or the girl who had worn it. I left her out of the story altogether.

'It was an undercover job – from my angle,' I said. 'If you know what I mean.' He reddened again, bit his teeth. I went on: 'I got back from the city hall without telling anybody I knew Waldo. In due time, when I decided they couldn't find out where he lived that night, I took the liberty of examining his apartment.'

'Looking for what?' the big man said thickly.

'For some letters. I might mention in passing there was nothing there at all – except a dead man. Strangled and hanging by a belt to the top of the wall-bed – well out of sight. A small man, about forty-five, Mexican or South American, well-dressed in a fawn-coloured – '

'That's enough,' the big man said. 'I'll bite, Dalmas. Was it a blackmail job you were on?'

'Yeah. The funny part was this little brown man had plenty of gun under his arm.'

'He wouldn't have five hundred bucks in twenties in his pocket, of course? Or are you saying?'

'He wouldn't. But Waldo had over seven hundred in currency when he was killed in the cocktail bar.'

'Looks like I underrated this Waldo,' the big man said calmly. 'He took my guy and his payoff money, gun and all. Waldo have a gun?'

'Not on him.'

'Get us a drink, honeybunch,' the big man said. 'Yes, I certainly did sell this Waldo person shorter than a bargain-counter shirt.'

The brunette unwound her legs and made two drinks with soda and ice. She took herself another gill without trimmings, wound herself back on the davenport. Her big glittering black eyes watched me solemnly.

'Well, here's how,' the big man said, lifting his glass in salute. 'I haven't murdered anybody, but I've got a divorce suit on my hands from now on. You haven't murdered anybody, the way you tell it, but you laid an egg down at police headquarters. What the hell! Life's a lot of trouble, anyway you look at it. I've still got honeybunch, here. She's a white Russian I met in Shanghai. She's safe as a vault and she looks as if she would cut your throat for a nickel. That's what I like about her. You get the glamour without the risk.'

'You talk damn foolish,' the girl spat at him.

'You look O.K. to me,' the big man went on ignoring her. 'That is, for a keyhole peeper. Is there an out?'

'Yeah. But it will cost a little money.'

'I expected that. How much?'

'Say another five hundred.'

'Goddam, thees hot wind make me dry like the ashes of love,' the Russian girl said bitterly.

'Five hundred might do,' the blond man said. 'What do I get for it?'

'If I swing it – you get left out of the story. If I don't – you don't pay.'

He thought it over. His face looked lined and tired now. The small beads of sweat twinkled in his short blond hair.

'This murder will make you talk,' he grumbled. 'The second one, I mean. And I don't have what I was going to buy. And if it's a hush, I'd rather buy it direct.'

'Who was the little brown man?' I asked.

'Name's Leon Valesanos, a Uruguayan. Another of my importations. I'm in a business that takes me a lot of places. He was working in the Spezzia Club in Chiseltown – you know, the strip of Sunset next to Beverly Hills. Working on roulette, I think. I gave him the five hundred to go down to this – this Waldo — and buy back some bills for stuff Miss Kolchenko had charged to my account and delivered here. That wasn't bright, was it? I had them in my brief case and this Waldo got a chance to steal them. What's your hunch about what happened?'

I sipped my drink and looked at him down my nose. 'Your Uruguayan pal probably talked cut and Waldo didn't listen good. Then the little guy thought maybe the Mauser might help his argument – and Waldo was too quick for him. I wouldn't say Waldo was a killer – not by intention. A black-mailer seldom is. Maybe he lost his temper and maybe he just held on to the little guy's neck too long. Then he had to take it on the lam. But he had another date, with more money coming up. And he worked the neighbourhood looking for the party. And accidentally he ran into a pal who was hostile enough and drunk enough to blow him down.'

'There's a hell of a lot of coincidence in all this business,' the big man said.

'It's the hot wind,' I grinned. 'Everybody's screwy to-night.'

'For the five hundred you guarantee nothing? If I don't

get my cover-up, you don't get your dough. Is that it?'

'That's it,' I said, smiling at him.

'Screwy is right,' he said, and drained his highball. 'I'm taking you up on it.'

'There are just two things,' I said softly, leaning forward in my chair. 'Waldo had a getaway car parked outside the cocktail bar where he was killed, unlocked with the motor running. The killer took it. There's always the chance of a kickback from that direction. You see, all Waldo's stuff must have been in that car.'

'Including my bills and your letters.'

'Yeah. But the police are reasonable about things like that – unless you're good for a lot of publicity. If you're not, I think I can eat some stale dog downtown and get by. If you are – that's the second thing. What did you say your name was?'

The answer was a long time coming. When it came I didn't get as much kick out of it as I thought I would. All at once it was too logical.

'Frank C. Barsaly,' he said.

After a while the Russian girl called me a taxi. When I left the party across the street was still doing all that a party could do. I noticed the walls of the house were still standing. That seemed a pity.

6

When I unlocked the glass entrance door of the Berglund I smelled policemen. I looked at my wrist watch. It was nearly 3 a.m. In the dark corner of the lobby a man dozed in a chair with a newspaper over his face. Large feet stretched out before him. A corner of the paper lifted an inch, dropped again. The man made no other movement.

I went on along the hall to the elevator and rode up to my floor. I soft-footed along the hallway, unlocked my door, pushed it wide and reached in for the light-switch.

A chain-switch tinkled and light glared from a standing-lamp by the easy chair, beyond the card table in which my chessmen were still scattered.

Copernik sat there with a stiff unpleasant grin on his face. The short dark man, Ybarra, sat across the room from him, on my left, silent, half-smiling as usual.

Copernik showed more of his big yellow horse teeth and said: 'Hi. Long time no see. Been out with the girls?'

I shut the door and took my hat off and wiped the back of my neck slowly, over and over again. Copernik went on grinning. Ybarra looked at nothing with his soft dark eyes.

'Take a seat, pal,' Copernik drawled. 'Make yourself at home. We got pow-pow to make. Boy, do I hate this night sleuthing. Did you know you were all out of hooch?'

'I could have guessed it,' I said. I leaned against the wall.

Copernik kept on grinning. 'I always did hate private dicks,' he said, 'but I never had a chance to twist one like I got to-night.'

He reached down lazily beside his chair and picked up a printed bolero jacket, tossed it on the card table. He reached down again and put a wide-brimmed hat beside it.

'I bet you look cuter than all hell with these on,' he said.

I took hold of a straight chair, twisted it around and straddled it, leaned my folded arms on the chair and looked at Copernik.

He got up very slowly – with an elaborate slowness – walked across the room and stood in front of me smoothing his coat down. Then he lifted his open right hand and hit me across the face with it – hard. It stung but I didn't move.

Ybarra looked at the wall, looked at the door, looked at nothing.

'Shame on you, pal,' Copernik said lazily. 'The way you was taking care of this nice exclusive merchandise. Waddled down behind your old shirts. You punk peepers always did make me sick.'

He stood there over me for a moment. I didn't move or speak. I looked into his glazed drinker's eyes. He doubled a fist at his side, then shrugged and turned and went back to the chair.

'O.K.,' he said. 'The rest will keep. Where did you get these things?'

'They belong to a lady.'

'Do tell. They belong to a lady. Ain't you the light-hearted – ! I'll tell you what lady they belong to. They belong to the lady a guy named Waldo asked about in a bar across the street – about two minutes before he got shot kind of dead. Or would that have slipped your mind?'

I didn't say anything.

'You was curious about her yourself,' Copernik sneered on. 'But you were smart, pal. You fooled me.'

'That wouldn't make me smart,' I said.

His face twisted suddenly and he started to get up. Ybarra laughed, suddenly and softly, almost under his breath. Copernik's eyes swung on him, hung there. Then he faced me again, blank-eyed.

'The guinea likes you,' he said. 'He thinks you're good.'

The smile left Ybarra's face, but no expression took its place. No expression at all.

Copernik said: 'You knew who the dame was all the time. You knew who Waldo was and where he lived. Right across the hall a floor below you. You knew this Waldo person had bumped a guy off and started to lam, only this broad came into his plans somewhere and he was anxious to meet up with her before he went away. Only he never got the chance. A heist guy from back East named Al Tessilore took care of that by taking care of Waldo. So you met the gal and hid her clothes and sent her on her way and kept your trap glued. That's the way guys like you make your beans. Am I right?'

'Yeah,' I said. 'Except that I only knew these things very recently. Who was Waldo?'

Copernik bared his teeth at me. Red spots burned high on his sallow cheeks. Ybarra, looking down at the floor, said very softly: 'Waldo Ratigan. We got him from Washington by teletype. He was a two-bit porch-climber with a few small terms on him. He drove a car in a bank stickup job in Detroit. He turned the gang in later and got a nolle prosse. One of the gang was this Al Tessilore. He hasn't talked a word, but we think the meeting across the street was purely accidental.'

Ybarra spoke in the soft quiet modulated voice of a man for whom sound have a meaning. I said: 'Thanks, Ybarra. Can I smoke – or would Copernik kick it out of my mouth?'

Ybarra smiled suddenly. 'You may smoke, sure,' he said.

'The guinea likes you all right,' Copernik jeered. 'You never know what a guinea will like, do you?'

I lit a cigarette. Ybarra looked at Copernik and said very softly.

'The word guinea – you overwork it. I don't like it so well applied to me.'

'The hell with what you like, guinea.'

Ybarra smiled a little more. 'You are making a mistake,' he said. He took a pocket nailfile out and began to use it, looking down.

Copernik blared: 'I smelled something rotten on you from the start, Dalmas. So when we made these two mugs, Ybarra and me think we'll drift over and dabble a few more words with you. I bring one of Waldo's morgue photos – nice work, the light just right in his eyes, his tie all straight and a white handkerchief showing just right in his pocket. Nice work. So on the way up, just as a matter of routine, we rout out the manager here and let him lamp it. And he knows the guy. He's here as A. B. Hummel, Apartment Thirty-one. So we go in there and find a stiff. Then we go round and round with that. Nobody knows him yet, but he's got some swell finger bruises under that strap and I hear they fit Waldo's fingers very nicely.'

'That's something,' I said. 'I thought maybe I murdered him.'

Copernik stared at me for a long time. His face had stopped grinning and was just a hard brutal face now. 'Yeah. We got something else even,' he said. 'We got Waldo's getaway car – and what Waldo had in it to take with him.'

I blew cigarette smoke jerkily. The wind pounded the shut windows. The air in the room was foul.

'Oh we're bright boys,' Copernik sneered. 'We never figured you with that much guts. Take a look at this.'

He plunged his bony hand into his coat pocket and drew something up slowly over the edge of the card table, drew it along the green top and left it there stretched out, gleaming. A string of white pearls with a clasp like a two-bladed propeller. They shimmered softly in the thick smoky air.

Lola Barsaly's pearls. The pearls the flier had given her. The guy who was dead, the guy she still loved.

I stared at them, but I didn't move. After a long moment Copernik said almost gravely: 'Nice, ain't they? Would you feel like telling us a story about now, Mis-ter Dalmas?'

I stood up and pushed the chair from under me, walked slowly across the room and stood looking down at the pearls. The largest was perhaps a third of an inch across. They were pure white, iridescent, with a mellow softness. I lifted them slowly off the card table from beside her clothes. They felt heavy, smooth, fine.

'Nice,' I said. 'A lot of the trouble was about these. Yeah, I'll talk now. They must be worth a lot of money.'

Ybarra laughed behind me. It was a very gentle laugh. 'About a hundred dollars,' he said. 'They're good phonies – but they're phony.'

I lifted the pearls again. Copernik's glassy eyes gloated at me. 'How do you tell?' I asked.

'I know pearls,' Ybarra said. 'These are good stuff, the kind women very often have made on purpose, as a kind of insurance. But they are slick like glass. Real pearls are gritty between the edges of the teeth. Try.'

I put two or three of them between my teeth and moved my teeth back and forth, then sideways. Not quite biting them. The beads were hard and slick.

'Yes. They are very good.' Ybarra said. 'Several even have little waves and flat spots, as real pearls might have.'

'Would they cost fifteen grand – if they were real?' I asked.

'Si. Probably. That's hard to say. It depends on a lot of things.'

'This Waldo wasn't so bad,' I said.

Copernik stood up quickly, but I didn't see him swing. I was still looking down at the pearls. His fist caught me on the side of the face, against the molars. I tasted blood at once. I staggered back and made it look like a worse blow than it was.

'Sit down and talk, you – !' Copernik almost whispered. I sat down and used a handkerchief to pat my cheek. I licked at the cut inside my mouth. Then I got up again and went over and picked up the cigarette he had knocked out of my mouth. I crushed it out in a tray and sat down again.

Ybarra filed at his nails and held one up against the lamp. There were beads of sweat on Copernik's eyebrows, at the inner ends.

'You found the beads in Waldo's car,' I said, looking at Ybarra. 'Find any papers?'

He shook his head without looking up.

'I'd believe *you*,' I said. 'Here it is. I never saw Waldo until he stepped into the cocktail bar to-night and asked about the girl. I knew nothing I didn't tell. When I got home and stepped out of the elevator this girl, in the printed bolero jacket and the wide hat and the blue silk crepe dress – all as he had described them – was waiting for the elevator, here, on my floor. And she looked like a nice girl.'

Copernik laughed jeeringly. It didn't make any difference to me. I had him cold. All he had to do was know that. He was going to know it now, very soon.

'I knew what she was up against as a police witness,' I said. 'And I suspected there was something else to it. But I didn't suspect for a minute that there was anything wrong with her. She was just a nice girl in a jam – and she didn't even know she was in a jam. I got her in here. She pulled a gun on me. But she didn't mean to use it.'

Copernik sat up very suddenly and he began to lick his lips. His face had a stony look now. A look like wet grey stone. He didn't make a sound.

'Waldo had been her chauffeur,' I went on. 'His name then was Joseph Choate. Her name is Mrs Frank C. Barsaly. Her husband is a big hydro-electric engineer. Some guy gave her the pearls once and she told her husband they were just store pearls. Waldo got wise somehow there was a romance behind them and when Barsaly came home from South America and fired him, because he was too good-looking, he lifted the pearls.'

Ybarra lifted his head suddenly and his teeth flashed. 'You mean he didn't know they were phony?'

'I thought he fenced the real ones and had imitations fixed up,' I said.

Ybarra nodded. 'It's possible.'

'He lifted something else,' I said. 'Some stuff from Barsaly's briefcase that showed he was keeping a woman – out in Brentwood. He was blackmailing wife and husband both, without either knowing about the other. Get it so far?'

'I get it,' Copernik said harshly, between his tight lips. His face was still wet grey stone. 'Get the hell on with it.'

'Waldo wasn't afraid of them,' I said. 'He didn't conceal where he lived. That was foolish, but it saved a lot of finagling, if he was willing to risk it. The girl came down here to-night with five grand to buy back her pearls. She never met Waldo. She came up here to look for him and walked up a floor before she went back down. A woman's idea of being cagey. So I met her. So I brought her in here. So she was in that dressing-room when Al Tessilore visited me to rub out a witness.' I pointed to the dressing-room door. 'So she came out with her little gun and stuck it in his back and saved my life,' I said.

Copernik didn't move. There was something horrible in his face now. Ybarra slipped his nailfile into a small leather case and slowly tucked it into his pocket.

'Is that all?' he asked gently.

I nodded. 'Except that she told me where Waldo's apartment was and I went in there and looked for the pearls. I found the dead man. In his pocket I found new car keys in a case from a Packard agency. And down on the street I found the Packard and took it to where it came from. Barsaly's kept woman. Barsaly had sent a friend from the Spezzia Club down to buy something and he had tried to buy it with his gun instead of the money Barsaly gave him. And Waldo beat him to the punch.'

'Is that all?' Ybarra asked softly.

'That's all,' I said, licking the torn place on the inside of my cheek.

Ybarra said slowly: 'What do you want?'

Copernik's face convulsed and he slapped his long hard thigh. 'This guy is good,' he jeered. 'He falls for a stray broad and breaks every law in the book and you ask him what does he want? I'll give him what he wants, guinea!'

Ybarra turned his head slowly and looked at him. 'I don't think you will,' he said. 'I think you'll give him a clean bill of health and anything else he wants. He's giving you a lesson on police work.'

Copernik didn't move or make a sound for a long minute. None of us moved. Then Copernik leaned forward and his coat fell open. The butt of his service gun looked out of its underarm holster.

'So what do you want?' he asked me.

'What's on the card table there. The jacket and hat and the phony pearls. And some names kept away from the papers. Is that too much?'

'Yeah – it's too much,' Copernik said almost gently. He swayed sideways and his gun jumped neatly into his hand. He rested his forearm on his thigh and pointed the gun at my stomach.

'I like better that you get a slug in the guts resisting arrest,' he said. 'I like that better, because of a report I made out on Al Tessilore's arrest and how I made the pinch. Because of some photos of me that are in the morning sheets going out about now. I like it better that you don't live long enough to laugh about that, baby.'

My mouth felt suddenly hot and dry. Far off I heard the wind booming. It seemed like the sound of guns.

Ybarra moved his feet on the floor and said coldly: 'You've got a couple of cases all solved, policeman. All you do for it is leave some junk here and keep some names from the papers. Which means from the D.A. If he gets them anyway, too bad for you.'

Copernik said: 'I like the other way.' The blue gun in his hand was like a rock. 'And God help you, if you don't back me up on it.'

Ybarra said: 'If the woman is brought out into the open, you'll be a liar on a police report and a chiseler on your own partner. In a week they won't even speak your name at headquarters. The taste of it would make them sick.'

The hammer clocked back on Copernik's gun and I watched his big bony finger slide in farther around the trigger. The back of my neck was as wet as a dog's nose.

Ybarra stood up. The gun jumped at him. He said: 'We'll see how yellow a guinea is. I'm telling you to put that gun up, Sam.'

He started to move. He moved four even steps. Copernik was a man without a breath of movement, a stone man.

Ybarra took one more step and quite suddenly the gun began to shake.

Ybarra said evenly: 'Put it up Sam. If you keep your head everything lies the way it is. If you don't – you're gone.'

He took one more step. Copernik's mouth opened wide and made a gasping sound and then he sagged in the chair as if he had been hit on the head. His eyelids drooped.

Ybarra jerked the gun out of his hand with a movement so quick it was no movement at all. He stepped back quickly, held the gun low at his side.

'It's the hot wind, Sam. Let's forget it,' he said in the same even, almost dainty voice.

Copernik's shoulders sagged lower and he put his face in his hands. 'O.K.,' he said between his fingers.

Ybarra went softly across the room and opened the door. He looked at me with lazy, half-closed eyes. 'I'd do a lot for a woman who saved my life, too,' he said. 'I'm eating this dish, but as a cop you can't expect me to like it.'

I said: 'The little man in the bed is called Leon Valesanos. He was a croupier at the Spezzia Club.'

'Thanks,' Ybarra said. 'Let's go, Sam.'

Copernik got up heavily and walked across the room and out of the open door and out of my sight. Ybarra stepped through the door after him and started to close it.

I said: 'Wait a minute.'

He turned his head slowly, his left hand on the door, the blue gun hanging down close to his right side.

'I'm not in this for money,' I said. 'The Barsalys live at Two-twelve Fremont Place. You can take the pearls to her. If Barsaly's name stays out of the paper, I get five C's. It goes to the Police Fund. I'm not so damn smart as you think. It just happened that way – and you had a heel for a partner.'

Ybarra looked across the room at the pearls on the card table. His eyes glistened. 'You take them,' he said. 'The five hundred's O.K. I think the fund has it coming.'

He shut the door quietly and in a moment I heard the elevator door clang.

7

I opened a window and stuck my head out into the wind and watched the squad car tool off down the block. The wind blew in hard and I let it blow. A picture fell off the wall and two chessmen rolled off the card table. The material of Lola Barsaly's bolero jacket lifted and shook.

I went out to the kitchenette and drank some Scotch and went back into the living-room and called her – late as it was.

She answered the phone herself, very quickly, with no sleep in her voice.

'Dalmas,' I said. 'O.K. your end?'

'Yes . . . yes,' she said. 'I'm alone.'

'I found something,' I said. 'Or rather the police did. But your dark boy gypped you. I have a string of pearls. They're not real. He sold the real ones, I guess, and made you up a string of ringers, with your clasp.'

She was silent for a long time. Then, a little faintly: 'The police found them?'

'In Waldo's car. But they're not telling. We have a deal. Look at the papers in the morning and you'll be able to figure out why.'

'There doesn't seem to be anything more to say,' she said. 'Can I have the clasp?'

'Yes. Can you meet me to-morrow at four in the Club Esquire bar?'

'You're rather sweet,' she said in a dragged out voice. 'I can. Frank is still at his meeting.'

'Those meetings – they take it out of a guy,' I said. We said good-bye.

I called a West Los Angeles number. He was still there, with the Russian girl.

'You can send me a cheque for five hundred in the morning,' I told him. 'Made out to the Police Fund, if you want to. Because that's where it's going.'

Copernik made the third page of the morning papers with two photos and a nice half-column. The little brown man in Apartment 31 didn't make the paper at all. The Apartment House Association has a good lobby too.

I went out after breakfast and the wind was all gone. It was soft, cool, a little foggy. The sky was close and comfortable and grey. I rode down to the boulevard and picked out the best jewellery store on it and laid a string of pearls on a black velvet mat under a daylight-blue lamp. A man in a wing collar and striped trousers looked down at them languidly.

'How good?' I asked.

'I'm sorry, sir. We don't make appraisals. I can give you the name of an appraiser.'

'Don't kid me,' I said. 'They're Dutch.'

He focused the light a little and leaned down and toyed with a few inches of the string.

'I want a string just like them, fitted to that clasp, and in a hurry,' I added.

'How, like them?' He didn't look up. 'And they're not Dutch. They're Bohemian.'

'O.K., can you duplicate them?'

He shook his head and pushed the velvet pad away as if it soiled him. 'In three months, perhaps. We don't blow glass like that in this country. If you wanted them matched – three months at least. And this house would not do that sort of thing at all.'

'It must be swell to be that snooty,' I said. I put a card under his black sleeve. 'Give me a name that will – and not in three months – and maybe not exactly like them.'

He shrugged, went away with the card, came back in five minutes and handed it back to me. There was something written on the back.

The old Levantine had a shop on Melrose, a junk shop with everything in the window from a folding baby carriage to a French horn, from a mother-of-pearl lorgnette in a faded plush case to one of those .44 Special Single Action Six-shooters they still make for Western peace officers whose grandfathers were tough.

The old Levantine wore a skull cap and two pairs of glasses and a full beard. He studied my pearls, shook his head sadly, and said: 'For twenty dollars, almost so good. Not so good, you understand. Not so good glass.'

'How like will they look?'

He spread his firm strong hands. 'I am telling you the truth,' he said. 'They would not fool a baby.'

'Make them up,' I said. 'With this clasp. And I want the others back too, of course.'

'Yah. Two o'clock,' he said.

Leon Valesanos, the little brown man from Uruguay, made the afternoon papers. He had been found hanging in an unnamed apartment. The police were investigating.

At four o'clock I walked into the long cool bar of the Club Esquire and prowled along the row of booths until I found one where a woman sat alone. She wore a hat like a shallow soup plate with a very wide edge, a brown tailormade suit with a severe mannish shirt and tie.

I sat down beside her and slipped a parcel along the seat. 'You don't open that,' I said. 'In fact you can slip it into the incinerator as it is, if you want to.'

She looked at me with dark tired eyes. Her fingers twisted a thin glass that smelled of peppermint. 'Thanks.' Her face was very pale.

I ordered a highball and the waiter went away. 'Read the papers?'

'Yes.'

'You understand now about this fellow Copernik who stole your act? That's why they won't change the story or bring you into it.'

'It doesn't matter now,' she said. 'Thank you, all the same. Please – please, show them to me.'

I pulled a string of pearls out of the loosely wrapped tissue paper in my pocket and slid them across to her. The silver propeller clasp winked in the light of the wall bracket. The little diamond winked. The pearls were as dull as white soap. They didn't even match in size.

'You were right,' she said tonelessly. 'They are not my pearls.'

The waiter came with my drink and she put her bag on them deftly. When he was gone she fingered them slowly once more, dropped them into the bag and gave me a dry mirthless smile.

'As you said – I'll keep the clasp.'

I said slowly: 'You don't know anything about me. You saved my life last night and we had a moment, but it was just a moment. You still don't know anything about me. There's a detective downtown named Ybarra, a Mexican of the nice sort, who was on the job when the pearls were found in Waldo's suitcase. That's in case you would like to make sure – '

She said, 'Don't be silly. It's all finished. It was a memory. I'm too young to nurse memories. It may be all for the best. I loved Stan Phillips – but he's gone – long gone.'

I stared at her, didn't say anything.

She added quietly: 'This morning my husband told me something I hadn't known. We are to separate. So I have very little to laugh about to-day.'

'I'm sorry,' I said lamely. 'There's nothing to say. I may see you sometime. Maybe not. I don't move much in your circle. Good luck.'

I stood up. We looked at each other for a moment. 'You haven't touched your drink,' she said.

'You drink it. That peppermint stuff will just make you sick.'

I stood there a moment with a hand hard on the table.

'If anybody ever bothers you,' I said, 'let me know.'

I went out of the bar without looking back at her, got into my car and drove west on Sunset and down all the way to the Coast Highway. Everywhere along the way gardens were full of withered and blackened leaves and flowers which the hot wind had burned.

But the ocean looked cool and languid and just the same as ever. I drove on almost to Malibu and then parked and went and sat on a big rock that was inside somebody's wire fence. It was about half-tide and coming in. The air smelled of kelp. I watched the water for a while and then I pulled a string of Bohemian glass imitation pearls out of my pocket and cut the knot at one end and slipped the pearls off one by one.

When I had them all loose in my left hand I held them like that for a while and thought. There wasn't really anything to think about. I was sure.

'To the memory of Mr Stan Phillips,' I said loud. 'Just another four-flusher.'

I flipped her pearls out into the water one by one, at the floating seagulls.

They made little splashes and the seagulls rose off the water and swooped at the splashes.

III

I'll be waiting

AT one o'clock in the morning, Carl, the night porter, turned down the last of three table lamps in the main lobby of the Windermere Hotel. The blue carpet darkened a shade or two and the walls drew back into remoteness. The chairs filled with shadowy loungers. In the corners were memories like cobwebs.

Tony Reseck yawned. He put his head on one side and listened to the frail, twittery music from the radio room beyond a dim arch at the far side of the lobby. He frowned. That should be his radio room after one a.m. Nobody should be in it. That red-haired girl was spoiling his nights.

The frown passed and a miniature of a smile quirked at the corners of his lips. He sat relaxed, a short, pale, paunchy, middle-aged man with long, delicate fingers clasped on the elk's tooth on his watch chain; the long delicate fingers of a sleight-of-hand artist, fingers with shiny, moulded nails and tapering first joints, fingers a little spatulate at the ends. Handsome fingers. Tony Reseck rubbed them gently to gether and there was peace in his quiet sea-grey eyes.

The frown came back on his face. The music annoyed him. He got up with a curious litheness, all in one piece, without moving his clasped hands from the watch chain. At one moment he was leaning back relaxed, and the next he was standing balanced on his feet, perfectly still, so that the movement of rising seemed to be a thing imperfectly perceived, an error of vision.

He walked with small, polished shoes delicately across the

blue carpet and under the arch. The music was louder. It contained the hot, acid blare, the frenetic, jittering runs of a jam session. It was too loud. The red-haired girl sat there and stared silently at the fretted part of the big radio cabinet as though she could see the band with its fixed professional grin and the sweat running down its back. She was curled up with her feet under her on a davenport which seemed to contain most of the cushions in the room. She was tucked among them carefully, like a corsage in the florist's tissue paper.

She didn't turn her head. She leaned there, one hand in a small fist on her peach-coloured knee. She was wearing lounging pyjamas of heavy ribbed silk embroidered with black lotus buds.

'You like Goodman, Miss Cressy?' Tony Reseck asked.

The girl moved her eyes slowly. The light in there was dim, but the violet of her eyes almost hurt. They were large, deep eyes without a trace of thought in them. Her face was classical and without expression.

She said nothing.

Tony smiled and moved his fingers at his sides, one by one, feeling them move. 'You like Goodman, Miss Cressy?' he repeated gently.

'Not to cry over,' the girl said tonelessly.

Tony rocked back on his heels and looked at her eyes. Large, deep, empty eyes. Or were they? He reached down and muted the radio.

'Don't get me wrong,' the girl said. 'Goodman makes money, and a lad that makes legitimate money these days is a lad you have to respect. But this jitterbug music gives me the backdrop of a beer flat. I like something with roses in it.'

'Maybe you like Mozart,' Tony said.

'Go on, kid me,' the girl said.

'I wasn't kidding you, Miss Cressy, I think Mozart was the greatest man that ever lived – and Toscanini is his prophet.'

'I thought you were the house dick.' She put her head back on a pillow and stared at him through her lashes. 'Make me some of that Mozart,' she added.

'It's too late,' Tony sighed. 'You can't get it now.'

She gave him another long lucid glance. 'Got the eye on me, haven't you, flatfoot?' She laughed a little, almost under her breath. 'What did I do wrong?'

Tony smiled his toy smile. 'Nothing, Miss Cressy. Nothing at all. But you need some fresh air. You've been five days in this hotel and you haven't been outdoors. And you have a tower room.'

She laughed again. 'Make me a story about it. I'm bored.'

'There was a girl here once had your suite. She stayed in the hotel a whole week, like you. Without going out at all, I mean. She didn't speak to anybody hardly. What do you think she did then?'

The girl eyed him gravely. 'She jumped her bill.'

He put his long delicate hand out and turned it slowly, fluttering the fingers, with an effect almost like a lazy wave breaking. 'Uh-uh. She sent down for her bill and paid it. Then she told the hop to be back in half an hour for her suitcases. Then she went out on her balcony.'

The girl leaned forward a little, her eyes still grave, one hand capping her peach-coloured knee. 'What did you say your name was?'

'Tony Reseck.'

'Sounds like a hunky.'

'Yeah,' Tony said. 'Polish.'

'Go on, Tony.'

'All the tower suites have private balconies, Miss Cressy. The walls of them are too low for fourteen stories above the street. It was a dark night, that night, high clouds.' He dropped his hand with a final gesture, a farewell gesture. 'Nobody saw her jump. But when she hit, it was like a big gun going off.'

'You're making it up, Tony.' Her voice was a clean dry whisper of sound.

He smiled his toy smile. His quiet sea-green eyes seemed almost to be smoothing the long waves of her hair. 'Eve Cressy,' he said musingly. 'A name waiting for lights to be in.'

'Waiting for a tall dark guy that's no good, Tony. You wouldn't care why. I was married to him once. I might be married to him again. You can make a lot of mistakes in just one lifetime.' The hand on her knee opened slowly until the fingers were strained back as far as they would go. Then they closed quickly and tightly, and even in that dim light the knuckles shone like little polished bones. 'I played him a low trick once. I put him in a bad place – without meaning to. You wouldn't care about that either. It's just that I owe him something.'

He leaned over softly and turned the knob on the radio. A waltz formed itself dimly on the warm air. A tinsel waltz, but a waltz. He turned the volume up. The music gushed from the loud-speaker in a swirl of shadowed melody. Since Vienna died, all waltzes are shadowed.

The girl put her head on one side and hummed three or four bars and stopped with a sudden tightening of her mouth.

'Eve Cressy,' she said. 'It was in lights once. At a bum night club. A dive. They raided it and the lights went out.'

He smiled at her almost mockingly. 'It was no dive while you were there, Miss Cressy. . . . That's the waltz the orchestra always played when the old porter walked up and down in front of the hotel entrance, all swelled up with his medals on his chest. The Last Laugh. Emil Jannings. You wouldn't remember that one, Miss Cressy.'

'Spring, Beautiful Spring,' she said. 'No, I never saw it.'

He walked three steps away from her and turned. 'I have to go upstairs and palm door-knobs. I hope I didn't bother you. You ought to go to bed now. It's pretty late.'

The tinsel waltz stopped and a voice began to talk. The

girl spoke through the voice. 'You really thought something like that – about the balcony?'

He nodded. 'I might have,' he said softly. 'I don't any more.'

'No chance, Tony.' Her smile was a dim lost leaf. 'Come and talk to me some more. Redheads don't jump, Tony. They hang on – and wither.'

He looked at her gravely for a moment and then moved away over the carpet. The porter was standing in the archway that led to the main lobby. Tony hadn't looked that way yet, but he knew somebody was there. He always knew if anybody was close to him. He could hear the grass grow like the donkey in The Blue Bird.

The porter jerked his chin at him urgently. His broad face above the uniform collar looked sweaty and excited. Tony stepped up close to him and they went together through the arch and out to the middle of the dim lobby.

'Trouble?' Tony asked wearily.

'There's a guy outside to see you, Tony. He won't come in. I'm doing a wipe-off on the plate glass of the doors and he comes up beside me, a tall guy. "Get Tony," he says, out of the side of his mouth.'

Tony said: 'Uh-huh,' and looked at the porter's pale blue eyes. 'Who was it?'

'Al, he said to say he was.'

Tony's face became as expressionless as dough. 'Okay.' He started to move off.

The porter caught his sleeve. 'Listen, Tony. You got any enemies?'

Tony laughed politely, his face still like dough.

'Listen, Tony.' The porter held his sleeve tightly. 'There's a big black car down the block, the other way from the hacks. There's a guy standing beside it with his foot on the running board. This guy that spoke to me, he wears a dark-coloured, wrap-around overcoat with a high collar turned up against his ears. His hat's way low. You can't hardly see

his face. He says, "Get Tony," out of the side of his mouth.
You ain't got any enemies, have you, Tony?'

'Only the finance company,' Tony said. 'Beat it.'

He walked slowly and a little stiffly across the blue carpet,
up the three shallow steps to the entrance lobby with the
three elevators on one side and the desk on the other. Only
one elevator was working. Beside the open doors, his arms
folded, the night operator stood silent in a neat blue uniform
with silver facings. A lean, dark Mexican named Gomez. A
new boy, breaking in on the night shift.

The other side was the desk, rose marble, with the night
clerk leaning on it delicately. A small neat man with a wispy
reddish moustache and cheeks so rosy they looked rouged.
He stared at Tony and poked a nail at his moustache.

Tony pointed a stiff index finger at him, folded the other
three fingers tight to his palm, and flicked his thumb up and
down on the stiff finger. The clerk touched the other side of
his moustache and looked bored.

Tony went on past the closed and darked news-stand and
the side entrance to the drugstore, out to the brass-bound
plate-glass doors. He stopped just inside them and took a
deep, hard breath. He squared his shoulders, pushed the
doors open and stepped out into the cold, damp night air.

The street was dark, silent. The rumble of traffic on Wil-
shire, two blocks away, had no body, no meaning. To the
left were two taxis. Their drivers leaned against a fender,
side by side, smoking. Tony walked the other way. The big
dark car was a third of a block from the hotel entrance. Its
lights were dimmed and it was only when he was almost up
to it that he heard the gentle sound of its engine turning
over.

A tall figure detached itself from the body of the car and
strolled towards him, both hands in the pockets of the dark
overcoat with the high collar. From the man's mouth a
cigarette tip glowed faintly, a rusty pearl.

They stopped two feet from each other.

The tall man said: 'Hi, Tony. Long time no see.'

'Hello, Al. How's it going?'

'Can't complain.' The tall man started to take his right hand out of his overcoat pocket, then stopped and laughed quietly. 'I forgot. Guess you don't want to shake hands.'

'That don't mean anything,' Tony said. 'Shaking hands. Monkeys can shake hands. What's on your mind, Al?'

'Still the funny little fat guy, eh, Tony?'

'I guess.' Tony winked his eyes tight. His throat felt tight.

'You like your job back there?'

'It's a job.'

Al laughed his quiet laugh again. 'You take it slow, Tony. I'll take it fast. So it's a job and you want to hold it. Oke. There's a girl named Eve Cressy flopping in your quiet hotel. Get her out. Fast and right now.'

'What's the trouble?'

The tall man looked up and down the street. A man behind in the car coughed lightly. 'She's hooked with a wrong number. Nothing against her personal, but she'll lead trouble to you. Get her out, Tony. You got maybe an hour.'

'Sure,' Tony said aimlessly, without meaning.

Al took his hand out of his pocket and stretched it against Tony's chest. He gave him a light, lazy push. 'I wouldn't be telling you just for the hell of it, little fat brother. Get her out of there.'

'Okay,' Tony said, without any tone in his voice.

The tall man took back his hand and reached for the car door. He opened it and started to slip in like a lean black shadow.

Then he stopped and said something to the men in the car and got out again. He came back to where Tony stood silent, his pale eyes catching a little dim light from the street.

'Listen, Tony. You always kept your nose clean. You're a good brother, Tony.'

Tony didn't speak.

Al leaned towards him, a long urgent shadow, the high

collar almost touching his ears. 'It's trouble business, Tony. The boys won't like it, but I'm telling you just the same. This Cressy was married to a lad named Johnny Ralls. Ralls is out of Quentin two, three days, or a week. He did a three-spot for manslaughter. The girl put him there. He ran down an old man one night when he was drunk, and she was with him. He wouldn't stop. She told him to go in and tell it, or else. He didn't go in. So the Johns come for him.'

Tony said, 'That's too bad.'

'It's kosher, kid. It's my business to know. This Ralls flapped his mouth in stir about how the girl would be waiting for him when he got out, all set to forgive and forget, and he was going straight to her.'

Tony said: 'What's he to you?' His voice had a dry, stiff crackle, like thick paper.

Al laughed. 'The trouble boys want to see him. He ran a table at a spot on the Strip and figured out a scheme. He and another guy took the house for fifty grand. The other lad coughed up, but we still need Johnny's twenty-five. The trouble boys don't get paid to forget.'

Tony looked up and down the dark street. One of the taxi drivers flicked a cigarette stub in a long arc over the top of one of the cabs. Tony watched it fall and spark on the pavement. He listened to the quiet sound of the big car's motor.

'I don't want any part of it,' he said. 'I'll get her out.'

Al backed away from him, nodding. 'Wise kid. How's mom these days?'

'Okay,' Tony said.

'Tell her I was asking for her.'

'Asking for her isn't anything,' Tony said.

Al turned quickly and got into the car. The car curved lazily in the middle of the block and drifted back toward the corner. Its lights went up and sprayed on a wall. It turned a corner and was gone. The lingering smell of its exhaust drifted past Tony's nose. He turned and walked back to the hotel, and into it. He went along to the radio room.

The radio still muttered, but the girl was gone from the davenport in front of it. The pressed cushions were hollowed out by her body. Tony reached down and touched them. He thought they were still warm. He turned the radio off and stood there, turning a thumb slowly in front of his body, his hand flat against his stomach. Then he went back through the lobby toward the elevator bank and stood beside a majolica jar of white sand. The clerk fussed behind a pebbled-glass screen at one end of the desk. The air was dead.

The elevator bank was dark. Tony looked at the indicator of the middle car and saw that it was at 14.

'Gone to bed,' he said under his breath.

The door of the porter's room beside the elevators opened and the little Mexican night operator came out in street clothes. He looked at Tony with a quiet sidewise look out of eyes the colour of dried-out chestnuts.

'Good night, boss.'

'Yeah,' Tony said absently.

He took a thin dappled cigar out of his vest pocket and smelled it. He examined it slowly, turning it around in his neat fingers. There was a small tear along the side. He frowned at that and put the cigar away.

There was a distant sound and the hand on the indicator began to steal around the bronze dial. Light glittered up in the shaft and the straight line of the car floor dissolved the darkness below. The car stopped and the doors opened, and Carl came out of it.

His eyes caught Tony's with a kind of jump and he walked over to him, his head on one side, a thin shine along his pink upper lip.

'Listen, Tony.'

Tony took his arm in a hard swift hand and turned him. He pushed him quickly, yet somehow casually, down the steps to the dim main lobby and steered him into a corner. He let go of the arm. His throat tightened again, for no reason he could think of.

'Well?' he said darkly. 'Listen to what?'

The porter reached into a pocket and hauled out a dollar bill. 'He gimme this,' he said loosely. His glittering eyes looked past Tony's shoulder at nothing. They winked rapidly. 'Ice and ginger ale.'

'Don't stall,' Tony growled.

'Guy in 14B,' the porter said.

'Lemme smell your breath.'

The porter leaned towards him obediently.

'Liquor,' Tony said harshly.

'He gimme a drink.'

Tony looked down at the dollar bill. 'Nobody's in 14B. Not on my list,' he said.

'Yeah. There is.' The porter licked his lips, and his eyes opened and shut several times. 'Tall dark guy.'

'All right,' Tony said crossly. 'All right. There's a tall dark guy in 14B and he gave you a buck and a drink. Then what?'

'Gat under his arm,' Carl said, and blinked.

Tony smiled, but his eyes had taken on the lifeless glitter of thick ice. 'You take Miss Cressy up to her room?'

Carl shook his head. 'Gomez, I saw her go up.'

'Get away from me,' Tony said between his teeth. 'And don't accept any more drinks from the guests.'

He didn't move until Carl had gone back into his cubbyhole by the elevators and shut the door. Then he moved silently up the three steps and stood in front of the desk, looking at the veined rose marble, the onyx pen set, the fresh registration card in its leather frame. He lifted a hand and smacked it down hard on the marble. The clerk popped out from behind the glass screen like a chipmunk coming out of its hole.

Tony took a flimsy out of his breast pocket and spread it on the desk. 'No 14B on this,' he said in a bitter voice.

The clerk wiped politely at his moustache. 'So sorry.

You must have been out to supper when he checked in.'

'Who?'

'Registered as James Watterson, San Diego.' The clerk yawned.

'Ask for anybody?'

The clerk stopped in the middle of the yawn and looked at the top of Tony's head. 'Why, yes. He asked for a swing band. Why?'

'Smart, fast, and funny,' Tony said. 'If you like 'em that way.' He wrote on his flimsy and stuffed it back into his pocket. 'I'm going upstairs and palm doorknobs. There's four tower rooms you ain't rented yet. Get up on your toes, son. You're slipping.'

'I make out,' the clerk drawled, and completed his yawn. 'Hurry back, pop. I don't know how I'll get through the time.'

'You could shave that pink fuzz off your lip,' Tony said, and went across to the elevators.

He opened up a dark one and lit the dome light and shot the car up to fourteen. He darkened it again, stepped out and closed the doors. This lobby was smaller than any other, except the one immediately below it. It had a single blue-panelled door in each of the walls other than the elevator wall. On each door was a gold number and letter with a gold wreath around it. Tony walked over to 14A and put his ear to the panel. He heard nothing. Eve Cressy might be in bed asleep, or in the bathroom, or out on the balcony. Or she might be sitting there in the room, a few feet from the door, looking at the wall. Well, he wouldn't expect to be able to hear her sit and look at the wall. He went over to 14B and put his ear to that panel. This was different. There was a sound in there. A man coughed. It sounded somehow like a solitary cough. There were no voices. Tony pressed the small nacre button beside the door.

Steps came without hurry. A thickened voice spoke through the panel. Tony made no answer, no sound. The thickened voice repeated the question. Lightly, maliciously, Tony pressed the bell again.

Mr James Watterson, of San Diego, should now open the door and give forth noise. He didn't. A silence fell beyond that door that was like the silence of a glacier. Once more Tony put his ear to the wood. Silence utterly.

He got out a master key on a chain and pushed it delicately into the lock of the door. He turned it, pushed the door inward three inches, and withdrew the key. Then he waited.

'All right,' the voice said harshly. 'Come in and get it.'

Tony pushed the door wide and stood there, framed against the light from the lobby. The man was tall, black-haired, angular, and white-faced. He held a gun. He held it as though he knew about guns.

'Step right in,' he drawled.

Tony went in through the door and pushed it shut with his shoulder. He kept his hands a little out from his sides, the clever fingers curled and slack. He smiled his quiet little smile.

'Mr Watterson?'

'And after that what?'

'I'm the house detective here.'

'It slays me.'

The tall, white-faced, somehow handsome and somehow not handsome man backed slowly into the room. It was a large room with a low balcony around two sides of it. French doors opened out on the little, private, open-air balcony that each of the tower rooms had. There was a grate set for a log fire behind a panelled screen in front of a cheerful davenport. A tall misted glass stood on a hotel tray beside a deep, cosy chair. The man backed toward this and stood in front of it. The large, glistening gun drooped and pointed at the floor.

'It slays me,' he said. 'I'm in the dump an hour and the house copper gives me the buzz. Okay, sweetheart, look in the closet and bathroom. But she just left.'

'You didn't see her yet,' Tony said.

The man's bleached face filled with unexpected lines. His thickened voice edged toward a snarl. 'Yeah? Who didn't I see yet?'

'A girl named Eve Cressy.'

The man swallowed. He put his gun down on the table beside the tray. He let himself down into the chair backwards, stiffly, like a man with a touch of lumbago. Then he leaned forward and put his hands on his kneecaps and smiled brightly between his teeth. 'So she got here, huh? I didn't ask about her yet. I'm a careful guy. I didn't ask yet.'

'She's been here five days,' Tony said. 'Waiting for you. She hasn't left the hotel a minute.'

The man's mouth worked a little. His smile had a knowing tilt to it. 'I got delayed a little up north,' he said smoothly. 'You know how it is. Visiting old friends. You seem to know a lot about my business, copper.'

'That's right, Mr Ralls.'

The man lunged to his feet and his hand snapped at the gun. He stood leaning over, holding it on the table, staring. 'Dames talk too much,' he said with a muffled sound in his voice, as though he held something soft between his teeth and talked through it.

'Not dames, Mr Ralls.'

'Huh?' The gun slithered on the hard wood of the table. 'Talk it up, copper. My mind reader just quit.'

'Not dames, Guys. Guys with guns.'

The glacier silence fell between them again. The man straightened his body slowly. His face was washed clean of expression, but his eyes were haunted. Tony leaned in front of him, a shortish plump man with a quiet, pale, friendly face and eyes as simple as forest water.

'They never run out of gas – those boys,' Johnny Ralls said, and licked at his lip. 'Early and late, they work. The old firm never sleeps.'

'You know who they are?' Tony said softly.

'I could maybe give nine guesses. And twelve of them would be right.'

'The trouble boys,' Tony said, and smiled a brittle smile.

'Where is she?' Johnny Ralls asked harshly.

'Right next door to you.'

The man walked to the wall and left his gun lying on the table. He stood in front of the wall, studying it. He reached up and gripped the grillwork of the balcony railing. When he dropped his hand and turned, his face had lost some of its lines. His eyes had a quieter glint. He moved back to Tony and stood over him.

'I've got a stake,' he said. 'Eve sent me some dough and I built it up with a touch I made up north. Case dough, what I mean. The trouble boys talk about twenty-five grand.' He smiled crookedly. 'Five C's I can count. I'd have a lot of fun making them believe that, I would.'

'What did you do with it?' Tony asked indifferently.

'I never had it, copper. Leave that lay. I'm the only guy in the world that believes it. It was a little deal I got suckered on.'

'I'll believe it,' Tony said.

'They don't kill often. But they can be awful tough.'

'Mugs,' Tony said with a sudden bitter contempt. 'Guys with guns. Just mugs.'

Johnny Ralls reached for his glass and drained it empty. The ice cubes tinkled softly as he put it down. He picked his gun up, danced it on his palm, then tucked it, nose down, into an inner breast pocket. He stared at the carpet.

'How come you're telling me this, copper?'

'I thought maybe you'd give her a break.'

'And if I wouldn't?'

'I kind of think you will,' Tony said.

Johnny Ralls nodded quietly. 'Can I get out of here?'

'You could take the service elevator to the garage. You could rent a car. I can give you a card to the garage-man.'

'You're a funny little guy,' Johnny Ralls said.

Tony took out a worn ostrich-skin billfold and scribbled on a printed card. Johnny Ralls read it, and stood holding it, tapping it against a thumbnail.

'I could take her with me,' he said, his eyes narrow.

'You could take a ride in a basket too,' Tony said. 'She's been here five days, I told you. She's been spotted. A guy I know called me up and told me to get her out of here. Told me what it was all about. So I'm getting you out instead.'

'They'll love that,' Johnny Ralls said. 'They'll send you violets.'

'I'll weep about it on my day off.'

Johnny Ralls turned his hand over and stared at the palm. 'I could see her, anyway. Before I blow. Next door to here, you said?'

Tony turned on his heel and started for the door. He said over his shoulder, 'Don't waste a lot of time, handsome. I might change my mind.'

The man said, almost gently: 'You might be spotting me right now, for all I know.'

Tony didn't turn his head. 'That's a chance you have to take.'

He went on to the door and passed out of the room. He shut it carefully, silently, looked once at the door of 14A and got into his dark elevator. He rode it down to the linen-room floor and got out to remove the basket that held the service elevator open at that floor. The door slid quietly shut. He held it so that it made no noise. Down the corridor, light came from the open door of the housekeeper's office. Tony got back into his elevator and went on down to the lobby.

The little clerk was out of sight behind his pebbled-glass screen, auditing accounts. Tony went through the main lobby and turned into the radio room. The radio was on again, soft. She was there, curled on the davenport again. The speaker hummed to her, a vague sound so low that what it said was as wordless as the murmur of trees. She turned her head slowly and smiled at him.

'Finished palming doorknobs? I couldn't sleep worth a nickel. So I came down again. Okay?'

He smiled and nodded. He sat down in a green chair and patted the plump brocade arms of it. 'Sure, Miss Cressy.'

'Waiting is the hardest kind of work, isn't it? I wish you'd talk to that radio. It sounds like a pretzel being bent.'

Tony fiddled with it, got nothing he liked, set it back where it had been.

'Beer-parlour drunks are all the customers now.'

She smiled at him again.

'I don't bother you being here, Miss Cressy?'

'I like it. You're a sweet little guy, Tony.'

He looked stiffly at the floor and a ripple touched his spine. He waited for it to go away. It went slowly. Then he sat back, relaxed again, his neat fingers clasped on his elk's tooth. He listened. Not to the radio – to far-off, uncertain things, menacing things. And perhaps to just the safe whirr of wheels going away into a strange night.

'Nobody's all bad,' he said out loud.

The girl looked at him lazily. 'I've met two or three I was wrong on, then.'

He nodded. 'Yeah,' he admitted judiciously. 'I guess there's some that are.'

The girl yawned and her deep violet eyes half closed. She nestled back into the cushions. 'Sit there a while, Tony. Maybe I could nap.'

'Sure. Not a thing for me to do. Don't know why they pay me.'

She slept quickly and with complete stillness, like a child. Tony hardly breathed for ten minutes. He just watched her, his mouth a little open. There was a quiet fascination in his limpid eyes, as if he was looking at an altar.

Then he stood up with infinite care and padded away under the arch to the entrance lobby and the desk. He stood at the desk listening for a little while. He heard a pen rustling out of sight. He went around the corner to the row of house phones in little glass cubbyholes. He lifted one and asked the night operator for the garage.

It rang three or four times and then a boyish voice answered: 'Windermere Hotel. Garage speaking.'

'This is Tony Reseck. That guy Watterson I gave a card to. He leave?'

'Sure, Tony. Half an hour almost. Is it your charge?'

'Yeah,' Tony said. 'My party. Thanks. Be seein' you.'

He hung up and scratched his neck. He went back to the desk and slapped a hand on it. The clerk wafted himself around the screen with his greeter's smile in place. It dropped when he saw Tony.

'Can't a guy catch up on his work?' he grumbled.

'What's the professional rate on 14B?'

The clerk stared morosely. 'There's no professional rate in the tower.'

'Make one. The fellow left already. Was there only an hour.'

'Well, well,' the clerk said airily. 'So the personality didn't click to-night. We get a skip-out.'

'Will five bucks satisfy you?'

'Friend of yours?'

'No. Just a drunk with delusions of grandeur and no dough.'

'Guess we'll have to let it ride, Tony. How did he get out?'

'I took him down the service elevator. You was asleep. Will five bucks satisfy you?'

'Why?'

The worn ostrich-skin wallet came out and a weedy five slipped across the marble. 'All I could shake him for,' Tony said loosely.

The clerk took the five and looked puzzled. 'You're the boss,' he said, and shrugged. The phone shrilled on the desk and he reached for it. He listened and then pushed it toward Tony. 'For you.'

Tony took the phone and cuddled it close to his chest. He put his mouth close to the transmitter. The voice was strange to him. It had a metallic sound. Its syllables were meticulously anonymous.

'Tony? Tony Reseck?'

'Talking.'

'A message from Al. Shoot?'

Tony looked at the clerk. 'Be a pal,' he said over the mouthpiece. The clerk flicked a narrow smile at him and went away. 'Shoot,' Tony said into the phone.

'We had a little business with a guy in your place. Picked him up scramming. Al had a hunch you'd run him out. Tailed him and took him to the kerb. Not so good. Backfire.'

Tony held the phone very tight and his temples chilled with the evaporation of moisture. 'Go on,' he said. 'I guess there's more.'

'A little. The guy stopped the big one. Cold. Al – Al said to tell you good-bye.'

Tony leaned hard against the desk. His mouth made a sound that was not speech.

'Get it?' The metallic voice sounded impatient, a little bored. 'This guy had him a rod. He used it. Al won't be phoning anybody any more.'

Tony lurched at the phone, and the base of it shook on the rose marble. His mouth was a hard dry knot.

The voice said: 'That's as far as we go, bud. G'night.' The phone clicked dryly, like a pebble hitting a wall.

Tony put the phone down in its cradle very carefully, so as not to make any sound. He looked at the clenched palm of his left hand. He took a handkerchief out and rubbed the palm softly and straightened the fingers out with his other hand. Then he wiped his forehead. The clerk came around the screen again and looked at him with glinting eyes.

'I'm off Friday. How about lending me that phone number?'

Tony nodded at the clerk and smiled a minute frail smile. He put his handkerchief away and patted the pocket he had put it in. He turned and walked away from the desk, across the entrance lobby, down the three shallow steps, along the shadowy reaches of the main lobby, and so in through the arch to the radio room once more. He walked softly, like a man moving in a room where somebody is very sick. He reached the chair he had sat in before and lowered himself into it inch by inch. The girl slept on, motionless, in that curled-up looseness achieved by some women and all cats. Her breath made not the slightest sound against the vague murmur of the radio.

Tony Reseck leaned back in the chair and clasped his hands on his elk's tooth and quietly closed his eyes.

IV

Goldfish

I

I WASN'T doing any work that day, just catching up on my foot-dangling. A warm gusty breeze was blowing in at the office window and the soot from the *Mansion House Hotel* oil-burners across the alley was rolling across the glass top of my desk in tiny particles, like pollen drifting over a vacant lot.

I was just thinking about going to lunch when Kathy Horne came in.

She was a tall, seedy, sad-eyed blonde who had once been a policewoman and had lost her job when she married a cheap little check-bouncer named Johnny Horne, to reform him. She hadn't reformed him, but she was waiting for him to come out so she could try again. In the meantime she ran the cigar counter at the *Mansion House*, and watched the grifters go by in a haze of nickel cigar smoke. And once in a while lent one of them ten dollars to get out of town. She was just that soft. She sat down and opened her big shiny bag and got out a package of cigarettes and lit one with my desk lighter. She blew a plume of smoke, wrinkled her nose at it.

'Did you ever hear of the Leander pearls?' she asked. 'Gosh, that blue serge shines. You must have money in the bank, the clothes you wear.'

'No,' I said, 'to both your ideas. I never heard of the Leander pearls and don't have any money in the bank.'

'Then you'd like to make yourself a cut of twenty-five grand maybe.'

I lit one of her cigarettes. She got up and shut the window, saying: 'I get enough of that hotel smell on the job.'

She sat down again, went on:

'It's nineteen years ago. They had the guy in Leavenworth fifteen and it's four since they let him out. A big lumberman from up north named Sol Leander bought them for his wife – the pearls, I mean – just two of them. They cost two hundred grand.'

'It must have taken a hand truck to move them,' I said.

'I see you don't know a lot about pearls,' Kathy Horne said. 'It's not just size. Anyhow they're worth more to-day and the twenty-five grand reward the Reliance people put out is still good.'

'I get it,' I said. 'Somebody copped them off.'

'Now you're getting yourself some oxygen.' She dropped her cigarette into a tray and let it smoke, as ladies will. I put it out for her. 'That's what the guy was in Leavenworth for, only they never proved he got the pearls. It was a mail-car job. He got himself hidden in the car somehow and up in Wyoming he shot the clerk, cleaned out the registered mail and dropped off. He got to B.C. before he was nailed. But they didn't get any of the stuff – not then. All they got was him. He got life.'

'If it's going to be a long story, let's have a drink.'

'I never drink until sundown. That way you don't get to be a heel.'

'Tough on the Eskimos,' I said. 'In the summertime, anyway.'

She watched me get my little flat bottle out. Then she went on:

'His name was Sype – Wally Sype. He did it alone. And he wouldn't squawk about the stuff, not a peep. Then after fifteen long years they offered him a pardon, if he would loosen up with the loot. He gave up everything but the pearls.'

'Where did he have it?' I asked. 'In his hat?'

'Listen, this isn't just a bunch of gag lines. I've got a lead to those marbles.'

I shut my mouth with my hand and looked solemn.

'He said he never had the pearls and they must have half-way believed him because they gave him the pardon. Yet the pearls were in the load, registered mail, and they were never seen again.'

My throat began to feel a little thick. I didn't say anything.

Kathy Horne went on:

'One time in Leavenworth, just one time in all those years, Wally Sype wrapped himself around a can of white shellac and got as tight as a fat lady's girdle. His cell mate was a little man they called Peeler Mardo. He was doing twenty-seven months for splitting twenty dollar bills. Sype told him he had the pearls buried somewhere in Idaho.'

I leaned forward a little.

'Beginning to get to you, eh?' she said. 'Well get this. Peeler Mardo is rooming at my house and he's a coke-hound and he talks in his sleep.'

I leaned back again. 'Good grief,' I said. 'And I was practically spending the reward money.'

She stared at me coldly. Then her face softened. 'All right,' she said a little hopelessly. 'I know it sounds screwy. All those years gone by and all the smart heads that must have worked on the case, postal men and private agencies and all. And then a coke-head to turn it up. But he's a nice little runt and somehow I believe him. He knows where Sype is.'

I said: 'Did he talk all this in his sleep?'

'Of course not. But you know me. An old policewoman's got ears. Maybe I was nosy, but I guessed he was an ex-con and I worried about him using the stuff so much. He's the only roomer I've got now and I'd kind of go in by his door and listen to him talking to himself. That way I got enough to brace him. He told me the rest. He wants help to collect.'

I leaned forward again. 'Where's Sype?'

Kathy Horne smiled, and shook her head. 'That's the one thing he wouldn't tell, that and the name Sype is using now. But it's somewhere up North, in or near Olympia, Washington. Peeler saw him up there and found out about him and he says Sype didn't see *him*.'

'What's Peeler doing down here?' I asked.

'Here's where they put the Leavenworth rap on him. You know an old con always goes back to look at the piece of sidewalk he slipped on. But he doesn't have any friends here now.'

I lit another cigarette and had another little drink.

'Sype has been out four years, you say. Peeler did twenty-seven months. What's he been doing with all the time since?'

Kathy Horne widened her china blue eyes pityingly. 'Maybe you think there's only one jailhouse he could get into.'

'Okay,' I said. 'Will he talk to me? I guess he wants help to deal with the insurance people, in case there are any pearls and Sype will put them right in Peeler's hand and so on. Is that it?'

Kathy Horne sighed. 'Yes, he'll talk to you. He's aching to. He's scared about something. Will you go out now, before he gets junked up for the evening?'

'Sure – if that's what you want.'

She took a flat key out of her bag and wrote an address on my pad. She stood up slowly.

'It's a double house. My side's separate. There's a door in between, with the key on my side. That's just in case he won't come to the door.'

'Okay,' I said. I blew smoke at the ceiling and stared at her.

She went towards the door, stopped, came back. She looked down at the floor.

'I don't rate much in it,' she said. 'Maybe not anything.

But if I could have a grand or two waiting for Johnny when he came out, maybe – '

'Maybe you could hold him straight,' I said. 'It's a dream, Kathy. It's all a dream. But if it isn't you cut an even third.'

She caught her breath and glared at me to keep from crying. She went towards the door, stopped and came back again.

'That isn't all,' she said. 'It's the old guy – Sype. He did fifteen years. He paid. Paid hard. Doesn't it make you feel kind of mean?'

I shook my head. 'He stole them, didn't he? He killed a man. What does he do for a living?'

'His wife has money,' Kathy Horne said. 'He just plays around with goldfish.'

'Goldfish?' I said. 'To hell with him.'

She went on out.

2

The last time I had been in the Gray Lake district I had helped a D.A.'s man named Bernie Obis shoot a gunman named Poke Andrews. But that was higher up the hill, further away from the lake. This house was on the second level, in a loop the street made rounding a spur of the hill. It stood by itself high up, with a cracked retaining wall in front and several vacant lots behind.

Being originally a double house it had two front doors and two sets of front steps. One of the doors had a sign tacked over the grating that masked the peep window: Ring 1432.

I parked my car and went up right-angle steps, passed between two lines of pinks, went up more steps to the side with the sign. That should be the roomer's side. I rang the bell. Nobody answered it, so I went across to the other door. Nobody answered that one either.

While I was waiting a grey Dodge coupé whished around the curve and a small neat girl in blue looked up at me for a second. I didn't see who else was in the car. I didn't pay much attention. I didn't know it was important.

I took out Kathy Horne's key and let myself into a closed living-room that smelled of cedar oil. There was just enough furniture to get by, net curtains, a quiet shaft of sunlight under the drapes in front. There was a tiny breakfast room, a kitchen, a bedroom in the back that was obviously Kathy's, a bathroom, another bedroom in front that seemed to be used as a sewing-room. It was this room that had the door cut through to the other side of the house.

I unlocked it and stepped, as it were, through a mirror. Everything was backwards, except the furniture. The living-room on that side had twin beds, didn't have the look of being lived in.

I went towards the back of the house, past the second bathroom, knocked at the shut door that corresponded to Kathy's bedroom.

No answer. I tried the knob and went in. The little man on the bed was probably Peeler Mardo. I noticed his feet first, because although he had on trousers and a shirt, his feet were bare and hung over the end of the bed. They were tied there by a rope around the ankles.

They had been burned raw on the soles. There was a smell of scorched flesh in spite of the open window. Also a smell of scorched wood. An electric iron on a desk was still connected. I went over and shut it off.

I went back to Kathy Horne's kitchen and found a pint of Brooklyn Scotch in the cooler. I used some of it and breathed deeply for a little while and looked out over the vacant lots. There was a narrow cement walk behind the house and green wooden steps down to the street.

I went back to Peeler Mardo's room. The coat of a brown suit with a red pin stripe hung over a chair with the pockets turned out and what had been in them on the floor.

He was wearing the trousers of the suit, and their pockets were turned out also. Some keys and change and a handkerchief lay on the bed beside him, and a metal box like a woman's compact, from which some glistening white powder had spilled. Cocaine.

He was a little man, not more than five feet four, with thin brown hair and large ears. His eyes had no particular colour. They were just eyes, and very wide open, and quite dead. His arms were pulled out from him and tied at the wrists by a rope that went under the bed.

I looked him over for bullet or knife wounds, didn't find any. There wasn't a mark on him except his feet. Shock or heart failure or a combination of the two must have done the trick. He was still warm. The gag in his mouth was both warm and wet.

I wiped off everything I had touched, looked out of Kathy's front window for a while before I left the house.

It was three-thirty when I walked into the lobby of the *Mansion House*, over to the cigar counter in the corner. I leaned on the glass and asked for Camels.

Kathy Horne flicked the pack at me, dropped the change into my outside breast pocket, and gave me her customer's smile.

'Well? You didn't take long,' she said, and looked sidewise along her eyes at a drunk who was trying to light a cigar with the old-fashioned flint and steel lighter.

'It's heavy,' I told her. 'Get set.'

She turned away quickly and flipped a pack of paper matches along the glass to the drunk. He fumbled for them, dropped both matches and cigar, scooped them angrily off the floor and went off looking back over his shoulder, as if he expected a kick.

Kathy looked past my head, her eyes cool and empty.

'I'm set,' she whispered.

'You cut a full half,' I said. 'Peeler's out. He's been bumped off – in his bed.'

Her eyes twitched. Two fingers curled on the glass near my elbow. A white line showed around her mouth. That was all.

'Listen,' I said. 'Don't say anything until I'm through. He died of shock. Somebody burned his feet with a cheap electric iron. Not yours. I looked. I'd say he died rather quickly and couldn't have said much. The gag was still in his mouth. When I went out there, frankly, I thought it was all hooey. Now I'm not so sure. If he gave up his dope, we're through, and so is Sype, unless I can find him first. Those workers didn't have any inhibitions at all. If he didn't give up, there's still time.'

Her head turned, her set eyes looked towards the revolving door of the lobby entrance. White patches glared in her cheeks.

'What do I do?' she breathed.

I poked at a box of wrapped cigars, dropped her key into it. Her long fingers got it out smoothly, hid it.

'When you get home you find him. You don't know a thing. Leave the pearls out, leave me out. When they check his prints they'll know he had a record and they'll just figure it was something caught up with him.'

I broke my cigarettes open and lit one, watched her for a moment. She didn't move an inch.

'Can you face it down?' I asked. 'If you can't, now's the time to speak.'

'Of course.' Her eyebrows arched. 'Do I look like a torturer?'

'You married a crook,' I said grimly.

She flushed, which was what I wanted. 'He isn't! He's just a damn fool! Nobody thinks any the worse of me, not even the boys down at Headquarters.'

'All right. I like it that way. It's not our murder, after all. And if we talk now, you can say good-bye to any share in any reward – even if one is ever paid.'

'Darn tootin'.,' Kathy Horne said pertly. 'Oh, the poor little runt,' she almost sobbed.

I patted her arm, grinned as heartily as I could and left the *Mansion House*.

3

The Reliance Indemnity Company had offices in the Graas Building, three small rooms that looked like nothing at all. They were a big enough outfit to be as shabby as they liked.

The resident manager was named Lutin, a middle-aged bald-headed man with quiet eyes, dainty fingers that caressed a dappled cigar. He sat behind a large, well-dusted desk and stared peacefully at my chin.

'Carmady, eh? I've heard of you.' He touched my card with a shiny little finger. 'What's on your mind?'

I rolled a cigarette around in my fingers and lowered my voice. 'Remember the Leander pearls?'

His smile was slow, a little bored. 'I'm not likely to forget them. They cost this company one hundred and fifty thousand dollars. I was a cocky young adjuster then.'

I said: 'I've got an idea. It may be all haywire. It very likely is. But I'd like to try it out. Is your twenty-five grand reward still good?'

He chuckled. 'Twenty grand, Carmady. We spent the difference ourselves. You're wasting time.'

'It's my time. Twenty it is then. How much co-operation can I get?'

'What kind of co-operation?'

'Can I have a letter identifying me to your other branches? In case I have to go out of the State. In case I need kind words from some local law.'

'Which way out of the State?'

I smiled at him. He tapped his cigar on the edge of a tray and smiled back. Neither of our smiles was honest.

'No letter,' he said. 'New York wouldn't stand for it. We have our own tie-up. But all the co-operation you can use, under the hat. And the twenty grand, if you click. Of course you won't.'

I lit my cigarette and leaned back, puffed smoke at the ceiling.

'No? Why not? You never got those marbles. They existed, didn't they?'

'Darn right they existed. And if they still do, they belong to us. But two hundred grand doesn't get buried for twenty years – and then get dug up.'

'All right. It's still my own time.'

He knocked a little ash off his cigar and looked down his eyes at me. 'I like your front,' he said, 'even if you are crazy. But we're a large organization. Suppose I have you covered from now on. What then?'

'I lose. I'll know I'm covered. I'm too long in the game to miss that. I'll quit, give up what I know to the law, and go home.'

'Why would you do that?'

I leaned forward over the desk again. 'Because,' I said slowly, 'the guy that had the lead got bumped off to-day.'

'Oh – oh.' Lutin rubbed his nose.

'I didn't bump him off,' I added.

We didn't talk any more for a little while. Then Lutin said:

'You don't want any letter. You wouldn't even carry it. And after your telling me that, you know damn well I won't dare give it to you.'

I stood up, grinned, started for the door. He got up himself, very fast, ran around the desk and put his small neat hand on my arm.

'Listen, I know you're crazy, but if you do get anything, bring it in through our boys. We need the advertising.'

'What the hell do you think I live on?' I growled.

'Twenty-five grand.'

'I thought it was twenty'.

'Twenty-five. And you're still crazy. Sype never had those pearls. If he had, he'd have made some kind of terms with us many years ago.'

'Okay,' I said. 'You've had plenty of time to make up your mind.'

We shook hands, grinned at each other like a couple of wise boys who know they're not kidding anybody, but won't give up trying.

It was a quarter to five when I got back to the office. I had a couple of short drinks and stuffed a pipe and sat down to interview my brains. The phone rang.

A woman's voice said: 'Carmady?' It was a small, tight, cold voice. I didn't know it.

'Yeah.'

'Better see Rush Madder. Know him?'

'No,' I lied. 'Why should I see him?'

There was a sudden tinkling, icy-cold laugh on the wire. 'On account of a guy had sore feet,' the voice said.

The phone clicked. I put my end of it aside, struck a match and stared at the wall until the flame burned my fingers.

Rush Madder was a shyster in the Quorn Building. An ambulance chaser, a small time fixer, an alibi builder-upper, anything that smelled a little and paid a little more. I hadn't heard of him in connexion with any big operations like burning people's feet.

4

It was getting toward quitting time on lower Spring Street. Taxis were dawdling close to the kerb, stenographers were getting an early start home, street cars were clogging up, and traffic cops were preventing people from making perfectly legal right turns.

The Quorn Building was a narrow front, the colour of dried mustard, with a large case of false teeth in the entrance. The directory held the names of painless dentists, people who teach you how to become a letter-carrier, just names, and numbers without any names. Rush Madder, Attorney-at-Law, was in Room 619.

I got out of a jolting open cage elevator, looked at a dirty spittoon on a dirty rubber mat, walked down a corridor that smelled of butts, and tried the knob below the frosted glass panel of 619. The door was locked. I knocked.

A shadow came against the glass and the door was pulled back with a squeak. I was looking at a thick-set man with a soft round chin, heavy black eyebrows, an oily complexion, and a Charlie Chan moustache that made his face look fatter than it was.

He put out a couple of nicotined fingers. 'Well, well, the old dog-catcher himself. The eye that never forgets. Carmady is the name, I believe?'

I stepped inside and waited for the door to squeak shut. A bare carpetless room paved in brown linoleum, a flat desk and a rolltop at right angles to it, a big green safe that looked as fireproof as a delicatessen bag, two filing cases, three chairs, a built-in closet, and washbowl in the corner by the door.

'Well, well, sit down,' Madder said. 'Glad to see you.' He fussed around behind his desk and adjusted a burst-out seat cushion, sat on it. 'Nice of you to drop around. Business?'

I sat down and put a cigarette between my teeth and looked at him. I didn't say a word. I watched him start to sweat. It started up in his hair. Then he grabbed a pencil and made marks on his blotter. Then he looked at me with a quick darting glance, down at his blotter again. He talked – to the blotter.

'Any ideas?' he asked softly.

'About what?'

He didn't look at me. 'About how we could do a little business together. Say, in stones.'

'Who was the wren?' I asked.

'Huh? What wren?' He still didn't look at me.

'The one that phoned me.'

'Did somebody phone you?'

I reached for his telephone, which was the old-fashioned gallows type. I lifted off the receiver and started to dial the number of Police Headquarters, very slowly. I knew he would know that number about as well as he knew his hat.

He reached over and pushed the hook down. 'Now, listen,' he complained. 'You're too fast. What you calling coppers for?'

I said slowly: 'They want to talk to you. On account of you know a broad that knows a man had sore feet.'

'Does it have to be that way?' His collar was too tight now. He yanked at it.

'Not from my side. But if you think I'm going to sit here and let you play with my reflexes, it does.'

Madder opened a flat tin of cigarettes and pushed one past his lips with a sound like somebody gutting a fish. His hand shook.

'All right,' he said thickly. 'All right. Don't get sore.'

'Just stop trying to count clouds with me,' I growled. 'Talk sense. If you've got a job for me, it's probably too dirty for me to touch. But I'll at least listen.'

He nodded. He was comfortable now. He knew I was bluffing. He puffed a pale swirl of smoke and watched it float up.

'That's all right,' he said evenly. 'I play dumb myself once in a while. The thing is we're wise. Carol saw you go to the house and leave it again. No law came.'

'Carol?'

'Carol Donovan. Friend of mine. She called you up.'

I nodded. 'Go ahead.'

He didn't say anything. He just sat there and looked at me owlishly.

I grinned and leaned across the desk a little and said: 'Here's what's bothering you. You don't know why I went to the house or why, having gone, I didn't yell police. That's easy. I thought it was a secret.'

'We're just kidding each other,' Madder said sourly.

'All right,' I said. 'Let's talk about pearls. Does that make it any easier?'

His eyes shone. He wanted to let himself get excited, but he didn't. He kept his voice down, said coolly:

'Carol picked him up one night, the little guy. A crazy little number, full of snow, but way back in his noodle an idea. He'd talk about pearls, about an old guy up in the northwest of Canada that swiped them a long time ago and still had them. Only he wouldn't say who the old guy was or where he was. Foxy about that. Holding out. I wouldn't know why.'

'He wanted to get his feet burned,' I said.

Madder's lips shook and another fine sweat showed in his hair.

'I didn't do that,' he said thickly.

'You or Carol, what's the odds? The little guy died. They can make murder out of it. You didn't find out what you wanted to know. That's why *I'm* here. You think I have information you didn't get. Forget it. If I knew enough, I wouldn't be here, and if you knew enough, you wouldn't want me here. Check?'

He grinned, very slowly, as if it hurt him. He struggled up in his chair and dragged a deep drawer out from the side of his desk, put a nicely moulded brown bottle up on the desk, and two striped glasses. He whispered:

'Two way split. You and me. I'm cutting Carol out. She's too damn' rough, Carmady. I've seen hard women, but she's the blueing on armour plate. And you'd never think it to look at her, would you?'

'Have I seen her?'

'I guess so. She says you did.'

'Oh, the girl in the Dodge.'

He nodded, and poured two good-sized drinks, put the bottle down and stood up. 'Water? I like it in mine.'

'No,' I said, 'but why cut me in? I don't know any more than you mentioned. Or very little. Certainly not as much as you must know to go that far.'

He leered across the glasses. 'I know where I can get fifty grand for the Leander pearls, twice what you could get. I can give you yours and still have mine. You've got the front I need to work in the open. How about the water?'

'No water,' I said.

He went across to the built-in wash place and ran the water and came back with his glass half full. He sat down again, grinned, lifted it.

We drank.

5

So far I had only made four mistakes. The first was mixing in it at all, even for Kathy Horne's sake. The second was staying mixed after I found Peeler Mardo dead. The third was letting Rush Madder see I knew what he was talking about. The fourth, the whisky, was the worst.

It tasted funny even on the way down. Then there was that sudden moment of sharp lucidity when I knew, exactly as though I had seen it, that he had switched his drink for a harmless one cached in the closet.

I sat still for a moment, with the empty glass at my finger's ends, gathering my strength. Madder's face began to get large and moony and vague. A fat smile jerked in and out under his Charlie Chan moustache as he watched me.

I reached back into my hip pocket and pulled out a loosely

wadded handkerchief. The small safe inside it didn't seem
to show. At least Madder didn't move, after his first grab
under the coat.

I stood up and swayed forward drunkenly and smacked
him square on the top of the head.

He gagged. He started to get up. I tapped him on the jaw.
He became limp and his hand sweeping down from under
his coat knocked his glass over on the desk top. I straightened
it, stood silent, listening, struggling with a rising wave of
nauseous stupor.

I went over to a communicating door and tried the knob.
It was locked. I was staggering by now. I dragged an office
chair to the entrance door and propped the back of it under
the knob. I leaned against the door panting, gritting my
teeth, cursing myself. I got handcuffs out and started back
towards Madder.

A very pretty black-haired, grey-eyed girl stepped out of
the clothes closet and poked a .32 at me.

She wore a blue suit cut with a lot of snap. An inverted
saucer of a hat came down in a hard line across her forehead.
Shiny black hair showed at the sides. Her eyes were slate-
grey, cold, and yet light-hearted. Her face was fresh and
young and delicate and as hard as a chisel.

'All right, Carmady. Lie down and sleep it off. You're
through.'

I stumbled towards her waving my sap. She shook her
head. When her face moved it got large before my eyes. Its
outlines changed and wobbled. The gun in her hand looked
like anything from a tunnel to a toothpick.

'Don't be a goof, Carmady,' she said. 'A few hours' sleep
for you, a few hours' start for us. Don't make me shoot. I
would.'

'Damn you,' I mumbled. 'I believe you would.'

'Right as rain, toots. I'm a lady that wants her own way.
That's fine. Sit down.'

The floor rose up and bumped me. I sat on it as on a raft

in a rough sea. I braced myself on flat hands. I could hardly feel the floor. My hands were numb. My whole body was numb.

I tried to stare her down. 'Ha-a! L-lady K-killer!' I giggled.

She threw a chilly laugh at me which I only just barely heard. Drums were beating in my head now, war drums from a far off jungle. Waves of light were moving, and dark shadows and a rustle as of a wind in tree-tops. I didn't want to lie down. I lay down.

The girl's voice came from very far off, an elfin voice.

'Two-way split, eh? He doesn't like my method, eh? Bless his big soft heart. We'll see about him.'

Vaguely as I floated off I seemed to feel a dull jar that might have been a shot. I hoped she had shot Madder, but she hadn't. She had merely helped me on my way out – with my own sap.

When I came around again it was night. Something clacked overhead with a heavy sound. Through the open window beyond the desk yellow light splashed on the high side walls of a building. The thing clacked again and the light went off. An advertising sign on the roof.

I got up off the floor like a man climbing out of thick mud. I waded over to the washbowl, splashed water on my face, felt the top of my head and winced, waded back to the door and found the light switch.

Strewn papers lay around the desk, broken pencils, envelopes, an empty brown whisky bottle, cigarette ends, and ashes. The debris of hastily emptied drawers. I didn't bother going through any of it. I left the office, rode down to the street in the shuddering elevator, slid into a bar and had a brandy, then got my car and drove on home.

I changed clothes, packed a bag, had some whisky, and answered the telephone. It was about nine-thirty.

Kathy Horne's voice said: 'So you're not gone yet. I hoped you wouldn't be.'

'Alone?' I asked, still thick in the voice.

'Yes, but I haven't been. The house has been full of coppers for hours. They were very nice, considering. Old grudge of some kind, they figured.'

'And the line is likely tapped now,' I growled. 'Where was I supposed to be going?'

'Well – you know. Your girl told me.'

'Little dark girl? Very cool? Name of Carol Donovàn?'

'She had your card. Why, wasn't it – '

'I don't have any girl,' I said simply. 'And I bet that just very casually, without thinking at all a name slipped past your lips – the name of a town up North. Did it?'

'Ye-es,' Kathy Horne admitted weakly.

I caught the night plane north.

It was a nice trip except that I had a sore head and a raging thirst for ice-water.

6

The *Snoqualmie Hotel* in Olympia was on Capital Way, fronting on the usual square city block of park. I left by the coffee shop door and walked down a hill to where the last, loneliest reach of Puget Sound dried and decomposed against a line of disused wharves. Corded firewood filled the foreground and old men pottered about in the middle of the stacks, or sat on boxes with pipes in their mouths and signs behind their heads reading: 'Firewood and Split Kindling. Free Delivery.'

Behind them a low cliff rose and the vast pines of the north loomed against a grey-blue sky.

Two of the old men sat on boxes about twenty feet apart, ignoring each other. I drifted near one of them. He wore corduroy pants and what had been a red and black mackinaw. His felt hat showed the sweat of twenty summers. One of his hands clutched a short black pipe, and with the grimed fingers of the other he slowly, carefully, ecstatically jerked at a long curling hair that grew out of his nose.

I set a box on end, sat down, filled my own pipe, lit it, puffed a cloud of smoke. I waved a hand at the water and said:

'You'd never think that ever met the Pacific Ocean.'

He looked at me.

I said: 'Dead end – quiet, restful, like your town. I like a town like this.' He went on looking at me.

'I'll bet,' I said, 'that a man that's been around a town like this knows everybody in it and in the country near it.'

He said: 'How much you bet?'

I took a silver dollar out of my pocket. They still had a few up there. The old man looked it over, nodded, suddenly yanked the long hair out of his nose and held it up against the light.

'You'd lose,' he said.

I put the dollar down on my knee. 'Know anybody around here that keeps a lot of goldfish?' I asked.

He stared at the dollar. The other old man near by was wearing overalls and shoes without any laces. He stared at the dollar. They both spat at the same instant. The first old man turned his head and yelled at the top of his voice:

'Know anybody keeps goldfish?'

The other old man jumped up off his box and seized a big axe, set a log on end and whanged the axe down on it, splitting it evenly. He looked at the first old man triumphantly and screamed:

'I ain't neither.'

The first old man said: 'Leetle deef,' He got up slowly and went over to a shack built of old boards of uneven lengths. He went into it, banged the door.

The second old man threw his axe down pettishly, spat in the direction of the closed door and went off among the stacks of cordwood.

The door of the shack opened, the man in the mackinaw poked his head out of it.

'Sewer crabs is all,' he said, and slammed the door again.

I put my dollar in my pocket and went back up the hill. I figured it would take too long to learn their language.

Capitol Way ran north and south. A dull green street car shuttled past on the way to a place called Tumwater. In the distance I could see the government buildings. Northward the street passed two hotels and some stores and branched right and left. Right went to Tacoma and Seattle. Left went over a bridge and out on to the Olympic Peninsula.

Beyond this right and left turn the street suddenly became old and shabby, with broken asphalt paving, a Chinese restaurant, a boarded-up movie house, a pawnbroker's establishment. A sign jutting over the dirty sidewalk said: 'Smoke Shop,' and in small letters underneath, as if it hoped nobody was looking, 'Pool'.

I went in past a rack of gaudy magazines and a cigar showcase that had flies inside it. There was a long wooden counter on the left, a few slot machines, a single pool table. Three kids fiddled with the slot machines and a tall thin man with a long nose and no chin played pool all by himself, with a dead cigar in his face.

I sat on a stool and a hard-eyed bald-headed man behind the counter got up from a chair, wiped his hands on a thick grey apron, showed me a gold tooth.

'A little rye,' I said. 'Know anybody that keeps goldfish?'

'Yeah,' he said. 'No.'

He poured something behind the counter and shoved a thick glass across.

'Two bits.'

I sniffed the stuff, wrinkled my nose. 'Was it the rye the "yeah" was for?'

The bald-headed man held up a large bottle with a label that said something about: 'Cream of Dixie Straight Rye Whiskey Guaranteed at Least Four Months Old.'

'Okay,' I said. 'I see it just moved in.'

I poured some water in it and drank it. It tasted like a

cholera culture. I put a quarter on the counter. The barman showed me a gold tooth on the other side of his face and
took hold of the counter with two hard hands and pushed
his chin at me.

'What was that crack?' he asked, almost gently.

'I just moved in,' I said. 'I'm looking for some goldfish
for the front window. Goldfish.'

The barman said very slowly: 'Do I look like a guy would
know a guy would have goldfish?' His face was a little white.

The long-nosed man who had been playing himself a
round of pool racked his cue and strolled over to the counter
beside me and threw a nickel on it.

'Draw me a drink before you wet yourself,' he told the
barman.

The barman prised himself loose from the counter with a
good deal of effort. I looked down to see if his fingers had
made any dents in the wood. He drew a coke, stirred it with
a swizzle-stick, dumped it on the bar top, took a deep
breath and let it out through his nose, grunted and went
away towards a door marked: 'Toilet'.

The long-nosed man lifted his coke and looked into the
smeared mirror behind the bar. The left side of his mouth
twitched briefly. A dim voice came from it, saying:

'How's Peeler?'

I pressed my thumb and forefinger together, put them to
my nose, sniffed, shook my head sadly.

'Hitting it high, huh?'

'Yeah,' I said. 'I didn't catch the name.'

'Call me Sunset. I'm always movin' west. Think he'll stay
clammed?'

'He'll stay clammed,' I said.

'What's your handle?'

'Dodge Willis, El Paso,' I said.

'Got a room somewhere?'

'Hotel.'

He put his glass down empty. 'Let's dangle.'

7

We went up to my room and sat down and looked at each other over a couple of glasses of Scotch and ginger ale. Sunset studied me with his close-set expressionless eyes, a little at a time, but very thoroughly in the end, adding it all up.

I sipped my drink and waited. At last he said in his lipless 'stir' voice:

'How come Peeler didn't come hisself?'

'For the same reason he didn't stay when he was here.'

'Meaning which?'

'Figure it out for yourself,' I said.

He nodded, just as though I had said something with a meaning. Then:

'What's the top price?'

'Twenty-five grand.'

'Nuts.' Sunset was emphatic, even rude.

I leaned back and lit a cigarette, puffed smoke at the open window and watched the breeze pick it up and tear it to pieces.

'Listen,' Sunset complained. 'I don't know you from last Sunday's sports section. You may be all to the silk. I just don't know.'

'Why'd you brace me?' I asked.

'You had the word, didn't you?'

This was where I took the dive. I grinned at him. 'Yeah. Goldfish was the password. The *Smoke Shop* was the place.'

His lack of expression told me I was right. It was one of those breaks you dream of, but don't handle right even in dreams.

'Well, what's the next angle?' Sunset inquired, sucking a piece of ice out of his glass and chewing on it.

I laughed. 'Okay, Sunset. I'm satisfied you're cagey. We could go on like this for weeks. Let's put our cards on the table. Where is the old guy?'

Sunset tightened his lips, moistened them, tightened them again. He set his glass down very slowly and his right hand hung lax on his thigh. I knew I had made a mistake, that Peeler knew where the old guy was, exactly. Therefore I should know.

Nothing in Sunset's voice showed I had made a mistake. He said crossly: 'You mean why don't I put my cards on the table and you just sit back and look 'em over. Nix.'

'Then how do you like this?' I growled. 'Peeler's dead.'

One eyebrow twitched, and one corner of his mouth. His eyes got a little blanker than before, if possible. His voice rasped lightly, like a finger on dry leather.

'How come?'

'Competition you two didn't know about.' I leaned back, smiled.

The gun made a soft metallic blur in the sunshine. I hardly saw where it came from. Then the muzzle was round and dark and empty looking at me.

'You're kidding the wrong guy,' Sunset said lifelessly. 'I ain't no soft spot for chiselers to lie on.'

I folded my arms, taking care that my right hand was outside, in view.

'I would be – if I was kidding. I'm not. Peeler played with a girl and she milked him – up to a point. He didn't tell her where to find the old fellow. So she and her top man went to see Peeler where he lived. They used a hot iron on his feet. He died of the shock.'

Sunset looked unimpressed. 'I got a lot of room in my ears yet,' he said.

'So have I,' I snarled, suddenly pretending anger. 'Just what the hell have you said that means anything – except that you know Peeler?'

He spun his gun on his trigger finger, watching it spin. 'Old man Sype's at Westport,' he said casually. 'That mean anything to you?'

'Yeah. Has he got the marbles?'

'How the hell would I know?' He steadied the gun again, dropped it to his thigh. It wasn't pointing at me now. 'Where's this competish you mentioned?'

'I hoped I ditched them,' I said. 'I'm not too sure. Can I put my hands down and take a drink?'

'Yeah, go ahead. How did you cut in?'

'Peeler roomed with the wife of a friend of mine who's in stir. A straight girl, one you can trust. He let her in and she passed it to me – afterwards.'

'After the bump? How many cuts your side? My half is set.'

I took my drink, shoved the empty glass away. 'The hell it is.'

The gun lifted an inch, dropped again. 'How many altogether?' he snapped.

'Three, now Peeler's out. If we can hold off the competition.'

'The feet-toasters? No trouble about that. What they look like?'

'Man named Rush Madder, a shyster down south, fifty, fat, thin down-curving moustache, dark hair thin on top, five-nine, a hundred and eighty, not much guts. The girl, Carol Donovan, black hair, long bob, grey eyes, pretty, small features, twenty-five to eight, five-two, hundred twenty, last seen wearing blue, hard as they come. The real iron in the combination.'

Sunset nodded indifferently and put his gun away. 'We'll soften her, if she pokes her snoot in,' he said. 'I've got a heap at the house. Let's take the air Westport way and look it over. You might be able to ease in on the goldfish angle. They say he's nuts about them. I'll stay under cover. He's too stir-wise for me. I smell of the bucket.'

'Swell,' I said heartily. 'I'm an old goldfish fancier myself.'

Sunset reached for the bottle, poured two fingers of Scotch and put it down. He stood up, twitched his collar straight, then shot his chinless jaw forward as far as it would go.

'But don't make no error, bo. It's goin' to take pressure. It's goin' to mean a run out in the deep woods and some thumb twisting. Snatch stuff, likely.'

'That's okay,' I said. 'The insurance people are behind us.'

Sunset jerked down the points of his vest and rubbed the back of his thin neck. I put my hat on, locked the Scotch in the bag by the chair I'd been sitting in, went over and shut the window.

We started towards the door. Knuckles rattled on it just as I reached for the knob. I gestured Sunset back along the wall. I stared at the door for a moment and then I opened it up.

The two guns came forward almost on the same level, one small – a .32, one a big Smith and Wesson. They couldn't come into the room abreast, so the girl came in first.

'Okay, hot shot,' she said dryly. 'Ceiling zero. See if you can reach it.'

8

I backed slowly into the room. The two visitors bored in on me, either side. I tripped over my bag and fell backwards, hit the floor and rolled on my side groaning.

Sunset said casually: 'H'ist 'm, folks. Pretty now!'

Two heads jerked away from looking down at me and then I had my gun loose, down at my side. I kept on groaning.

There was a silence. I didn't hear any guns fall. The door of the room was still wide open and Sunset was flattened against the wall more or less behind it.

The girl said between her teeth: 'Cover the shamus, Rush – and shut the door. Skinny can't shoot here. Nobody can.'

Then, in a whisper I barely caught, she added: 'Slam it!'

Rush Madder waddled backwards across the room keeping the Smith and Wesson pointed my way. His back was to Sunset and the thought of that made his eyes roll. I could have shot him easily enough, but it wasn't the play. Sunset stood with his feet spread and his tongue showing. Something that could have been a smile wrinkled his flat eyes.

He stared at the girl and she stared at him. Their guns stared at each other.

Rush Madder reached the door, grabbed the edge of it and gave it a hard swing. I knew exactly what was going to happen. As the door slammed the .32 was going to go off. It wouldn't be heard if it went off at the right instant. The explosion would be lost in the slamming of the door.

I reached out and took hold of Carol Donovan's ankle and jerked it hard.

The door slammed. Her gun went off and chipped the ceiling.

She whirled on me kicking. Sunset said in his tight but somehow penetrating drawl:

'If this is it, this it it. Let's go!' The hammer clicked back on his Colt.

Something in his voice steadied Carol Donovan. She relaxed, let her automatic fall to her side and stepped away from me with a vicious look back.

Madder turned the key in the door and leaned against the wood, breathing noisily. His hat had tipped over one ear and the end of two strips of adhesive showed under the brim.

Nobody moved while I had these thoughts. There was no sound of feet outside in the hall, no alarm, I got up on my knees, slid my gun out of sight, rose on my feet and went over to the window. Nobody down on the sidewalk was staring up at the upper floors of the *Snoqualmie Hotel*.

I sat on the broad old-fashioned sill and looked faintly embarrassed, as though the minister had said a bad word.

The girl snapped at me: 'Is this lug your partner?'

I didn't answer. Her face flushed slowly and her eyes burned. Madder put a hand out and fussed:

'Now listen, Carol, now listen here. This sort of act ain't the way – '

'Shut up!'

'Yeah,' Madder said in a clogged voice. 'Sure.'

Sunset looked the girl over lazily for the third or fourth time. His gunhand rested easily against his hip bone and his whole attitude was of complete relaxation. Having seen him pull his gun once I hoped the girl wasn't fooled.

He said slowly: 'We've heard about you two. What's your offer? I wouldn't listen even, only I can't stand a shooting rap.'

The girl said:' There's enough it in for four.' Madder nodded his big head vigorously, almost managed a smile.

Sunset glanced at me. I nodded. 'Four it is,' he sighed. 'But that's the top. We'll go to my place and gargle. I don't like it here.'

'We must look simple,' the girl said nastily.

'Kill-simple,' Sunset drawled. 'I've met lots of them. That's why we're going to talk it over. It's not a shooting play.'

Carol Donovan slipped a suede bag from under her left arm and tucked her .32 into it. She smiled. She was pretty when she smiled.

'My ante is in,' she said quietly. 'I'll play. Where is the place?'

'Out Water Street. We'll go in a hack.'

'Lead on, sport.'

We went out of the room and down in the elevator, four friendly people walking out through a lobby full of antlers and stuffed birds and pressed wildflowers in glass frames. The taxi went out Capitol Way, past the square, past a big red apartment house that was too big for the town except when the Legislature was sitting. Along car tracks past the distant capitol buildings and the high closed gates of the governor's mansion.

Oak trees bordered the sidewalks. A few largish residences showed behind garden walls. The taxi shot past them and veered on to a road that led towards the tip of the Sound. In a short while a house showed in a narrow clearing between tall trees. Water glistened far back behind the tree trunks. The house had a roofed porch, a small lawn rotten with weeds and overgrown bushes. There was a shed at the end of a dirt driveway and an antique touring car squatted under the shed.

We got out and I paid the taxi. All four of us carefully watched it out of sight. Then Sunset said:

'My place is upstairs. There's a schoolteacher lives down below. She ain't at home. Let's go up and gargle.'

We crossed the lawn to the porch and Sunset threw a door open, pointed up narrow steps.

'Ladies first. Lead on, beautiful. Nobody locks a door in this town.'

The girl gave him a cool glance and passed him to go up the stairs. I went next, then Madder, Sunset last.

*

The single room that made up most of the second floor was dark from the trees, had a dormer window, a wide day-bed pushed back under the slope of the roof, a table, some wicker chairs, a small radio, and a round black stove in the middle of the floor.

Sunset drifted into a kitchenette and came back with a square bottle and some glasses. He poured drinks, lifted one and left the others on the table.

We helped ourselves and sat down.

Sunset put his drink down in a lump, leaned over to put his glass on the floor and came up with his Colt out.

I heard Madder's gulp in the sudden cold silence. The girl's mouth twitched as if she were going to laugh. Then she leaned forward, holding her glass on top of her bag with her left hand.

Sunset slowly drew his lips into a thin straight line. He said slowly and carefully:

'Feet-burners, huh? Burned my pal's feet, huh?'

Madder choked, started to spread his fat hands. The Colt flicked at him. He put his hands on his knees and clutched his kneecaps.

'And suckers at that,' Sunset went on tiredly. 'Burn a guy's feet to make him sing and then walk right into the parlour of one of his pals. You couldn't tie that with Christmas ribbon.'

Madder said jerkily: 'All r-right. W-what's the p-pay-off?'

The girl smiled slightly but she didn't say anything.

Sunset grinned. 'Rope,' he said softly. 'A lot of rope tied in hard knots, with water on it. Then me and my pal trundle off to catch fireflies – pearls to you – and when we come back –' he stopped, drew his left hand across the front of his throat. 'Like the idea?' he glanced at me.

'Yeah, but don't make a song about it,' I said. 'Where's the rope?'

'Bureau,' Sunset answered, and pointed with one ear at the corner.

I started in that direction, by way of the walls. Madder made a sudden thin whimpering noise and his eyes turned up in his head and he fell straight forward off the chair on his face, in a dead faint.

That jarred Sunset. He hadn't expected anything so foolish. His right hand jerked around until the Colt was pointing down at Madder's back.

The girl slipped her hand under her bag. The bag lifted an inch. The gun that was caught there in a trick clip – the gun that Sunset thought was inside the bag – spat and flamed briefly.

Sunset coughed. His Colt boomed and a piece of wood detached itself from the back of the chair Madder had been sitting in. Sunset dropped the Colt and put his chin down on his chest and tried to look at the ceiling. His long legs slid out in front of him and his heels made a rasping sound on the floor. He sat like that, limp, his chin on his chest, his eyes looking upward. Dead as a pickled walnut.

I kicked Miss Donovan's chair out from under her and she banged down on her side in a swirl of silken legs. Her hat went crooked on her head. She yelped. I stood on her hand and then shifted suddenly and kicked her gun clear across the attic. I sent her bag after it – with her other gun inside it. She screamed at me.

'Get up,' I snarled.

She got up slowly, backed away from me biting her lip, savage-eyed, suddenly a nasty-faced little brat at bay. She kept on backing until the wall stopped her. Her eyes glittered in a ghastly face.

I glanced down at Madder, went over to a closed door. A bathroom was behind it. I reversed a key and gestured at the girl.

'In.'

She walked stiff-legged across the floor and passed in front of me, almost touching me.

'Listen a minute, shamus – '

I pushed her through the door and slammed it and turned the key. It was all right with me if she wanted to jump out of the window. I had seen the windows from below.

I went across to Sunset, felt him, felt the small hard lump of keys on a ring in his pocket, and got them out without quite knocking him off his chair. I didn't look for anything else.

There were car keys on the ring.

I looked at Madder again, noticed that his fingers were as white as snow. I went down the narrow dark stairs to the porch, around to the side of the house and got into the old touring car under the shed. One of the keys on the ring fitted its ignition lock.

The car took a beating before it started up and let me back it down the dirt driveway to the kerb. Nothing moved in the house that I saw or heard. The tall pines behind and beside the house stirred their upper branches listlessly and a cold heartless sunlight sneaked through them intermittently as they moved.

I drove back to Capitol Way and downtown again as fast as I dared, past the square and the *Snoqualmie Hotel* and over the bridge towards the Pacific Ocean and Westport.

9

An hour's fast driving through thinned-out timberland, interrupted by three stops for water and punctuated by the cough of a head gasket leak, brought me within sound of surf. The broad white road, striped with yellow down the centre, swept around the flank of a hill, a distinct cluster of buildings loomed up in front of the shine of the ocean, and the road forked. The left fork was sign-posted: 'Westport – 9 Miles,' and didn't go towards the buildings. It crossed a rusty cantilever bridge and plunged into a region of wind-distorted apple orchards.

Twenty minutes more and I chugged into Westport, a sandy spit of land with scattered frame houses dotted over rising ground behind it. The end of the spit was a long narrow pier, and the end of the pier a cluster of sailing boats with half-lowered sails flapping against their single masts. And beyond them a buoyed channel and a long irregular line where the water creamed on a hidden sandbar.

Beyond the sandbar the Pacific rolled over to Japan. This was the last outpost of the coast, the farthest west a man could go and still be on the mainland of the United States. A swell place for an ex-convict to hide out with a couple of somebody else's pearls the size of new potatoes – if he didn't have any enemies.

I pulled up in front of a cottage that had a sign in the yard: 'Luncheons, Teas, Dinners.' A small rabbit-faced man with freckles was waving a garden rake at two black chickens. The chickens appeared to be sassing him back. He turned when the engine of Sunset's car coughed itself still.

I got out, went through a wicket gate, pointed to the sign. 'Luncheon ready?'

He threw the rake at the chickens, wiped his hands on his trousers and leered. 'The wife put that up,' he confided to me in a thin, impish voice. 'Ham and eggs is what it means.'

'Ham and eggs get along with me,' I said.

We went into the house. There were three tables covered with patterned oilcloth, some chromos on the walls, a full-rigged ship in a bottle on the mantel. I sat down. The host went away through a swing door and somebody yelled at him and a sizzling noise was heard from the kitchen. He came back and leaned over my shoulder, put some cutlery and a paper napkin on the oilcloth.

'Too early for apple brandy, ain't it?' he whispered.

I told him how wrong he was. He went away again and came back with glasses and a quart of clear amber fluid. He sat down with me and poured. A rich baritone voice in the kitchen was singing 'Chloe' over the sizzling.

We clinked glasses and drank and waited for the heat to crawl up our spines.

'Stranger, ain't you?' the little man asked.

I said I was.

'From Seattle maybe? That's a nice piece of goods you got on.'

'Seattle,' I agreed.

'We don't git many strangers,' he said, looking at my left ear. 'Ain't on the way to nowheres. Now before repeal – ' he stopped, shifted his sharp, woodpecker gaze to my other ear.

'Ah, before repeal,' I said with a large gesture, and drank knowingly.

He leaned over and breathed on my chin. 'Hell, you could load up in any fish stall on the pier. The stuff come in under catches of crabs and oysters. Hell, Westport was lousy with it. They give the kids cases of Scotch to play with. There wasn't a car in this town that slept in a garage, mister. The garages was all full to the roof of Canadian hooch. Hell, they had a coastguard cutter off the pier watchin' the boats unload one day every week. Friday. Always the same day.' He winked.

I puffed a cigarette and the sizzling noise and the baritone rendering of 'Chloe' went on in the kitchen.

'But hell, you wouldn't be in the liquor business,' he said.

'Hell, no, I'm a goldfish buyer,' I said.

'Okay,' he said sulkily.

*

I poured us another round of the apple brandy. 'This bottle is on me,' I said, 'And I'm taking a couple more with me.'

He brightened up. 'What did you say the name was?'

'Carmady. You think I'm kidding you about the goldfish. I'm not.'

'Hell, there ain't a livin' in them little fellers, is there?'

I held my sleeve out. 'You said it was a nice piece of goods. Sure there's a living out of the fancy brands. New brands, new types all the time. My information is there's an old guy down here somewhere that has a real collection. Maybe would sell it. Some he's bred himself.'

I poured us another round of the apple brandy. A large woman with a moustache kicked the swing door open a foot and yelled: 'Pick up the ham and eggs!'

My host scuttled across and came back with my food. I ate. He watched me minutely. After a time he suddenly smacked his skinny leg under the table.

'Old Wallace,' he chuckled. 'Sure, you come to see old Wallace. Hell, we don't know him right well. He don't act neighbourly.'

He turned around in his chair and pointed out through the sleazy curtains at a distant hill. On top of the hill was a yellow and white house that shone in the sun.

'Hell, that's where he lives. He's got a mess of them. Gold-fish, huh? Hell, you could bend me with an eye-dropper.'

That ended my interest in the little man. I gobbled my food, paid off for it and for three quarts of apple brandy at a dollar a quart, shook hands and went back out to the touring car.

There didn't seem to be any hurry. Rush Madder would come out of his faint, and he would turn the girl loose. But they didn't know anything about Westport. Sunset hadn't mentioned the name in their presence. They didn't know it when they reached Olympia, or they would have gone there at once. And if they had listened outside my room at the hotel, they would have known I wasn't alone. They hadn't acted as if they knew that when they charged in.

I had lots of time. I drove down to the pier and looked it over. It looked tough. There were fishstalls, drinking dives, a tiny honkytonk for the fishermen, a pool-room, an arcade of slot machines, and smutty peep-shows. Bait fish squirmed and darted in big wooden tanks down in the water along the piles. There were loungers and they looked like trouble for anyone that tried to interfere with them. I didn't see any law enforcement around.

I drove back up the hill to the yellow and white house. It stood very much alone, four blocks from the next nearest dwelling. There were flowers in front, a trimmed green lawn, a rock garden. A woman in a brown and white print dress was popping at aphids with a spray-gun.

I let my heap stall itself, got out and took my hat off.

'Mister Wallace live here?'

She had a handsome face, quiet, firm-looking. She nodded.

'Would you like to see him?' She had a quiet firm voice, a good accent.

It didn't sound like the voice of a train-robber's wife.

I gave her my name, said I'd been hearing about his fish down in the town. I was interested in fancy goldfish.

She put the spray-gun down and went into the house. Bees buzzed around my head, large fuzzy bees that wouldn't mind the cold wind off the sea. Far off like background music the surf pounded on the sandbars. The northern sunshine seemed bleak to me, had no heat in the core of it.

The woman came out of the house and held the door open.

'He's at the top of the stairs,' she said, 'if you'd like to go up.'

I went past a couple of rustic rockers and into the house of the man who had stolen the Leander pearls.

10

Fish tanks were all around the big room, two tiers of them on braced shelves, big oblong tanks with metal frames, some with lights over them and some with lights down in them. Water grasses were festooned in careless patterns behind the algae-coated glass and the water held a ghostly greenish light and through the greenish light moved fish of all the colours of the rainbow.

There were long slim fish like golden darts and Japanese Veiltails with fantastic trailing tails, and X-ray fish as transparent as coloured glass, tiny guppies half an inch long, calico popeyes spotted like a bride's apron, and big lumbering Chinese Moors with telescope eyes, froglike faces and unnecessary fins, waddling through the green water like fat men going to lunch.

Most of the light came from a big sloping skylight. Under the skylight at a bare wooden table a tall gaunt man stood

with a squirming red fish in his left hand, and in his right
hand a safety razor blade backed with adhesive tape.

He looked at me from under wide grey eyebrows. His eyes
were sunken, colourless, opaque. I went over beside him
and looked down at the fish he was holding.

'Fungus?' I asked.

He nodded slowly. 'White fungus.' He put the fish down
on the table and carefully spread its dorsal fin. The fin was
ragged and split and the ragged edges had a mossy white
colour.

'White fungus,' he said, 'ain't so bad. I'll trim this feller
up and he'll be right as rain. What can I do for you, Mister?'

I rolled a cigarette around in my fingers and smiled at
him.

'Like people,' I said. 'The fish, I mean. They get things
wrong with them.'

He held the fish against the wood and trimmed off the
ragged part of the fin. He spread the tail and trimmed that.
The fish had stopped squirming.

'Some you can cure,' he said, 'and some you can't. You
can't cure swimming-bladder disease, for instance.' He
glanced up at me. 'This don't hurt him, case you think it
does,' he said. 'You can shock a fish to death but you can't
hurt it like a person.'

He put the razor blade down and dipped a cotton swab in
some purplish liquid, painted the cut places. Then he
dipped a finger in a jar of white vaseline and smeared that
over. He dropped the fish in a small tank off to one side of
the room. The fish swam around peacefully, quite content.

The gaunt man wiped his hands, sat down at the edge of
a bench and stared at me with lifeless eyes. He had been
good-looking once, a long time ago.

'You interested in fish?' he asked. His voice had the quiet
careful murmur of the cell block and the exercise yard.

I shook my head. 'Not particularly. That was just an
excuse. I came a long way to see you, Mister Sype.'

He moistened his lips and went on staring at me. When his voice came again it was tired and soft.

'Wallace is the name, Mister.'

I puffed a smoke ring and poked my finger through it. 'For my job it's got to be Sype.'

He leaned forward and dropped his hands between his spread bony knees, clasped them together. Big gnarled hands that had done a lot of hard work in their time. His head tipped up at me and his dead eyes were cold under the shaggy brows. But his voice stayed soft.

'Haven't seen a dick in a year. To talk to. What's your lay?'

'Guess,' I said.

His voice got still softer. 'Listen, dick. I've got a nice home here, quiet. Nobody bothers me any more. Nobody's got a right to. I got a pardon straight from the White House. I've got the fish to play with and a man gets fond of anything he takes care of. I don't owe the world a nickel. I paid up. My wife's got enough dough for us to live on. All I want is to be left alone, dick.' He stopped talking, shook his head once. 'You can't burn me up – not any more.'

I didn't say anything. I smiled a little and watched him.

'Nobody can touch me,' he said. 'I got a pardon straight from the President's study. I just want to be let alone.'

I shook my head and kept on smiling at him. 'That's the one thing you can never have – until you give in.'

'Listen,' he said softly. 'You may be new on this case. It's kind of fresh to you. You want to make a rep for yourself. But me, I've had almost twenty years of it, and so have a lot of other people, some of 'em pretty smart people too. They know I don't have nothing that don't belong to me. Never did have. Somebody else got it.'

'The mail clerk,' I said. 'Sure.'

'Listen,' he said, still softly. 'I did my time. I know all the angles. I know they ain't going to stop wondering – long as anybody's alive that remembers. I know they're going to send some punk out once in a while to kind of stir it up

That's okay. No hard feelings. Now what do I do to get you to go home again?'

I shook my head and stared past his shoulder at the fish drifting in their big silent tanks. I felt tired. The quiet of the house made ghosts in my brain, ghosts of a lot of years ago. A train pounding through the darkness, a stickup hidden in a mail car, a gun flash, a dead clerk on the floor, a silent drop off at some water tank, a man who had kept a secret for nineteen years – almost kept it.

*

You made one mistake,' I said slowly. 'Remember a fellow named Peeler Mardo?'

He lifted his head. I could see him searching in his memory. The name didn't seem to mean anything to him.

'A fellow you knew in Leavenworth.' I said. 'A little runt that was in there for splitting twenty-dollar bills and putting phony backs on them.'

'Yeah,' he said. 'I remember.'

'You told him you had the pearls,' I said.

I could see he didn't believe me. 'I must have been kidding him,' he said slowly, emptily.

'Maybe. But here's the point. He didn't think so. He was up in this country a while ago with a pal, a guy who called himself Sunset. They saw you somewhere and Peeler recognized you. He got to thinking how he could make himself some jack. But he was a coke hound and he talked in his sleep. A girl got wise and then another girl and a shyster. Peeler got his feet burned and he's dead.'

Sype stared at me unblinkingly. The lines at the corners of his mouth deepened.

I waved my cigarette and went on:

'We don't know how much he told, but the shyster and a girl are in Olympia. Sunset's in Olympia, only he's dead. They killed him. I don't know if they know where you are or not. But they will sometime, or others like them. You can wear the cops down, if they can't find the pearls and you don't try to sell them. You can wear the insurance company down and even the postal men.'

Sype didn't move a muscle. His big knotty hands clenched between his knees didn't move. His dead eyes just stared.

'But you can't wear the chiselers down,' I said. 'They'll never lay off. There'll always be a couple or three with time enough and money enough and meanness enough to bear down. They'll find out what they want to know some way. They'll snatch your wife or take you out in the woods and give you the works. And you'll have to come through . . . Now I've got a decent, square proposition.'

'Which bunch are you?' Sype asked suddenly. 'I thought you smelled of dick, but I ain't so sure now.'

'Insurance,' I said. 'Here's the deal. Twenty-five grand reward in all. Five grand to the girl that passed me the info. She got it on the square and she's entitled to that cut. Ten grand to me. I've done all the work and looked into all the guns. Ten grand to you, through me. You couldn't get a nickel direct. Is there anything in it? How does it look?'

'It looks fine,' he said gently. 'Except for one thing. I don't have no pearls, dick.'

I scowled at him. That was my wad. I didn't have any more. I straightened away from the wall and dropped a cigarette end on the wood floor, crushed it out. I turned to go.

He stood up and put a hand out. 'Wait a minute,' he said gravely, 'and I'll prove it to you.'

He went across the floor in front of me and out of the room. I stared at the fish and chewed my lip. I heard the sound of a car engine somewhere, not very close. I heard a draw open and shut, apparently in a near-by room.

Sype came back into the fish room. He had a shiny Colt .45 in his gaunt fist. It looked as long as a man's forearm.

He pointed it at me and said: 'I got pearls in this, six of them. Lead pearls. I can comb a fly's whiskers at sixty yards. You ain't no dick. Now get up and blow – and tell your redhot friends I'm ready to shoot their teeth out any day of the week and twice on Sunday.'

I didn't move. There was a madness in the man's dead eyes. I didn't dare move.

'That's grandstand stuff,' I said slowly. 'I can prove I'm a dick. You're an ex-con and it's felony just having that rod. Put it down and talk sense.'

The car I had heard seemed to be stopping outside the house. Brakes whined on drums. Feet clattered up a walk, up steps. Sudden sharp voices, a caught exclamation.

Sype backed across the room until he was between the table and a big twenty or thirty gallon tank. He grinned at me, the wide clear grin of a fighter at bay.

'I see your friends kind of caught up with you,' he drawled. 'Take your gat out and drop it on the floor while you still got time – and breath.'

I didn't move. I looked at the wiry hair above his eyes. I looked into his eyes. I knew if I moved – even to do what he told me – he would shoot.

Steps came up the stairs. They were clogged, shuffling steps, with a hint of struggle in them.

Three people came into the room.

II

Mrs Sype came in first, stiff-legged, her eyes glazed, her arms bent rigidly at the elbows and the hands clawing straight forward at nothing, feeling for something that wasn't there. There was a gun in her back, one of Carol Donovan's small .32s, held efficiently in Carol Donovan's small ruthless hand.

Madder came last. He was drunk, brave from the bottle, flushed and savage. He threw the Smith and Wesson down on me and leered.

Carol Donovan pushed Mrs Sype aside. The older woman stumbled over into the corner and sank down on her knees, blank-eyed.

Sype stared at the Donovan girl. He was rattled because she was a girl and young and pretty. He hadn't been used to the type. Seeing her took the fire out of him. If men had come in he would have shot them to pieces.

The small dark white-faced girl faced him coldly, said in her tight chilled voice:

'All right, Dad. Shed the heater. Make it smooth now.'

Sype leaned down slowly, not taking his eyes off her. He put his enormous frontier Colt on the floor.

'Kick it away from you, Dad.'

Sype kicked it. The gun skidded across the bare boards, over towards the centre of the room.

'That's the way, old-timer. You hold on him, Rush, while I unrod the dick.'

The two guns swivelled and the hard grey eyes were looking at me now. Madder went a little way towards Sype and pointed his Smith and Wesson at Sype's chest.

The girl smiled, not a nice smile. 'Bright boy, eh? You sure stick your neck out all the time, don't you? Made a beef, shamus. Didn't frisk your skinny pal. He had a little map in one shoe.'

'I didn't need one,' I said smoothly, and grinned at her.

I tried to make the grin appealing, because Mrs Sype was moving her knees on the floor, and every move took her nearer to Sype's Colt.

'But you're all washed up now, you and your big smile. Hoist the mitts while I get your iron. Up, Mister.'

She was a girl, about five feet two inches tall, and weighed around a hundred and twenty. Just a girl. I was five-eleven and a half, weighed one-ninety-five. I put my hands up and hit her on the jaw.

That was crazy, but I had all I could stand of the Donovan—Madder act, the Donovan—Madder guns, the Donovan—Madder tough talk. I hit her on the jaw.

She went back a yard and her popgun went off. A slug burned my ribs. She started to fall. Slowly, like a slow-motion picture, she fell. There was something silly about it.

Mrs Sype got the Colt and shot her in the back.

Madder whirled and the instant he turned Sype rushed him. Madder jumped back and yelled and covered Sype again. Sype stopped cold and the wide crazy grin came back on his gaunt face.

The slug from the Colt knocked the girl forward as though a door had whipped in a high wind. A flurry of blue cloth, something thumped my chest – her head. I saw her face for a moment as she bounced back, a strange face that I had never seen before.

Then she was a huddled thing on the floor at my feet, small, deadly, extinct, with redness coming out from under her, and the tall quiet woman behind her with the smoking Colt held in both hands.

Madder shot Sype twice. Sype plunged forward still grinning and hit the end of the table. The purplish liquid he had used on the sick fish sprayed up over him. Madder shot him again as he was falling.

I jerked my Lüger out and shot Madder in the most painful place I could think of that wasn't likely to be fatal – the back of the knee. He went down exactly as if he had tripped over a hidden wire. I had cuffs on him before he even started to groan.

I kicked guns here and there and went over to Mrs Sype and took the big Colt out of her hands.

It was very still in the room for a little while. Eddies of smoke drifted towards the skylight, filmy grey, pale in the afternoon sun. I heard the surf booming in the distance. Then I heard a whistling sound close at hand.

It was Sype trying to say something. His wife crawled across to him, still on her knees, huddled beside him. There was blood on his lips and bubbles. He blinked hard, trying to clear his head. He smiled up at her. His whistling voice said very faintly:

'The Moors, Hattie – the Moors.'

Then his neck went loose and the smile melted off his face. His head rolled to one side on the bare floor.

Mrs Sype touched him, then got very slowly to her feet and looked at me, calm, dry-eyed.

She said in a low clear voice: 'Will you help me carry him to the bed? I don't like him here with these people.'

I said: 'Sure. What was that he said?'

'I don't know. Some nonsense about his fish, I think.'

I lifted Sype's shoulders and she took his feet and we carried him into the bedroom and put him on the bed. She folded his hands on his chest and shut his eyes. She went over and pulled the blinds down.

'That's all, thank you,' she said, not looking at me. 'The telephone is downstairs.'

She sat down in a chair beside the bed and put her head down on the coverlet near Sype's arm.

I went out of the room and shut the door.

12

Madder's leg was bleeding slowly, not dangerously. He stared at me with fear-crazed eyes while I tied a tight handkerchief above his knee. I figured he had a cut tendon and maybe a chipped kneecap. He might walk a little lame when they came to hang him.

I went downstairs and stood on the porch looking at the two cars in front, then down the hill towards the pier. Nobody could have told where the shots came from, unless he happened to be passing. Quite likely nobody had even noticed them. There was probably shooting in the woods around there a good deal.

I went back into the house and looked at the crank telephone on the living-room wall, but didn't touch it yet. Something was bothering me. I lit a cigarette and stared out of the window and a ghost voice said in my ears: 'The Moors, Hattie. The Moors.'

I went back upstairs into the fish room. Madder was groaning now, thick panting groans. What did I care about a torturer like Madder?

The girl was quite dead. None of the tanks was hit. The fish swam peacefully in their green water, slow and peaceful and easy. They didn't care about Madder either.

The tank with the black Chinese Moors in it was over in the corner, about ten gallon size. There were just four of them, big fellows, about four inches body length, coal black all over. Two of them were sucking oxygen on top of the water and two were waddling sluggishly on the bottom. They had thick deep bodies with a lot of spreading tail and high dorsal fins and their bulging telescope eyes that made them look like frogs when they were head towards you.

I watched them fumbling around in the green stuff that was growing in the tank. A couple of red pond snails were window-cleaning. The two on the bottom looked thicker and more sluggish than the two on the top. I wondered why.

There was a long-handled strainer made of woven string lying between two of the tanks. I got it and fished down in the tank, trapped one of the big Moors and lifted it out. I turned it over in the net, looked at its faintly silver belly. I saw something that looked like a suture. I felt the place. There was a hard lump under it.

I pulled the other one off the bottom. Same suture, same hard round lump. I got one of the two that had been sucking air on top. No suture, no hard round lump. It was harder to catch too.

I put it back in the tank. My business was with the other

two. I like goldfish as well as the next man, but business is business and crime is crime. I took my coat off and rolled my sleeves up and picked the razor blade backed with adhesive off the table.

It was a very messy job. It took about five minutes. Then they lay in the palm of my hand, three-quarters of an inch in diameter, heavy, perfectly round, milky white and shimmering with that inner light no other jewel had. The Leander pearls.

I washed them off, wrapped them in my handkerchief, rolled down my sleeves and put my coat back on. I looked at Madder, at his little pain- and fear-tortured eyes, the sweat on his face. I didn't care anything about Madder. He was a killer, a torturer.

I went out of the fish room. The bedroom door was still shut. I went down below and cranked the wall telephone.

'This is the Wallace place at Westport,' I said. 'There's been an accident. We need a doctor and we'll have to have the police. What can you do?'

The girl said: 'I'll try and get you a doctor, Mr Wallace. It may take a little time though. There's a town marshal at Westport. Will he do?'

'I suppose so,' I said and thanked her and hung up. There were points about a country telephone after all.

*

I lit another cigarette and sat down in one of the rustic rockers on the porch. In a little while there were steps and Mrs Sype came out of the house. She stood a moment looking off down the hills, then she sat down in the other rocker beside her. Her dry eyes looked at me steadily.

'You're a detective, I suppose,' she said slowly, diffidently.

'Yes, I represent the company that insured the Leander pearls.'

She looked off into the distance. 'I thought he would have

peace here,' she said. 'That nobody would bother him any more. That this place would be a sort of sanctuary.'

'He ought not to have tried to keep the pearls.'

She turned her head, quickly this time. She looked blank now, then she looked scared.

I reached down in my pocket and got out the wadded handkerchief, opened it up on the palm of my hand. They lay there together on the white linen, two hundred grand worth of murder.

'He could have had his sanctuary,' I said. 'Nobody wanted to take it away from him. But he wasn't satisfied with that.'

She looked slowly, lingeringly at the pearls. Then her lips twitched. Her voice got hoarse.

'Poor Wally,' she said. 'So you did find them. You're pretty clever, you know. He killed dozens of fish before he learned how to do that trick. She looked up into my face. A little wonder showed at the back of her eyes.

She said: 'I always hated the idea. Do you remember the old Bible theory of the scapegoat?'

I shook my head, no.

'The animal on which the sins of a man were laid and then it was driven off into the wilderness. The fish were his scapegoat.'

She smiled at me. I didn't smile back.

She said, still smiling faintly: 'You see, he once had the pearls, the real ones, and suffering seemed to him to make them his. But he couldn't have had any profit from them, even if he had found them again. It seems some landmark changed, while he was in prison, and he never could find the spot in Idaho where they were buried.'

An icy finger was moving slowly up and down my spine. I opened my mouth and something I supposed might be my voice said:

'Huh?'

She reached a finger out and touched one of the pearls. I

was still holding them out, as if my hand was a shelf nailed to the wall.

'So he got these,' she said. 'In Seattle. They're hollow, filled with white wax. I forget what they call the process. They look very fine. Of course I never saw any really valuable pearls.'

'What did he get them for?' I croaked.

'Don't you see? They were his sin. He had to hide them in the wilderness, this wilderness. He hid them in the fish. And do you know – ' she leaned towards me again and her eyes shone. She said very slowly, very earnestly:

'Sometimes I think that in the very end, just the last year or so, he actually believed they were the real pearls he was hiding. Does all this mean anything to you?'

I looked down at my pearls. My hand and the handkerchief closed over them slowly.

I said: 'I'm a plain man, Mrs Sype. I guess the scapegoat idea is a bit over my head. I'd say he was just trying to kid himself a bit – like any heavy loser.'

She smiled again. She was handsome when she smiled. Then she shrugged, quite lightly.

'Of course, you would see it that way. But me – ' she spread her hands. 'Oh, well, it doesn't matter much now. May I have them for a keepsake?'

'Have them?'

'The – the phony pearls. Surely you don't – '

I stood up. An old Ford roadster without a top was chugging up the hill. A man in it had a big star on his vest. The chatter of the motor was like the chatter of some old angry bald-headed ape in the zoo.

Mrs Sype was standing beside me, with her hand half out, a thin, beseeching look on her face.

I grinned at her with sudden ferocity.

'Yeah, you were pretty good in there for a while,' I said. 'I damn near fell for it. And was I cold down the back, lady! But you helped. "Phony" was a shade out of charac-

ter for you. Your work with the Colt was fast and kind of
ruthless. Most of all Sype's last words queered it. "The
Moors, Hattie – the Moors." He wouldn't have bothered
with that if the stones had been ringers. And he wasn't
sappy enough to kid himself all the way.'

For a moment her face didn't change at all. Then it did.
Something horrible showed in her eyes. She put her lips out
and spat at me. Then she slammed into the house.

I tucked twenty-five thousand dollars into my vest pocket.
Twelve thousand five hundred for me and twelve thousand
five hundred for Kathy Horne. I could see her eyes when
I brought her the cheque, and when she put it in the bank,
to wait for Johnny to get paroled from Quentin.

The Ford had pulled up behind the other cars. The man
driving spat over the side, yanked his emergency brake on,
got out without using the door. He was a big fellow in shirt
sleeves.

I went down the steps to meet him.

V

Guns at Cyrano's

I

TED MALVERN liked the rain; liked the feel of it, the sound of it, the smell of it. He got out of his LaSalle coupé and stood for a while by the side entrance to the *Carondelet*, the high collar of his blue suede ulster tickling his ears, his hands in his pockets and a limp cigarette sputtering between his lips. Then he went in past the barber shop and the drugstore and the perfume shop with its rows of delicately lighted bottles, ranged like the ensemble in the finale of a Broadway musical.

He rounded a gold-veined pillar and got into an elevator with a cushioned floor.

' 'Lo, Albert. A swell rain. Nine.'

The slim tired-looking kid in pale blue and silver held a white gloved hand against the closing doors, said:

'Jeeze, you think I don't know your floor, Mister Malvern?'

He shot the car up to nine without looking at his signal light, whooshed the doors open, then leaned suddenly against the cage and closed his eyes.

Malvern stopped on his way out, flicked a sharp glance from bright brown eyes. 'What's the matter, Albert? Sick?'

The boy worked a pale smile on his face. 'I'm workin' double shift. Corky's sick. He's got boils. I guess maybe I didn't eat enough.'

The tall, brown-eyed man fished a crumpled five-spot out of his pocket, snapped it under the boy's nose. The boy's eyes bulged. He heaved upright.

'Jeeze, Mister Malvern. I didn't mean – '

'Skip it, Albert. What's a fin between pals? Eat some extra meals on me.'

He got out of the car and started along the corridor. Softly, under his breath, he said:

'Sucker . . . '

The running man almost knocked him off his feet. He rounded the turn fast, lurched past Malvern's shoulder, ran for the elevator.

'Down!' He slammed through the closing doors.

Malvern saw a white set face under a pulled-down hat that was wet with rain; two empty black eyes set very close. Eyes in which there was a peculiar stare he had seen before. A load of dope.

The car dropped like lead. Malvern looked at the place where it had been for a long moment, then he went on down the corridor and around the turn.

He saw the girl lying half in and half out of the open door of 914.

She lay on her side, in a sheen of steel grey lounging pyjamas, her cheek pressed into the nap of the hall carpet, her head a mass of thick corn blonde hair, waved with glassy precision. Not a hair looked out of place. She was young, very pretty, and she didn't look dead.

Malvern slid down beside her, touched her cheek. It was warm. He lifted the hair softly away from her head and saw the bruise.

'Sapped.' His lips pressed back against his teeth.

He picked her up in his arms, carried her through a short hallway to the living-room of a suite, put her down on a big velour davenport in front of some gas logs.

She lay motionless, her eyes shut, her face bluish behind the make-up. He shut the outer door and looked through the apartment, then went back to the hallway and picked up something that gleamed white against the baseboard. It was a bone-handled .22 automatic, seven-shot. He sniffed it, dropped it into his pocket and went back to the girl

He took a big hammered silver flask out of his inside breast pocket and unscrewed the top, opened her mouth with his fingers and poured whisky against her small white teeth. She gagged and her head jerked out of his hand. Her eyes opened. They were deep blue, with a tint of purple. Light came into them and the light was brittle.

He lit a cigarette and stood looking down at her. She moved a little more. After a while she whispered:

'I like your whisky. Could I have a little more?'

He got a glass from the bathroom, poured whisky into it. She sat up very slowly, touched her head, groaned. Then she took the glass out of his hand and put the liquor down with a practised flip of the wrist.

'I still like it,' she said. 'Who are you?'

She had a deep soft voice. He liked the sound of it. He said:

'Ted Malvern. I live down the hall in 937.'

'I – I got a dizzy spell, I guess.'

'Uh-huh. You got sapped, angel.' His bright eyes looked at her probingly. There was a smile tucked to the corner of his lips.

Her eyes got wider. A glaze came over them, the glaze of a protective enamel.

He said: 'I saw the guy. He was snowed to the hairline. And here's your gun.'

He took it out of his pocket, held it on the flat of his hand.

'I suppose that makes me think up a bedtime story,' the girl said slowly.

'Not for me. If you're in a jam, I might help you. It all depends.'

'Depends on what?' Her voice was colder, sharper.

'On what the racket is,' he said softly. He broke the magazine from the small gun, glanced at the top cartridge. 'Copper-nickel, eh? You know your ammunition, angel.'

'Do you have to call me angel?'

'I don't know your name.'

He grinned at her, then walked over to a desk in front of the windows, put the gun down on it. There was a leather photo frame on the desk, with two photos side by side. He looked at them casually at first, then his gaze tightened. A handsome dark woman and a thin blondish cold-eyed man whose high stiff collar, large knotted tie and narrow lapels dated the photo back many years. He stared at the man.

The girl was talking behind him. 'I'm Jean Adrian. I do a number at *Cyrano's*, in the floor show.'

Malvern still stared at the photo. 'I know Benny Cyrano pretty well,' he said absently. 'These your parents?'

He turned and looked at her. She lifted her head slowly. Something that might have been fear showed in her deep blue eyes.

'Yes. They've been dead for years,' she said dully. 'Next question?'

He went quickly back to the davenport and stood in front of her. 'Okay,' he said thinly. 'I'm nosey. So what? This is my town. My dad used to run it. Old Marcus Malvern, the People's Friend. This is my hotel. I own a piece of it. That snowed-up hoodlum looked like a life-taker to me. Why wouldn't I want to help out?'

The blonde girl stared at him lazily. 'I still like your whisky,' she said. 'Could I – '

'Take it from the neck, angel. You get it down faster,' he grunted.

She stood up suddenly and her face got a little white. 'You talk to me as if I was a crook,' she snapped. 'Here it is, if you have to know. A boy friend of mine has been getting threats. He's a fighter, and they want him to drop a fight. Now they're trying to get at him through me. Does that satisfy you a little?'

Malvern picked his hat off a chair, took the cigarette end out of his mouth and rubbed it out in a tray. He nodded quietly, said in a changed voice:

'I beg your pardon.' He started towards the door.

The giggle came when he was half-way there. The girl said behind him softly:

'You have a nasty temper. And you've forgotten your flask.'

He went back and picked the flask up. Then he bent suddenly, put a hand under the girl's chin and kissed her on the lips.

'To hell with you, angel. I like you,' he said softly.

He went back to the hallway and out. The girl touched her lips with one finger, rubbed it slowly back and forth. There was a shy smile on her face.

2

Tony Acosta, the bell captain, was slim and dark and slight as a girl, with small delicate hands and velvety eyes and a hard little mouth. He stood in the doorway and said:

'Seventh row was the best I could get, Mister Malvern. This Deacon Werra ain't bad and Duke Targo's the next light heavy champ.'

Malvern said: 'Come in and have a drink, Tony.' He went over to the window, stood looking out at the rain. 'If they buy it for him,' he added over his shoulder.

'Well – just a short one, Mister Malvern.'

The dark boy mixed a highball carefully at a tray on an imitation Sheraton desk. He held the bottle against the light and gauged his drink carefully, tinkled ice gently with a long spoon, sipped, smiled, showing small white teeth.

'Targo's a lu, Mister Malvern. He's fast, clever, got a sock in both mitts, plenty guts, don't ever take a step back.'

'He has to hold up the bums they feed him,' Malvern drawled.

'Well, they ain't fed him no lion meat yet,' Tony said.

The rain beat against the glass. The thick drops flattened out and washed down the pane in tiny waves.

Malvern said: 'He's a bum. A bum with colour and looks, but still a bum.'

Tony sighed deeply. 'I wisht I was goin'. It's my night off, too.'

Malvern turned slowly and went over to the desk, mixed a drink. Two dusky spots showed in his cheeks and his voice was tired, drawling.

'So that's it. What's stopping you?'

'I got a headache.'

'You're broke again,' Malvern almost snarled.

The dark boy looked sidewise under his long lashes, said nothing.

Malvern clenched his left hand, unclenched it slowly. His eyes were sullen.

'Just ask Ted,' he sighed. 'Good old Ted. He leaks dough. He's soft. Just ask Ted. Okay, Tony, take a ducat back and get a pair together.'

He reached into his pocket, held a bill out. The dark boy looked hurt.

'Jeeze, Mister Malvern, I wouldn't have you think – '

'Skip it! What's a fight ticket between pals? Get a couple and take your girl. To hell with this Targo.'

Tony Acosta took the bill. He watched the older man carefully for a moment. Then his voice was very soft, saying:

'I'd rather go with you, Mister Malvern. Targo knocks them over, and not only in the ring. He's got a peachy blonde right on this floor. Miss Adrian, in 914.'

Malvern stiffened. He put his glass down slowly, turned it on the top of the desk. His voice got a little hoarse.

'He's still a bum, Tony. Okay, I'll meet you for dinner, in front of your hotel at seven.'

'Jeeze, that's swell, Mister Malvern.'

Tony Acosta went out softly, closed the outer door without a sound.

Malvern stood by the desk, his finger-tips stroking the top of it, his eyes on the floor. He stood like that for a long time.

'Ted Malvern, the All-American sucker,' he said grimly, out loud. 'A guy that plays with the help and carries the torch for stray broads. Yeah.'

He finished his drink, looked at his wrist-watch, put on his hat and the blue suede raincoat, went out. Down the corridor in front of 914 he stopped, lifted his hand to knock, then dropped it without touching the door.

He went slowly on to the elevators and rode down to the street and his car.

*

The *Tribune* office was at Fourth and Spring. Malvern parked around the corner, went in at the employees' entrance and rode to the fourth floor in a rickety elevator operated by an old man with a dead cigar in his mouth and a rolled magazine which he held six inches from his nose while he ran the elevator.

On the fourth floor big double doors were lettered 'City Room'. Another old man sat outside them at a small desk with a call box.

Malvern tapped on the desk, said: 'Adams. Ted Malvern calling.'

The old man made noises into the box, released a key pointed with his chin.

Malvern went through the doors, past a horseshoe copy desk, then past a row of small desks at which typewriters were being banged. At the far end a lanky red-haired man was doing nothing with his feet on a pulled-out drawer, the back of his neck on the back of a dangerously tilted swivel chair and a big pipe in his mouth pointed straight at the ceiling.

When Malvern stood beside him he moved his eyes down without moving any other part of his body and said around the pipe:

'Greetings. Teddy. How's the idle rich?'

Malvern said: 'How's a glance at your clips on a guy named Courtway? State Senator John Myerson Courtway, to be precise.'

Adams put his feet on the floor. He raised himself erect by pulling on the edge of his desk. He brought his pipe down level, took it out of his mouth and spat into a waste basket. He said:

'That old icicle? When was he ever news? Sure.' He stood up wearily, added: 'Come along, Uncle,' and started along the end of the room.

They went along another row of desks, past a fat girl in smudged make-up who was typing and laughing at what she was writing.

They went through a door into a big room that was mostly six-foot tiers of filing cases with an occasional alcove in which there was a small table and a chair.

Adams prowled the filing cases, jerked one out and set a folder on a table.

'Park yourself. What's the graft?'

Malvern leaned on the table on an elbow, scuffed through a thick wad of cuttings. They were monotonous, political in nature, not front page. Senator Courtway said this and that on this and that matter of public interest, addressed this and that meeting, went to or returned from this and that place. It all seemed very dull.

He looked at a few half-tone cuts of a thin, white-haired man with a blank, composed face, deep set dark eyes in which there was no light or warmth. After a while he said:

'Got a print I could sneeze? A real one, I mean.'

Adams sighed, stretched himself, disappeared down the line of file walls. He came back with a shiny narrow black and white photograph, tossed it down on the table.

'You can keep it,' he said. 'We got dozens. The guy lives for ever. Shall I have it autographed for you?'

Malvern looked at the photo with narrow eyes, for a long

time. 'It's right,' he said slowly. 'Was Courtway ever married?'

'Not since I left off my diapers,' Adams growled. 'Probably not ever. Say, what'n hell's the mystery?'

Malvern smiled slowly at him. He reached his flask out, set it on the table beside the folder. Adams' face brightened swiftly and his long arm reached.

'Then he never had a kid,' Malvern said.

Adams leered over the flask. 'Well – not for publication, I guess. If I'm any judge of a mug, not at all.' He drank deeply, wiped his lips, drank again.

'And that,' Malvern said, 'is very funny indeed. Have three more drinks – and forget you ever saw me.'

3

The fat man put his face close to Malvern's face. He said with a wheeze:

'You think it's fixed, neighbour?'

'Yeah. For Werra.'

'How much says so?'

'Count your poke.'

'I got five yards that want to grow.'

'Take it,' Malvern said tonelessly, and kept on looking at the back of a corn-blonde head in a ringside seat. A white wrap with white fur was below the glassily waved hair. He couldn't see the face. He didn't have to.

The fat man blinked his eyes and got a thick wallet carefully out of a pocket inside his vest. He held it on the edge of his knee, counted out ten fifty-dollar bills, rolled them up, edged the wallet back against his ribs.

'You're on, sucker,' he wheezed. 'Let's see your dough.'

Malvern brought his eyes back, reached out a flat pack of

new hundreds, ruffled them. He slipped five from under the printed band, held them out.

'Boy, this is from home,' the fat man said. He put his face close to Malvern's face again. 'I'm Skeets O'Neal. No little powders, huh?'

Malvern smiled very slowly and pushed his money into the fat man's hand. 'You hold it, Skeets. I'm Ted Malvern. Old Marcus Malvern's son. I can shoot faster than you can run – and fix it afterwards.'

The fat man took a long hard breath and leaned back in his seat. Tony Acosta stared soft-eyed at the money in the fat man's pudgy tight hand. He licked his lips and turned a small embarrassed smile on Malvern.

'Gee, that's lost dough, Mister Malvern,' he whispered. 'Unless – unless you got something inside.'

'Enough to be worth a five-yard plunge,' Malvern growled.

The buzzer sounded for the sixth.

The first five had been anybody's fight. The big blond boy, Duke Targo, wasn't trying. The dark one, Deacon Werra, a powerful, loose-limbed Polack with bad teeth and only two cauliflower ears, had the physique but didn't know anything but rough clinching and a giant swing that started in the basement and never connected. He had been good enough to hold Targo off so far. The fans razzed Targo a good deal.

When the stool swung back out of the ring Targo hitched at his black and silver trunks, smiled with a small tight smile at the girl in the white wrap. He was very good-looking, without a mark on him. There was blood on his left shoulder from Werra's nose.

The bell rang and Werra charged across the ring, slid off Targo's shoulder, got a left hook in. Targo got more of the hook than was in it. He piled back into the ropes, bounced out, clinched.

Malvern smiled quietly in the darkness.

The referee broke them easily. Targo broke clean. Werra tried for an uppercut and missed. They sparred for a minute. There was waltz music from the gallery. Then Werra started a swing from his shoetops. Targo seemed to wait for it, to wait for it to hit him. There was a queer strained smile on his face. The girl in the white wrap stood up suddenly.

Werra's swing grazed Targo's jaw. It barely staggered him. Targo lashed a long right that caught Werra over the eye. A left hook smashed into Werra's jaw, then a right cross almost to the same spot.

The dark boy went down on his hands and knees, slipped slowly all the way to the floor, lay with both gloves under him. There were catcalls as he was counted out.

The fat man struggled to his feet, grinning hugely. He said:

'How you like it, pal? Still think it was a set piece?'

'It came unstuck,' Malvern said in a voice as toneless as a police radio.

The fat man said: 'So long, pal. Come around lots.' He kicked Malvern's ankle climbing over him.

Malvern sat motionless, watched the auditorium empty. The fighters and their handlers had gone down the stairs under the ring. The girl in the white wrap had disappeared in the crowd. The lights went out and the barnlike structure looked cheap, sordid.

Tony Acosta fidgeted, watching a man in striped overalls picking up papers between the seats.

*

Malvern stood up suddenly, said: 'I'm going to talk to that bum, Tony. Wait outside in the car for me.'

He went swiftly up the slope to the lobby, through the remnants of the gallery crowd to a grey door marked: 'No Admittance'. He went through that and down a ramp to another door marked the same way. A special cop in faded and unbuttoned khaki stood in front of it, with a bottle of beer in one hand and a hamburger in the other.

Malvern flashed a police card and the cop lurched out of the way without looking at the card. He hiccoughed peacefully as Malvern went through the door, then along a narrow passage with numbered doors lining it. There was noise behind the doors. The fourth door on the left had a scribbled card with the name 'Duke Targo' fastened to the panel by a thumbtack.

Malvern opened it into the heavy sound of a shower going, out of sight.

In a narrow and utterly bare room a man in a white sweater was sitting on the end of a rubbing table that had clothes scattered on it. Malvern recognized him as Targo's chief second.

He said: 'Where's the Duke?'

The sweatered man jerked a thumb towards the shower noise. Then a man came around the door and lurched very close to Malvern. He was tall and had curly brown hair with hard grey colour in it. He had a big drink in his hand. His face had the flat glitter of extreme drunkenness. His hair was damp, his eyes bloodshot. His lips curled and uncurled in rapid smiles without meaning. He said thickly: 'Scramola umpchay.'

Malvern shut the door calmly and leaned against it and started to get his cigarette case from his vest pocket, inside his open blue raincoat. He didn't look at the curly-haired man at all.

The curly-haired man lunged his free right hand up suddenly, snapped it under his coat, out again. A blue steel gun shone dully against his light suit. The glass in his left hand slopped liquor.

'None of that!' he snarled.

Malvern brought the cigarette case out very slowly, showed it in his hand, opened it and put a cigarette between his lips. The blue gun was very close to him, not very steady.

The hand holding the glass shook in a sort of jerky rhythm.

Malvern said loosely: 'Yeah. You *ought* to be looking for trouble.'

The sweatered man got off the rubbing table. Then he stood very still and looked at the gun. The curly-haired man said:

'We like trouble. Frisk him, Mike.'

The sweatered man said: 'I don't want any part of it, Shenvair. For Pete's sake, take it easy. You're lit like a ferry boat.'

Malvern said: 'It's okay to frisk me. I'm not rodded.'

'Nix,' the sweatered man said. 'This guy is the Duke's bodyguard. Deal me out.'

The curly-haired man said: 'Sure, I'm drunk,' and giggled.

'You're a friend of the Duke?' the sweatered man asked.

'I've got some information for him,' Malvern said.

'About what?'

Malvern didn't say anything. 'Okay,' the sweatered man said. He shrugged bitterly.

'Know what, Mike?' the curly-haired man said suddenly and violently. 'I think this — wants my job. Hell, yes. He looks like a bum. You ain't a shamus, are you, mister?' He 'punched Malvern with the muzzle of the gun.

'Yeah,' Malvern said. 'And keep your iron next your own belly.'

The curly-haired man turned his head a little and grinned back over his shoulder.

'What d'you know about that, Mike? He's a shamus. Sure he wants my job. Sure he does.'

'Put the heater up, you fool,' the sweatered man said disgustedly.

The curly-haired man turned a little more. 'I'm his protection, ain't I?' he complained.

Malvern knocked the gun aside almost casually, with the hand that held his cigarette case. The curly-haired man snapped his head around again. Malvern slid close to him, sank a stiff punch in his stomach, holding the gun away with his forearm. The curly-haired man gagged, sprayed liquor down the front of Malvern's raincoat. His glass shattered on the floor. The blue gun left his hand and went over in a corner. The sweatered man went after it.

The noise of the shower had stopped unnoticed and the blond fighter came out towelling himself vigorously. He stared open-mouthed at the tableau.

Malvern said: 'I don't need this any more.'

He heaved the curly-haired man away from him and laced his jaw with a hard right as he went back. The curly-haired man staggered across the room, hit the wall, slid down it and sat on the floor.

The sweatered man snatched the gun up and stood rigid, watching Malvern.

Malvern got out a handkerchief and wiped the front of his coat, while Targo shut his large well-shaped mouth slowly and began to move the towel back and forth across his chest. After a moment he said:

'Just who the hell may you be?'

Malvern said: 'I used to be a private dick. Malvern's the name. I think you need help.'

Targo's face got a little redder than the shower had left it. 'Why?'

'I heard you were supposed to throw it, and I think you tried to. Werra was too lousy. You couldn't help yourself. That means you're in a jam.'

Targo said very slowly: 'People get their teeth kicked in for saying things like that.'

The room was very still for a moment. The drunk sat up on the floor and blinked, tried to get his feet under him, and gave it up.

Malvern added quietly: 'Benny Cyrano is a friend of mine. He's your backer, isn't he?'

The sweatered man laughed harshly. Then he broke the

gun and slid the shells out of it, dropped the gun on the floor. He went to the door, went out, slammed the door shut.

Targo looked at the shut door, looked back at Malvern. He said very slowly:

'What did you hear?'

'Your friend Jean Adrian lives in my hotel, on my floor. She got sapped by a hood this afternoon. I happened by and saw the hood running away, picked her up. She told me a little of what it was all about.'

Targo had put on his underwear and socks and shoes. He reached into a locker for a black satin shirt, put that on. He said:

'She didn't tell me.'

'She wouldn't – before the fight.'

Targo nodded slightly. Then he said: 'If you know Benny, you may be all right. I've been getting threats. Maybe it's a lot of birdseed and maybe it's some Spring Street punter's idea of how to make himself a little easy dough. I fought my fight the way I wanted to. Now you can take the air, mister.'

He put on high-waisted black trousers and knotted a white tie on his black shirt. He got a white serge coat trimmed with black braid out of the locker, put that on. A black and white handkerchief flared from the pocket in three points.

Malvern stared at the clothes, moved a little towards the door and looked down at the drunk.

'Okay,' he said. 'I see you've got a bodyguard. It was just an idea I had. Excuse it, please.'

He went out, closed the door gently, and went back up the ramp to the lobby, out to the street. He walked through the rain around the corner of the building to a big gravelled parking lot.

The lights of a car blinked at him and his coupé slid along the wet gravel and pulled up. Tony Acosta was at the wheel.

Malvern got in at the right side and said: 'Let's go out to Cyrano's and have a drink, Tony.'

'Jeeze, that's swell. Miss Adrian's in the floor show there. You know, the blonde I told you about.'

Malvern said: 'Yeah. I saw Targo. I kind of liked him — but I didn't like his clothes.'

4

Gus Neishacker was a two-hundred-pound fashion plate with very red cheeks and thin, exquisitely pencilled eyebrows – eyebrows from a Chinese vase. There was a red carnation in the lapel of his wide-shouldered dinner jacket and he kept sniffing at it while he watched the head waiter seat a party of guests. When Malvern and Tony Acosta came through the flyer arch he flashed a sudden smile and went to them with his hand out.

'How's a boy, Ted? Party?'

Malvern said: 'Just the two of us. Meet Mister Acosta. Gus Neishacker, Cyrano's floor manager.'

Gus Neishacker shook hands with Tony without looking at him. He said: 'Let's see, the last time you dropped in – '

'She left town,' Malvern said. 'We'll sit near the ring but not too near. We don't dance together.'

Gus Neishacker jerked a menu from under the head waiter's arm and led the way down five crimson steps, along the tables that skirted the oval dance floor.

They sat down. Malvern ordered rye highballs and Denver sandwiches. Neishacker gave the order to a waiter, pulled a chair out and sat down at the table. He took a pencil out and made triangles on the inside of a match cover.

'See the fights?' he asked carelessly.

'Was that what they were?'

Gus Neishacker smiled indulgently. 'Benny talked to the

Duke. He says you're wise.' He looked suddenly at Tony Acosta.

'Tony's all right,' Malvern said.

'Yeah. Well do us a favour, will you? See it stops right here. Benny likes this boy. He wouldn't let him get hurt. He'd put protection all around him – *real* protection – if he thought that threat stuff was anything but some pool-hall bum's idea of a very funny joke. Benny never backs but one boxfighter at a time, and he picks them damn' careful.'

Malvern lit a cigarette, blew smoke from a corner of his mouth, said quietly: 'It's none of my business, but I'm telling you it's screwy. I have a nose for that sort of thing.'

Gus Neishacker stared at him a minute, then shrugged. He said: 'I hope you're right,' stood up quickly and walked away among the tables. He bent to smile here and there, and speak to a customer.

Tony Acosta's velvet eyes shone. He said: 'Jeeze, Mister Malvern, you think it's rough stuff?'

Malvern nodded, didn't say anything. The waiter put their drinks and sandwiches on the table, went away. The band on the stage at the end of the oval floor blared out a long chord and a slick, grinning M.C. slid out on the stage and put his lips to a small open mike.

The floor show began. A line of half naked girls ran out under a rain of coloured lights. They coiled and uncoiled in a long sinuous line, their bare legs flashing, their navels little dimples of darkness in soft white, very nude flesh.

A hard-boiled red-head sang a hard-boiled song in a voice that could have been used to split firewood. The girls came back in black tights and silk hats, did the same dance with a slightly different exposure.

The music softened and a tall high yaller torch singer drooped under an amber light and sang of something very far away and unhappy, in a voice like old ivory.

Malvern sipped his drink, poked at his sandwich in the

dim light. Tony Acosta's hard young face was a small tense blur beside him.

The torch singer went away and there was a little pause and then suddenly all the lights in the place went out except the lights over the music racks of the band and the little pale amber lights at the entrances to the radiating aisles of booths beyond the tables.

There were squeals in the thick darkness. A single white spot winked on, high up under the roof, settled on a runway beside the stage. Faces were chalk white in the reflected glare. There was the red glow of a cigarette tip here and there. Four tall black men moved in the light, carrying a white mummy case on their shoulders. They came slowly, in rhythm, down the runway. They wore white Egyptian head-dresses and loincloths of white leather and white sandals laced to the knees. The black smoothness of their limbs was like black marble in the moonlight.

They reached the middle of the dance-floor and slowly upended the mummy case until the cover tipped forward and fell and was caught. Then slowly, very slowly, a swathed white figure tipped forward and fell – slowly, like the last leaf from a dead tree. It tipped in the air, seemed to hover, then plunged towards the floor under a shattering roll of drums.

The light went off, went on. The swathed figure was upright on the floor, spinning, and one of the blacks was spinning the opposite way, winding the white shroud around his body. Then the shroud fell away and a girl was all tinsel and smooth white limbs under the hard light and her body shot through the air glittering and was caught and passed around swiftly among the four black men, like a baseball handled by a fast infield.

Then the music changed to a waltz and she danced among the black men slowly and gracefully, as though among four bony pillars, very close to them but never touching them.

The act ended. The applause rose and fell in thick waves. The light went out and it was dark again, and then all the

lights went up and the girl and the four black men were
gone.

'Keeno,' Tony Acosta breathed. 'Oh, keeno. That was
Miss Adrian, wasn't it?'

Malvern said slowly: 'Yeah. A little daring.' He lit another cigarette, looking around. 'There's another black and
white number, Tony. The Duke himself, in person.'

Duke Targo stood applauding violently at the entrance
to one of the radiating booth aisles. There was a loose grin
on his face. He looked as if he might have had a few drinks.

An arm came down over Malvern's shoulders. A hand
planted itself in the ashtray at his elbow. He smelled Scotch
in heavy gusts. He turned his head slowly, looked up at the
liquor-shiny face of Shenvair, Duke Targo's drunken bodyguard.

'Smokes and a white gal,' Shenvair said thickly. 'Lousy.
Crummy. Godawful crummy.'

Malvern smiled slowly, moved his chair a little. Tony
Acosta stared at Shenvair round-eyed, his little mouth a thin
line.

'Blackface, Mister Shenvair. Not real smokes. I liked
it.'

'And who the hell cares what you like?' Shenvair wanted
to know.

Malvern smiled delicately, laid his cigarette down on the
edge of a plate. He turned his chair a little more.

'Still think I want your job, Shenvair?'

'Yeah. I owe you a smack in the puss too.' He took his
hand out of the ashtray, wiped it off on the tablecloth. He
doubled it into a fist. 'Like it now?'

A waiter caught him by the arm, spun him around.

'You lost your table, sir? This way.'

Shenvair patted the waiter on the shoulder, tried to put
an arm around his neck. 'Swell, let's go nibble a drink. I
don't like these people.'

They went away, disappeared among the tables.

Malvern said: 'To hell with this place, Tony,' and stared
moodily towards the band stage. Then his eyes became
intent.

*

A girl with corn-blonde hair, in a white wrap with a white
fur collar, appeared at the edge of the shell, went behind it,
reappeared nearer. She came along the edge of the booths
to the place where Targo had been standing. She slipped in
between the booths there, disappeared.

Malvern said: 'Yeah. To hell with this place. Let's go,
Tony,' in a low angry voice. Then very softly, in a tensed
tone: 'No – wait a minute. I see another guy I don't
like.'

The man was on the far side of the dance-floor, which was
empty at the moment. He was following its curve around,
past the tables that fringed it. He looked a little different
without his hat. But he had the same flat white expressionless face, the same close-set eyes. He was youngish, not more
than thirty, but already having trouble with his bald spot.
The slight bulge of a gun under his left arm was barely
noticeable. He was the man who had run away from Jean
Adrian's apartment in the *Carondelet*.

He reached the aisle into which Targo had gone, into
which a moment before Jean Adrian had gone. He went
into it.

Malvern said sharply: 'Wait here, Tony.' He kicked his
chair back and stood up.

Somebody rabbit-punched him from behind. He swivelled,
close to Shenvair's grinning sweaty face.

'Back again, pal,' the curly-haired man chortled, and hit
him on the jaw.

It was a short jab, well placed for a drunk. It caught Malvern off balance, staggered him. Tony Acosta came to his
feet snarling, catlike. Malvern was still rocking when Shenvair let go with the other fist. That was too slow, too wide.

Malvern slid inside it, uppercut the curly-haired man's nose
savagely, got a handful of blood before he could get his hand
away. He put most of it back on Shenvair's face.

Shenvair wobbled, staggered back a step and sat down on
the floor, hard. He clapped a hand to his nose.

'Keep an eye on this bird, Tony,' Malvern growled
swiftly.

Shenvair took hold of the nearest tablecloth and yanked
it. It came off the table. Silver and glasses and china followed it to the floor. A man swore and a woman squealed.
A waiter ran towards them with a livid, furious face.

Malvern almost didn't hear the two shots.

They were small and flat, close together, a small calibre
gun. The rushing waiter stopped dead, and a deeply-etched
white line appeared around his mouth as instantly as though
the lash of a whip had cut it there.

A dark woman with a sharp nose opened her mouth to
yell and no sound came from her. There was that instant
when nobody makes a sound, when it almost seems as if
there will never again be any sound – after the sound of a
gun. Then Malvern was running.

He bumped into people who stood up and craned their
necks. He reached the entrance to the aisle into which the
white-faced man had gone. The booths had high walls and
swing doors not so high. Heads stuck out over the doors, but
no one was in the aisle yet. Malvern charged up a shallow
carpeted slope, at the far end of which booth doors stood
wide open.

Legs in dark cloth showed past the doors, slack on the
floor, the knees sagged. The toes of black shoes were pointed
into the booth.

Malvern shook an arm off, reached the place.

The man lay across the end of a table, his stomach and
one side of his face on the white cloth, his left hand dropped
between the table and the padded seat. His right hand on
top of the table didn't quite hold a big black gun, a .45 with

cut barrel. The bald spot on his head glistened under the light, and the oily metal of the gun glistened beside it.

Blood leaked from under his chest, vivid scarlet on the white cloth, seeping into it as into blotting paper.

Duke Targo was standing up, deep in the booth. His left arm in the white serge coat was braced on the end of the table. Jean Adrian was sitting down at his side. Targo looked at Malvern blankly, as if he had never seen him before. He pushed his big right hand forward.

A small white-handled automatic lay on his palm.

'I shot him,' he said thickly. 'He pulled a gun on us and shot him.'

Jean Adrian was scrubbing her hands together on a scrap of handkerchief. Her face was strained, cold, not scared. Her eyes were dark.

'I shot him,' Targo said. He threw the small gun down on the cloth. It bounced, almost hit the fallen man's head. 'Let's – let's get out of here.'

Malvern put a hand against the side of the sprawled man's neck, held it there a second or two, took it away.

'He's dead,' he said. 'When a citizen drops a redhot – that's news.'

Jean Adrian was staring at him stiff-eyed. He flashed a smile at her, put a hand against Targo's chest, pushed him back.

'Sit down, Targo. You're not going any place.'

Targo said: 'Well – okay. I shot him, see.'

'That's all right,' Malvern said. 'Just relax.'

People were close behind him now, crowding him. He leaned back against the press of bodies and kept on smiling at the girls' white face.

5

Benny Cyrano was shaped like two eggs, a little one that
was his head on top of a big one that was his body. His small
dapper legs and feet in patent leather shoes were pushed
into the kneehole of a dark sheenless desk. He held a corner
of a handkerchief tightly between his teeth and pulled
against it with his left hand and held his right hand out
pudgily in front of him, pushing against the air. He was
saying in a voice muffled by the handkerchief.

'Now wait a minute, boys. Now wait a minute.'

There was a striped built-in sofa in one corner of the
office, and Duke Targo sat in the middle of it, between two
Headquarters dicks. He had a dark bruise over his cheek-
bone, his thick blond hair was tousled and his black satin
shirt looked as if somebody had tried to swing him by it.

One of the dicks, the grey-haired one, had a split lip. The
young one with hair as blond as Targo's had a black eye.
They both looked mad, but the blond one looked madder.

Malvern straddled a chair against the wall and looked
sleepily at Jean Adrian, near him in a leather rocker. She
was twisting a handkerchief in her hands, rubbing her palms
with it. She had been doing this for a long time, as if she had
forgotten she was doing it. Her small firm mouth was angry.

Gus Neishacker leaned against the closed door smoking.

'Now wait a minute, boys,' Cyrano said. 'If you didn't
get tough with him, he wouldn't fight back. He's a good boy
– the best I ever had. Give him a break.'

Blood dribbled from one corner of Targo's mouth, in a
fine thread down to his jutting chin. It gathered there and
glistened. His face was empty, expressionless.

Malvern said coldly: 'You wouldn't want the boys to stop
playing blackjack pinochle, would you, Benny?'

The blond dick snarled: 'You still got that private dick
licence, Malvern?'

'It's lying around somewhere, I guess,' Malvern said.

'Maybe we could take it away from you,' the blond dick snarled.

'Maybe you could do a fan dance, copper. You might be all kinds of a smart guy for all I'd know.'

The blond dick started to get up. The older one said: 'Leave him be. Give him six feet. If he steps over that, we'll take the screws out of him.'

Malvern and Gus Neishacker grinned at each other. Cyrano made helpless gestures in the air. The girl looked at Malvern under her lashes. Targo opened his mouth and spat blood straight before him on the blue carpet.

Something pushed against the door and Neishacker stepped to one side, opened it a crack, then opened it wide. McChesney came in.

McChesney was a lieutenant of detectives, tall, sandy-haired, fortyish, with pale eyes and a narrow suspicious face. He shut the door and turned the key in it, went slowly over and stood in front of Targo.

'Plenty dead,' he said. 'One under the heart, one in it. Nice snap shooting. In any league?'

'When you've got to deliver you've got to deliver,' Targo said dully.

'Make him?' the grey-haired dick asked his partner, moving away along the sofa.

McChesney nodded. 'Torchy Plant. A gun for hire. I haven't seen him around for all of two years. Tough as an ingrowing toenail with his right load. A bindle punk.'

'He'd have to be that to throw his party in here,' the grey-haired dick said.

McChesney's long face was serious, not hard. 'Got a permit for the gun, Targo?'

Targo said: 'Yes. Benny got me one two weeks ago. I been getting a lot of threats.'

'Listen, Lieutenant,' Cyrano chirped, 'some gamblers try to scare him into a dive, see? He wins nine straight fights by

knockouts so they get a swell price. I told him he should take
one at that maybe.'

'I almost did,' Targo said sullenly.

'So they sent the redhot to him,' Cyrano said.

McChesney said: 'I wouldn't say no. How'd you beat his
draw, Targo? Where was your gun?'

'On my hip.'

'Show me.'

Targo put his hand back into his right hip pocket and
jerked a handkerchief out quickly, stuck his finger through
it like a gun barrel.

'That handkerchief in the pocket?' McChesney asked
'With the gun?'

Targo's big reddish face clouded a little. He nodded.

McChesney leaned forward casually and twitched the
handkerchief from his hand. He sniffed at it, unwrapped it
sniffed at it again, folded it and put it away in his own
pocket. His face said nothing.

'What did he say, Targo?'

'He said: "I got a message for you, punk, and this is it."
Then he went for the gat and it stuck a little in the clip. I
got mine out first.'

McChesney smiled faintly and leaned far back, teetering
on his heels. His faint smile seemed to slide off the end of his
long nose. He looked Targo up and down.

'Yeah,' he said softly. 'I'd call it damn' nice shooting with
a .22. But you're fast for a big guy . . . Who got these threats?'

'I did,' Targo said. 'Over the phone.'

'Know the voice?'

'It might have been this same guy. I'm not just positive.'

McChesney walked stiff-legged to the other end of the
office, stood a moment looking at a hand-tinted sporting
print. He came back slowly, drifted over to the door.

'A guy like that don't mean a lot,' he said quietly, 'but we
got to do our job. The two of you will have to come down
town and make statements. Let's go.'

He went out. The two dicks stood up, with Duke Targo between them. The grey-haired one snapped:

'You goin' to act nice, bo?'

Targo sneered: 'If I get to wash my face.'

They went out. The blond dick waited for Jean Adrian to pass in front of him. He swung the door, snarled back at Malvern:

'As for you – nuts!'

Malvern said softly: 'I like them. It's the squirrel in me, copper.'

Gus Neishacker laughed, then shut the door and went to the desk.

'I'm shaking like Benny's third chin,' he said. 'Let's all have a shot of cognac.'

He poured three glasses a third full, took one over to the striped sofa and spread his long legs out on it, leaned his head back and sipped the brandy.

Malvern stood up and downed his drink. He got a cigarette out and rolled it around in his fingers, staring at Cyrano's smooth white face with an up-from-under look.

'How much would you say changed hands on that fight to-night?' he asked softly. 'Bets.'

Cyrano blinked, massaged his lips with a fat hand. 'A few grand. It was just a regular weekly show. It don't listen, does it?'

Malvern put the cigarette in his mouth and leaned over the desk to strike a match. He said:

'If it does, murder's getting awfully cheap in this town.'

Cyrano didn't say anything. Gus Neishacker sipped the last of his brandy and carefully put the empty glass down on a round cork table beside the sofa. He stared at the ceiling, silently.

After a moment Malvern nodded at the two men, crossed the room and went out, closed the door behind him. He went along a corridor off which dressing-rooms opened, dark now. A curtained archway let him out at the back of the stage.

In the foyer the head waiter was standing at the glass doors, looking out at the rain and the back of a uniformed policeman. Malvern went into the empty cloak room, found his hat and coat, put them on, came out to stand beside the head waiter.

He said: 'I guess you didn't notice what happened to the kid I was with?'

The head waiter shook his head and reached forward to unlock the door.

'There was four hundred people here – and three hundred scrammed before the Law checked in. I'm sorry.'

Malvern nodded and went out into the rain. The uniformed man glanced at him casually. He went along the street to where the car had been left. It wasn't there. He looked up and down the street, stood for a few moments in the rain, then walked towards Melrose.

After a little while he found a taxi.

6

The ramp of the *Carondelet* garage curved down into semi-darkness and chilled air. The dark bulks of stalled cars looked ominous against the whitewashed walls, and the single droplight in the small office had the relentless glitter of the death house.

A big Negro in stained overalls came out rubbing his eyes, then his face split in an enormous grin.

'Hello, there, Mistuh Malvu'n. You kinda restless to-night?'

Malvern said: 'I get a little wild when it rains. I bet my heap isn't here.'

'No, it ain't, Mistuh Malvu'n. I been all around wipin' off and yours ain't here aytall.'

Malvern said woodenly: 'I lent it to a pal. He probably wrecked it . . . '

He flicked a half-dollar through the air and went back up the ramp to the side street. He turned towards the back of the hotel, came to an alley-like street one side of which was the rear wall of the *Carondelet*. The other side had two frame houses and a four-storey brick building. *Hotel Blaine* was lettered on a round milky globe over the door.

Malvern went up three cement steps and tried the door. It was locked. He looked through the glass panel into a small dim empty lobby. He got out two pass-keys; the second one moved the lock a little. He pulled the door hard towards him, tried the first one again. That snicked the bolt back far enough for the loosely-fitted door to open.

He went in and looked at an empty counter with a sign: 'Manager' beside a plunger bell. There was an oblong of empty numbered pigeon-holes on the wall. Malvern went around the counter and fished a leather register out of a space under the top. He read names back three pages, found the boyish scrawl: 'Tony Acosta', and a room number in another writing.

He put the register away and went past the automatic elevator and upstairs to the fourth floor.

The hallway was very silent. There was weak light from a ceiling fixture. The last door but one on the left-hand side had a crack of light showing around its transom. That was the door – 411. He put his hand out to knock, then withdrew it without touching the door.

The door-knob was heavily smeared with something that looked like blood.

Malvern's eyes looked down and saw what was almost a pool of blood on the stained wood before the door, beyond the edge of the runner.

His hand suddenly felt clammy inside his glove. He took

the glove off, held the hand stiff, clawlike for a moment, then shook it slowly. His eyes had a sharp strained light in them.

He got a handkerchief out, grasped the door-knob inside it, turned it slowly. The door was unlocked. He went in.

He looked across the room and said very softly: 'Tony . . . oh, Tony.'

Then he shut the door behind him and turned a key in it, still with the handkerchief.

There was light from the bowl that hung on three brass chains from the middle of the ceiling. It shone on a made-up bed, some painted, light-coloured furniture, a dull green carpet, a square writing desk of eucalyptus wood.

Tony Acosta sat at the desk. His head was slumped forward on his left arm. Under the chair on which he sat, between the legs of the chair and his feet, there was a glistening brownish pool.

Malvern walked across the room so rigidly that his ankles ached after the second step. He reached the desk, touched Tony Acosta's shoulder.

'Tony,' he said thickly, in a low, meaningless voice. 'My God, Tony!'

Tony didn't move. Malvern went around to his side. A blood-soaked bath towel glared against the boy's stomach, across his pressed-together thighs. His right hand was crouched against the front edge of the desk, as if he was trying to push himself up. Almost under his face there was a scrawled envelope.

Malvern pulled the envelope towards him slowly, lifted it like a thing of weight, read the wandering scrawl of words.

'Tailed him . . . woptown . . . 28 Court Street . . . over garage . . . shot me . . . think I got . . . him . . . your car . . .'

The line trailed over the edge of the paper, became a blot there. The pen was on the floor. There was a bloody thumb print on the envelope.

Malvern folded it meticulously to protect the print, put

the envelope in his wallet. He lifted Tony's head, turned it a little towards him. The neck was still warm; it was beginning to stiffen. Tony's soft dark eyes were open and they held the quiet brightness of a cat's eyes. They had that effect the eyes of the new dead have of almost, but not quite, looking at you.

Malvern lowered the head gently on the outstretched left arm. He stood laxly, his head on one side, his eyes almost sleepy. Then his head jerked straight and his eyes hardened.

He stripped off his raincoat and the suitcoat underneath, rolled his sleeves up, wet a face towel in the basin in the corner of the room and went to the door. He wiped the knobs off, bent down and wiped up the smeared blood from the floor outside.

He rinsed the towel and hung it up to dry, wiped his hands carefully, put his coat on again. He used his handkerchief to open the transom, to reverse the key and lock the door from the outside. He threw the key in over the top of the transom, heard it tinkle inside.

He went downstairs and out of the *Hotel Blaine*. It still rained. He walked to the corner, looked along a tree-shaded block. His car was a dozen yards from the intersection, parked carefully, the lights off, the keys in the ignition. He drew them out, felt the seat under the wheel. It was wet, sticky. Malvern wiped his hand off, ran the windows up and locked the car. He left it where it was.

Going back to the *Carondelet* he didn't meet anybody. The hard slanting rain still pounded down into the empty streets.

7

There was a thin thread of light under the door of 914. Malvern knocked lightly, looking up and down the hall, moved his gloved finger softly on the panel while he waited.

He waited a long time. Then a voice spoke wearily behind the wood of the door.

'Yes? What is it?'

'Ted Malvern, angel. I have to see you. It's strictly business.'

The door clicked, opened. He looked at a tired white face, dark eyes that were slatelike, not violet-blue. There were smudges under them as though mascara had been rubbed into the skin. The girl's strong little hand twitched on the edge of the door.

'You,' she said wearily. 'It would be you. Yes . . . Well, I've simply got to have a shower. I smell of policemen.'

'Fifteen minutes?' Malvern asked casually, but his eyes were very sharp on her face.

She shrugged slowly, then nodded. The closing door seemed to jump at him. He went along to his own rooms, threw off his hat and coat, poured whisky into a glass and went into the bathroom to get icewater from the small tap over the basin.

He drank slowly, looking out of the windows at the dark breadth of the boulevard. A car slid by now and then, two beams of white light attached to nothing emanating from nowhere.

He finished the drink, stripped to the skin, went under a shower. He dressed in fresh clothes, refilled his big flask and put it in his inner pocket, took a snubnosed automatic out of a suit-case and held it in his hand for a minute staring at it. Then he put it back in the suit-case, lit a cigarette and smoked it through.

He got a dry hat and a tweed coat and went back to 914. The door was almost insidiously ajar. He slipped in with a light knock, shut the door, went on into the living-room and looked at Jean Adrian.

She was sitting on the davenport, with a freshly scrubbed look, in loose plum-coloured pyjamas and a Chinese coat. tendril of damp hair drooped over one temple. Her small even features had the cameo-like clearness that tiredness gives to the very young.

Malvern said: 'Drink?'

She gestured emptily. 'I suppose so.'

He got glasses, mixed whisky and ice water, went to the davenport with them.

'Are they keeping Targo on ice?'

She moved her chin an eighth of an inch, staring into her glass.

'He cut loose again, knocked two cops half-way through the wall. They love that boy.'

Malvern said: 'He has a lot to learn about cops. In the morning the cameras will be all set for him. I can think of some nice headlines, such as: "Well-known Fighter too Fast for Gunmen. Duke Targo Puts Crimp in Underworld Hot Rod." '

The girl sipped her drink. 'I'm tired,' she said. 'And my foot itches. Let's talk about what makes this your business.'

'Sure.' He flipped his cigarette case open, held it under her chin. Her hand fumbled at it and while it still fumbled he said: 'When you light that tell me why you shot him.'

Jean Adrian put the cigarette between her lips, bent her head to the match, inhaled and threw her head back. Colour awakened slowly in her eyes and a small smile curved the line of her pressed lips. She didn't answer.

Malvern watched her for a minute, turning his glass in his hands. Then he stared at the floor, said:

'It was your gun – the gun I picked up here in the afternoon. Targo said he drew it from his hip pocket, the slowest draw in the world. Yet he's supposed to have shot twice, accurately enough to kill a man, while the man wasn't even getting his gun loose from a shoulder-holster. That's hooey. But you, with the gun in a bag in your lap, and knowing the hood, might just have managed it. He would have been watching Targo.'

The girl said emptily: 'You're a private dick, I hear.

You're the son of a boss politician. They talked about you downtown. They act a little afraid of you, of people you might know. Who sicked you on to me?'

Malvern said: 'They're not afraid of me, angel. They just talked like that to see how you'd react, if I was involved, and so on. They don't know what it's all about.'

'They were told plainly enough what it was all about.'

Malvern shook his head. 'A cop never believes what he gets without a struggle. He's too used to cooked-up stories. I think McChesney's wise you did the shooting. He knows by now if that handkerchief of Targo's had been in a pocket with a gun.'

Her limp fingers discarded her cigarette half-smoked. A curtain eddied at the window and loose flakes of ash crawled around in the ashtray. She said slowly:

'All right. I shot him. Do you think I'd hesitate after this afternoon?'

Malvern rubbed the lobe of his ear. 'I'm playing this too light,' he said softly. 'You don't know what's in my heart. Something has happened, something nasty. Do you think the hood meant to kill Targo?'

'I thought so – or I wouldn't have shot a man.'

'I think maybe it was just a scare. Like the other one. After all a night-club is a poor place for a get-away.'

She said sharply: 'They don't do many low tackles on forty-fives. He'd have got away all right. Of course he meant to kill somebody. And of course I didn't mean Duke to front for me. He just grabbed the gun out of my hand and slammed into his act. What did it matter? I knew it would all come out in the end.'

She poked absently at the still burning cigarette in the tray, kept her eyes down. After a moment she said, almost in a whisper: 'Is that all you wanted to know?'

Malvern let his eyes crawl sideways, without moving his head, until he could just see the firm curve of her cheek, the strong line of her throat. He said thickly:

'Shenvair was in on it. The fellow I was with at Cyrano's followed Shenvair to a hideout. Shenvair shot him. He's dead. He's dead, angel – just a young kid that worked here in the hotel. Tony, the bell captain. The cops don't know that yet.'

The muffled clang of elevator doors was heavy through the silence. A horn tooted dismally out in the rain on the boulevard. The girl sagged forward suddenly, then sideways, fell across Malvern's knees. Her body was half-turned and she lay almost on her back across his thighs, her eyelids flickering. The small blue veins in them stood out rigid in the soft skin.

He put his arms around her slowly, loosely, then they tightened, lifted her. He brought her face close to his own face. He kissed her on the side of the mouth.

Her eyes opened, stared blankly, unfocused. He kissed her again, tightly, then pushed her upright on the davenport.

He said quietly: 'That wasn't just an act, was it?'

She leaped to her feet, spun around. Her voice was low, tense, and angry.

'There's something horrible about you! Something – satanic. You come here and tell me another man has been killed – and then you kiss me. It isn't real.'

Malvern said dully: 'There's something horrible about any man that goes suddenly gaga over another man's woman.'

'I'm not his woman!' she snapped. 'I don't even like him – and I don't like you.'

Malvern shrugged. They stared at each other with bleak hostile eyes. The girl clicked her teeth shut, then said almost violently:

'Get out! I can't talk to you any more. I can't stand you around. Will you get out?'

Malvern said: 'Why not?' He stood up, went over and got his hat and coat.

The girl sobbed once sharply, then she went in light quick

strides across the room to the windows, became motionles
with her back to him.

Malvern looked at her back, went over near her and stoo
looking at the soft hair low down on her neck. He said:

'Why the hell don't you let me help? I know there's some
thing wrong. I wouldn't hurt you.'

The girl spoke to the curtain in front of her face, savagely

'Get out! I don't want your help. Go away and stay away
I won't be seeing you – ever.'

Malvern said slowly: 'I think you've got to have help
Whether you like it or not. That man in the photoframe o
the desk there – I think I know who he is. And I don't thin
he's dead.'

The girl turned. Her face now was as white as paper. He
eyes strained at his eyes. She breathed thickly, harshly. Afte
what seemed a long time she said:

'I'm caught. Caught. There's nothing you can do abou
it.'

Malvern lifted a hand and drew his fingers slowly dow
her cheek, down the angle of her tight jaw. His eyes held
hard brown glitter, his lips a smile. It was a cunning, almos
a dishonest smile.

He said: 'I'm wrong, angel. I don't know him at al
Good night.'

He went back across the room, through the little hallway
opened the door. When the door opened the girl clutche
at the curtain and rubbed her face against it slowly.

Malvern didn't shut the door. He stood quite still hal
way through it, looking at two men who stood there wit
guns.

They stood close to the door, as if they had been about t
knock. One was thick, dark saturnine. The other one was a
albino with sharp red eyes, a narrow head that showe
shining snow-white hair under a rain-spattered dark hat. H
had the thin sharp teeth and the drawn-back grin of a ra

Malvern started to close the door behind him. The albin

aid: 'Hold it, rube. The door, I mean. We're goin' in.'

The other man slid forward and pressed his left hand up and down Malvern's body carefully. He stepped away, said: 'No gat, but a swell flask under his arm.'

The albino gestured with his gun. 'Buck up, rube. We want the broad, too.'

Malvern said tonelessly: 'It doesn't take a gun, Critz. I know you and I know your boss. If he wants to see me, I'll be glad to talk to him.'

He turned and went back into the room with the two gunmen behind him.

Jean Adrian hadn't moved. She stood by the window sill, the curtain against her cheek, her eyes closed, as if she hadn't heard the voices at the door at all.

Then she heard them come in and her eyes snapped open. She turned slowly, stared past Malvern at the two gunmen. The albino walked to the middle of the room, looked around at without speaking, went into the bedroom and bathroom. Doors opened and shut. He came back on quiet cat-like feet, pulled his overcoat open and pushed his hat back on his head.

'Get dressed, sister. We have to go for a ride in the rain. Okay?'

The girl stared at Malvern now. He shrugged, smiled a little, spread his hands.

'That's how it is, angel. Might as well fall in line.'

The lines of her face got thin and contemptuous. She said slowly: 'You – you – .' Her voice trailed off into a sibilant, meaningless mutter. She went across the room stiffly and out of it into the bedroom.

The albino slipped a cigarette between his sharp lips, chuckled with a wet, gurgling sound, as if his mouth was all of saliva.

'She don't seem to like you, rube.'

Malvern frowned. He walked slowly to the writing desk, leaned his hips against it, stared at the floor.

'She thinks I sold her out,' he said dully.

'Maybe you did, rube,' the albino drawled.

Malvern said: 'Better watch her. She's neat with a gun.'

His hands, reaching casually behind him on the desk,
tapped the top of it lightly, then without apparent change
of movement folded the leather photo frame down on its side
and edged it under the blotter.

8

There was a padded arm rest in the middle of the rear seat of
the car, and Malvern leaned an elbow on it, cupped his chin
in his hand, stared through the half-misted windows at the
rain. It was thick white spray in the headlights, and the noise
of it on the top of the car was like drum-fire very far off.

Jean Adrian sat on the other side of the arm rest, in the
corner. She wore a black hat and a grey coat with tufts of
silky hair on it, longer than caracul and not so curly. She
didn't look at Malvern or speak to him.

The albino sat on the right of the thick dark man, who
drove. They went through the silent streets, past blurred
houses, blurred trees, the blurred shine of street lights. There
were neon signs behind thick curtains of mist. There was
no sky.

Then they climbed and a feeble arc light strung over an
intersection threw light on a sign post, and Malvern read
the name 'Court Street'.

He said softly: 'This is woptown, Critz. The big guy can't
be so dough-heavy as he used to be.'

Light flickered from the albino's eyes as he glanced back.
'You should know, rube.'

The car slowed in front of a big frame house with
trellised porch, walls finished in round shingles, blind, light-
less windows. Across the street a stencil sign on a brick build-

ng built to the sidewalk said: 'Paolo Perrugini Funeral Parlours.'

The car swung out to make a wide turn into a gravel driveway. Lights splashed into an open garage. They went n, slid to a stop beside a big shiny undertaker's ambulance.

The Albino snapped: 'All out!'

Malvern said: 'I see our next trip is all arranged for.'

'Funny guy,' the albino snarled. 'A wise monkey.'

'Uh-huh. I just have nice scaffold manners,' Malvern drawled.

The dark man cut the motor and snapped on a big flash, hen cut the lights, got out of the car. He shot the beam of he flash up a narrow flight of wooden steps in the corner. The albino said:

'Up you go, rube. Push the girl ahead of you. I'm behind with my rod.'

Jean Adrian got out of the car past Malvern, without ooking at him. She went up the steps stiffly, and the three nen made a procession behind her.

There was a door at the top. The girl opened it and hard white light came out at them. They went into a bare attic vith exposed studding, a square window in front and rear. hut tight, the glass painted black. A bright bulb hung on a drop cord over a kitchen table and a big man sat at the table with a saucer of cigarette butts at his elbow. Two of them till smoked.

A thin loose-lipped man sat on a bed with a Lüger beside his left hand. There was a worn carpet on the floor, a few ticks of furniture, a half-open clapboard door in the corner hrough which a toilet seat showed, and one end of a big old-ashioned bathtub standing up from the floor on iron legs.

The man at the kitchen table was large but not handsome. He had carroty hair and eyebrows a shade darker, a square aggressive face, a strong jaw. His thick lips held his cigarette brutally. His clothes looked as if they had cost a great deal of money and had been slept in.

He glanced carelessly at Jean Adrian, said around the cigarette:

'Park the body, sister. Hi, Malvern. Gimme that rod, Lefty, and you boys drop down below again.'

The girl went quietly across the attic and sat down in a straight wooden chair. The man on the bed stood up, put the Lüger at the big man's elbow on the kitchen table. The three gunmen went down the stairs, leaving the door open.

The big man touched the Lüger, stared at Malvern, said sarcastically:

'I'm Doll Conant. Maybe you remember me.'

Malvern stood loosely by the kitchen table, with his legs spread wide, his hands in his overcoat pockets, his head tilted back. His half-closed eyes were sleepy, very cold.

He said: 'Yeah. I helped my dad hang the only rap on you that ever stuck.'

'It didn't stick, mug. Not with the Court of Appeals.'

'Maybe this one will,' Malvern said carelessly. 'Kidnapping is apt to be a sticky rap in this State.'

Conant grinned without opening his lips. His expression was grimly good-humoured. He said:

'Let's not barber. We got business to do and you know better than that last crack. Sit down – or rather take a look at Exhibit One first. In the bathtub behind you. Yeah, take a look at that. Then we can get down to tacks.'

Malvern turned, went across to the clapboard door, pushed through it. There was a bulb sticking out of the wall with a key-switch. He snapped it on, bent over the tub.

For a moment his body was quite rigid and his breath was held rigidly. Then he let it out very slowly, and reached his left hand back and pushed the door almost shut. He bent further over the big iron tub.

It was long enough for a man to stretch out in, and a man was stretched out in it, on his back. He was fully dressed, even to a hat, although his hat didn't look as if he had put it on himself. He had thick, grey-brown curly hair. There was blood on his face and there was a gouged, red-rimmed hole at the inner corner of his left eye.

He was Shenvair and he was long since dead.

Malvern sucked in his breath and straightened slowly, then suddenly he bent forward still further until he could see into the space between the tub and the wall. Something blue and metallic glistened down there in the dust. A blue steel gun. A gun like Shenvair's gun.

Malvern glanced back quickly. The not quite shut door showed him a part of the attic, the top of the stairs, one of Doll Conant's feet square and placid on the carpet, under the kitchen table. He reached his arm out slowly down behind the tub, gathered the gun up. The four exposed chambers had steeljacketed bullets in them.

Malvern opened his coat, slipped the gun down inside the waistband of his trousers, tightened his belt, and buttoned his coat again. He went out of the bathroom, shut the clapboard door carefully.

Doll Conant gestured at a chair across the table from him: 'Sit down.'

Malvern glanced at Jean Adrian. She was staring at him with a kind of rigid curiosity, her eyes dark and colourless in a stone white face under the black hat.

He gestured at her, smiling faintly. 'It's Mister Shenvair, angel. He met with an accident. He's – dead.'

The girl stared at him without any expression at all. Then she shuddered once, violently. She stared at him again, made no sound of any kind.

Malvern sat down in the chair across the table from Conant.

Conant eyed him, added a smoking stub to the collection in the white saucer, lit a fresh cigarette, streaking the match the whole length of the kitchen table.

He puffed, said casually: 'Yeah, he's dead. You shot him.'

Malvern shook his head very slightly, smiled. 'No.'

'Skip the baby eyes, feller. You shot him. Perrugini, the

wop undertaker across the street, owns this place, rents it out now and then to a right boy for a quick dust. Incidentally, he's a friend of mine, does me a lot of good among the other wops. He rented it to Shenvair. Didn't know him, but Shenvair got a right ticket into him. He heard shooting over here to-night, took a look out of his window, saw a guy make it to a car. He saw the licence number on the car. Your car.'

Malvern shook his head again. 'But I didn't shoot him, Conant.'

'Try and prove ... The wop ran over and found Shenvair half-way up the stairs, dead. He dragged him up and stuck him in the bathtub. Some crazy idea about the blood, I suppose. Then he went through him, found a police card, a private dick licence, and that scared him. He got me on the phone and when I got the name, I came steaming.'

Conant stopped talking, eyed Malvern steadily. Malvern said very softly:

'You hear about the shooting at Cyrano's to-night?'

Conant nodded.

Malvern went on:

'I was there, with a kid friend of mine from the hotel. Just before the shooting this Shenvair threw a punch at me. The kid followed Shenvair here and they shot at each other. Shenvair was drunk and scared and I'll bet he shot first. I didn't even know the kid had a gun. Shenvair shot him through the stomach. He got home, died there. He left me a note. I have the note.'

After a moment Conant said:

'You killed Shenvair, or hired that boy to do it. Here's why. He tried to copper his bet on your blackmail racket. He sold out to Courtway.'

Malvern looked startled. He snapped his head around to look at Jean Adrian. She was leaning forward, staring at him with colour in her cheeks, a shine in her eyes. She said very softly:

'I'm sorry – angel, I had you wrong.'

Malvern smiled a little, turned back to Conant. He said:

'She thought I was the one that sold out. Who's Court-way? Your bird dog, the State Senator?'

Conant's face turned a little white. He laid his cigarette down very carefully in the saucer, leaned across the table and hit Malvern in the mouth with his fist. Malvern went over backwards in the rickety chair. His head struck the floor.

Jean Adrian stood up quickly and her teeth made a sharp clicking sound. Then she didn't move.

Malvern rolled over on his side and got up and set the chair upright. He got a handkerchief out, patted his mouth, looked at the handkerchief.

Steps clattered on the stairs and the albino poked his narrow head into the room, poked a gun still further in.

'Need any help, Boss?'

Without looking at him Conant said: 'Get out – and shut that door – and stay out!'

*

The door was shut. The albino's steps died down the stairs. Malvern put his left hand on the back of the chair and moved it slowly back and forth. His right hand still held the handkerchief. His lips were getting puffed and darkish. His eyes looked at the Lüger by Conant's elbow.

Conant picked up his cigarette and put it in his mouth. He said:

'Maybe you think I'm going to neck this blackmail racket. I'm not, brother. I'm going to kill it – so it'll stay killed. You're going to spill your guts. I have three boys downstairs who need exercise. Get busy and talk.'

Malvern said: 'Yeah – but your three boys are downstairs. He slipped the handkerchief inside his coat. His hand came out with the blue gun in it. He said: 'Take that Lüger by the barrel and push it across the table so I can reach it.'

Conant didn't move. His eyes narrowed to slits. His hard

mouth jerked the cigarette in it once. He didn't touch the Lüger. After a moment he said:

'Guess you know what will happen to you now.'

Malvern shook his head slightly. He said: 'Maybe I'm not particular about that. If it does happen, I promise you *you* won't know anything about it.'

Conant stared at him, didn't move. He stared at him for quite a long time, stared at the blue gun. 'Where did you get it? Didn't the heels frisk you?'

Malvern said: 'They did. This is Shenvair's gun. Your wop friend must have kicked it behind the bathtub. Careless.'

Conant reached two thick fingers forward and turned the Lüger around and pushed it to the far edge of the table. He nodded and said tonelessly:

'I lose this hand. I ought to have thought of that. That makes me do the talking.'

Jean Adrian came quickly across the room and stood at the end of the table. Malvern reached forward across the chair and took the Lüger in his left hand and slipped it down into his overcoat pocket, kept his hand on it. He rested the hand holding the blue gun on the top of the chair.

Jean Adrian said: 'Who is this man?'

'Doll Conant, a local bigtimer. Senator John Myerson Courtway is his pipe line into the State Senate. And Senator Courtway, angel, is the man in your photo frame on your desk. The man you said was your father, that you said was dead.'

The girl said very quietly: 'He *is* my father. I knew he wasn't dead. I'm blackmailing him – for a hundred grand. Shenvair and Targo and I. He never married my mother, so I'm illegitimate. But I'm still his child. I have rights and he won't recognize them. He treated my mother abominably, left her without a nickel. He had detectives watch me for years. Shenvair was one of them. He recognized my photos when I came here and met Targo. He remembered.

He went up to San Francisco and got a copy of my birth certificate. I have it here.'

She fumbled at her bag, felt around it, opened a small zipper pocket in the lining. Her hand came out with a folded paper. She tossed it on the table.

Conant stared at her, reached a hand for the paper, spread it out and studied it. He said slowly:

'This doesn't prove anything.'

Malvern took his left hand out of his pocket and reached for the paper. Conant pushed it towards him.

It was a certified copy of a birth certificate, dated originally in 1912. It recorded the birth of a girl child, Adriana Gianni Myerson, to John and Antonina Gianni Myerson. Malvern dropped the paper again.

He said: 'Adriana Gianni – Jean Adrian. Was that the tip-off, Conant?'

Conant shook his head. 'Shenvair got cold feet. He tipped Courtway. He was scared. That's why he had this hideout lined up. I thought that was why he got killed. Targo couldn't have done it, because Targo's still in the can. Maybe I had you wrong, Malvern.'

Malvern stared at him woodenly, didn't say anything. Jean Adrian said:

'It's my fault. I'm the one that's to blame. It was pretty rotten. I see that now. I want to see him and tell him I'm sorry and that he'll never hear from me again. I want to make him promise he won't do anything to Duke Targo. May I?'

Malvern said: 'You can do anything you want to, angel. I have two guns that say so. But why did you wait so long? And why didn't you go at him through the courts? You're in show business. The publicity would have made you – even if he beat you out.'

The girl bit her lip, said in a low voice: 'My mother never really knew who he was, never knew his last name even. He was John Myerson to her. I didn't know until I came here and happened to see a picture in the local paper. He had changed, but I knew the face. And of course the first part of his name – '

Conant said sneeringly: 'You didn't go at him openly because you knew damn well you weren't his kid. That your mother just wished you on to him like any cheap broad who sees herself out of a swell meal ticket. Courtway says he can prove it, and that he's going to prove it and put you where you belong. And believe me, sister, he's just the stiff-necked kind of sap who would kill himself in public life raking up a twenty-year-old scandal to do that little thing.'

The big man spat his cigarette stub out viciously, added: 'It cost me money to put him where he is and I aim to keep him there. That's why I'm in it. No dice, sister. I'm putting the pressure on. You're going to take a lot of air and keep on taking it. As for your two-gun friend – maybe he didn't know, but he knows now and that ties him up in the same package.'

Conant banged on the table top, leaned back, looking calmly at the blue gun in Malvern's hand.

Malvern stared into the big man's eyes, said very softly: 'That hood at Cyrano's to-night – he wasn't your idea of putting on the pressure by any chance, Conant, was he?'

Conant grinned harshly, shook his head. The door at the top of the stairs opened a little, silently. Malvern didn't see it. He was staring at Conant. Jean Adrian saw it.

Her eyes widened and she stepped back with a startled exclamation, that jerked Malvern's eyes to her.

The albino stepped softly through the door with a gun levelled.

His red eyes glistened, his mouth was drawn wide in a snarling grin. He said:

'The door's kind of thin, Boss. I listened. Okay? . . . Shed the heater, rube, or I blow you both in half.'

Malvern turned slightly and opened his right hand and let the blue gun bounce on the thin carpet. He shrugged, spread his hands out wide, didn't look at Jean Adrian.

The albino stepped clear of the door, came slowly forward and put his gun against Malvern's back.

Conant stood up, came around the table, took the Lüger out of Malvern's coat pocket and hefted it. Without a word or a change of expression he slammed it against the side of Malvern's jaw.

Malvern sagged drunkenly, then went down on the floor on his side.

Jean Adrian screamed, clawed at Conant. He threw her off, changed the gun to his left hand and slapped the side of her face with a hard palm.

'Pipe down, sister. You've had all your fun.'

The albino went to the head of the stairs and called down it. The two other gunmen came up into the room, stood grinning.

Malvern didn't move on the floor. After a little while Conant lit another cigarette and rattled a knuckle on the table top beside the birth certificate. He said gruffly:

'She wants to see the old man. Okay, she can see him. We'll all go see him. There's still something in this that stinks.' He raised his eyes, looked at the stocky man. 'You and Lefty go downtown and spring Targo, get him out to the Senator's place as soon as you can. Step on it.'

The two hoods went back down the stairs.

Conant looked down at Malvern, kicked him in the ribs lightly, kept on kicking them until Malvern opened his eyes and stirred.

9

The car waited at the top of a hill, before a pair of tall wrought-iron gates, inside which there was a lodge. A door of the lodge stood open and yellow light framed a big man in an overcoat and a pulled-down hat. He came forward slowly into the rain, his hands down in his pockets.

The rain slithered about his feet and the albino leaned against the uprights of the gate, clicking his teeth. The big man said:

'What yuh want? I can see yuh.'

'Shake it up, rube. Mister Conant wants to call on your boss.'

The man inside spat into the wet darkness. 'So what? Know what time it is?'

Conant opened the car door suddenly and went over to the gates. The rain made noise between the car and the voices.

Malvern turned his head slowly and patted Jean Adrian's hand. She pushed his hand away from her quickly.

Her voice said softly: 'You fool – oh, you fool!'

Malvern sighed. 'I'm having a swell time, angel. A swell time.'

The man inside the gates took out keys on a long chain, unlocked the gates and pushed them back until they clicked on the chocks. Conant and the albino came back to the car.

Conant stood in the rain with a heel hooked on the running board. Malvern took his big flask out of his pocket, felt it over to see if it was dented, then unscrewed the top. He held it out towards the girl, said:

'Have a little bottle courage.'

She didn't answer him, didn't move. He drank from the flask, put it away, looked past Conant's broad back at acres of dripping trees, a cluster of lighted windows that seemed to hang in the sky.

A car came up the hill stabbing the wet dark with its headlights, pulled behind the sedan and stopped. Conant went over to it, put his head into it and said something. The car backed, turned into the driveway, and its lights splashed on retaining walls, disappeared, reappeared at the top of the drive as a hard white oval against a stone *porte-cochère*.

Conant got into the sedan and the albino swung it into the driveway after the other car. At the top in a cement parking circle ringed with cypresses, they all got out.

At the top of the steps a big door was open and a man in a bathrobe stood in it. Targo, between two men who leaned hard against him, was half-way up the steps. He was bare-headed and without an overcoat. His big body in the white coat looked enormous between the two gunmen.

The rest of the party went up the steps and into the house and followed the bathrobed butler down a hall lined with portraits of somebody's ancestors, through a stiff oval foyer to another hall and into a panelled study with soft lights and heavy drapes and deep leather chairs.

A man stood behind a big dark desk that was set in an alcove made by low, outjutting bookcases. He was enormously tall and thin. His white hair was so thick and fine that no single hair was visible in it. He had a small straight bitter mouth, black eyes without depth in a whitelined face. He stooped a little and a blue corduroy bathrobe faced with satin was wrapped around his almost freakish thinness.

The butler shut the door and Conant opened it again and jerked his chin at the two men who had come in with Targo. They went out. The albino stepped behind Targo and pushed him down into a chair. Targo looked dazed, stupid. There was a smear of dirt on one side of his face and his eyes had a drugged look.

The girl went over to him quickly, said: 'Oh, Duke – are you all right, Duke?'

Targo blinked at her, half-grinned. 'So you had to rat, huh? Skip it. I'm fine.' His voice had an unnatural sound.

Jean Adrian went away from him and sat down and hunched herself together as if she was cold.

The tall man stared coldly at everyone in the room in turn, then said lifelessly: 'Are these the blackmailers – and was it necessary to bring them here in the middle of the night?'

Conant shook himself out of his coat, threw it on the floor behind a lamp. He lit a fresh cigarette and stood spread-legged in the middle of the room, a big, rough, rugged man very sure of himself. He said:

'The girl wanted to see you and tell you she was sorry and wants to play ball. The guy in the ice cream coat is Targo, the fighter. He got himself in a shooting scrape at a night spot and acted so wild downtown they fed him sleep tablets to quiet him. The other guy is Ted Malvern, old Marcus Malvern's boy. I don't figure him yet.'

Malvern said dryly: 'I'm a private detective, Senator. I'm here in the interests of my client, Miss Adrian.' He laughed.

The girl looked at him suddenly, then looked at the floor.

Conant said gruffly, 'Shenvair, the one you know about, got himself bumped off. Not by us. That's still to straighten out.'

The tall man nodded coldly. He sat down at his desk and picked up a white quill pen, tickled one ear with it.

'And what is your idea of the way to handle this matter, Conant?' he asked thinly.

Conant shrugged. 'I'm a rough boy, but I'd handle this one legal. Talk to the D.A., toss them in a coop on suspicion of extortion. Cook up a story for the papers, then give it time to cool. Then dump these birds across the State line and tell them not to come back – or else.'

Senator Courtway moved the quill around to his other ear. 'They could attack me again, from a distance,' he said icily. 'I'm in favour of a showdown, put them where they belong.'

'You can't try them, Courtway. It would kill you politically.'

'I'm tired of public life, Conant. I'll be glad to retire.' The tall thin man curved his mouth into a faint smile.

'The hell you are,' Conant growled. He jerked his head around, snapped: 'Come here, sister.'

Jean Adrian stood up, came slowly across the room, stood in front of the desk.

'Make her?' Conant snarled.

Courtway stared at the girl's set face for a long time, without a trace of expression. He put his quill down on the desk, opened a drawer and took out a photograph. He looked from the photo to the girl, back to the photo, said tonelessly:

'This was taken a number of years ago, but there's a very strong resemblance. I don't think I'd hesitate to say it's the same face.'

He put the photo down on the desk and with the same unhurried motion took an automatic out of the drawer and put it down on the desk beside the photo.

Conant stared at the gun. His mouth twisted. He said thickly: 'You won't need that, Senator. Listen, your showdown idea is all wrong. I'll get detailed confessions from these people and we'll hold them. If they ever act up again, it'll be time enough then to crack down with the big one.'

Malvern smiled a little and walked across the carpet until he was near the end of the desk. He said: 'I'd like to see that photograph,' and leaned over suddenly and took it.

Courtway's thin hand dropped to the gun, then relaxed. He leaned back in his chair and stared at Malvern.

*

Malvern stared at the photograph, lowered it, said softly to Jean Adrian: 'Go sit down.'

She turned and went back to her chair, dropped into it wearily.

Malvern said: 'I'd like your showdown idea, Senator. It's clean and straightforward and a wholesome change in policy for Mr Conant. But it won't work.' He snicked a fingernail at the photo. 'This has a superficial resemblance, no more. I don't think it's the same girl at all myself. Her ears are differently shaped and lower on her head. Her eyes are closer together than Miss Adrian's eyes, the line of her jaw is longer. Those things don't change. So what have you got? An extortion letter. Maybe, but you can't tie it to anyone or you'd have done it already. The girl's name. Just coincidence. What else?'

Conant's face was granite hard, his mouth bitter. His voice shook a little, saying: 'And how about the certificate the gal took out of her purse, wise guy?'

Malvern smiled faintly, rubbed the side of his jaw with his fingertips. 'I thought you got that from Shenvair?' he said slyly. 'And Shenvair is dead.'

Conant's face was a mask of fury. He balled his fist, took a jerky step forward. 'Why you – damn' louse – '

Jean Adrian was leaning forward, staring round-eyed at Malvern. Targo was staring at him, with a loose grin, pale hard eyes. Courtway was staring at him. There was no expression of any kind on Courtway's face. He sat cold, relaxed, distant.

Conant laughed suddenly, snapped his fingers. 'Okay toot your horn,' he grunted.

Malvern said slowly: 'I'll tell you another reason why there'll be no showdown. That shooting at *Cyrano's*. Those threats to make Targo drop an unimportant fight. That hood that went to Miss Adrian's hotel room and sapped her left her lying on her doorway. Can't you use your big noodle at all? Can't you tie all that in, Conant? *I* can.'

Courtway leaned forward suddenly and placed his hand on his gun, folded it around the butt. His black eyes were holes in a white frozen face.

Conant didn't move, didn't speak.

Malvern went on: 'Why did Targo get those threats, and after he didn't drop the fight, why did a gun go to see him at *Cyrano's*, a night-club a very bad place for that kind of play? Because at *Cyrano's* he was with the girl, and Cyrano was his backer, and if anything happened at *Cyrano's* the law

would get the threat story before they had time to think of
anything else. That's why. The threats were a build-up for
a killing. When the shooting came off Targo was to be with
the girl, so the hood could get the girl and it would look as
if Targo was the one he was after.

'He would have tried for Targo, too, of course, but above
all he would have got the girl. Because she was the dynamite
behind this shakedown. Without her it meant nothing, and
with her it could always be made over into a legitimate
paternity suit, if it didn't work the other way. You knew
about her and about Targo, because Shenvair got cold feet
and sold out. And Shenvair knew about the hood – because
when the hood showed, and I saw him – and Shenvair knew
I knew him, because he had heard me tell Targo about him
– then Shenvair tried to pick a drunken fight with me and
keep me from trying to interfere.'

Malvern stopped, rubbed the side of his head again, very
slowly, very gently. He watched Conant with an up from
under look.

Conant said slowly, very harshly: 'I don't play those
games, buddy. Believe it or not – I don't.'

Malvern said: 'Listen. The hood could have killed the
girl at the hotel with his sap. He didn't, because Targo
wasn't there and the fight hadn't been fought, and the build-
up would have been all wasted. He went there to have a
close look at her, without make-up. And she was scared
about something, and had a gun with her. So he sapped her
down and ran away. That visit was just a finger.'

Conant said again: 'I don't play those games, buddy.'
Then he took the Lüger out of his pocket and held it down
at his side.

Malvern shrugged, turned his head to stare at Senator
Courtway.

'No, but *he* does,' he said softly. 'He had the motive, and
the play wouldn't look like him. He cooked it up with
Shenvair – and if it went wrong, as it did, Shenvair would

have breezed and if the law got wise, big tough Doll Conant is the boy whose nose would be in the mud.'

Courtway smiled a little and said in an utterly dead voice

'The young man is very ingenious, but surely – '

Targo stood up. His face was a stiff mask. His lips moved slowly and he said:

'It sounds pretty good to me. I think I'll twist your damn neck, Mister Courtway.'

The albino snarled. 'Sit down, punk,' and lifted his gun

Targo turned slightly and slammed the albino on the jaw He went over backwards, smashed his head against the wall The gun sailed along the floor from his limp hand.

Targo started across the room.

Conant looked at him sideways and didn't move. Targo went past him, almost touching him. Conant didn't move a muscle. His big face was blank, his eyes narrowed to a faint glitter between the heavy lids.

Nobody moved but Targo. Then Courtway lifted his gun and his finger whitened on the trigger and the gun roared

Malvern moved across the room very swiftly and stood in front of Jean Adrian, between her and the rest of the room

Targo looked down at his hands. His face twisted into a silly smile. He sat down on the floor and pressed both his hands against his chest.

Courtway lifted his gun again and then Conant moved The Lüger jerked up, flamed twice. Blood flowed down Courtway's hand. His gun fell behind his desk. His long body seemed to swoop down after the gun. It jack-knifed until only his shoulders showed humped above the line of the desk.

Conant said: 'Stand up and take it, — — double-crossing swine!'

There was a shot behind the desk. Courtway's shoulder went down out of sight.

After a moment Conant went around behind the desk stooped, straightened.

'He ate one,' he said very calmly. 'Through the mouth . . . And I lose a nice clean senator.'

Targo took his hands from his chest and fell over sideways on the floor and lay still.

The door of the room slammed open. The butler stood in it, tousled-headed, his mouth gaping. He tried to say something, saw the gun in Conant's hand, saw Targo slumped on the floor. He didn't say anything.

The albino was getting to his feet, rubbing his chin, feeling his teeth, shaking his head. He went slowly along the wall and gathered up his gun.

Conant snarled at him: 'Swell gun you turned out to be. Get on the phone. Get Malloy, the night captain – and snag it up!'

Malvern turned, put his hand down and lifted Jean Adrian's cold chin.

'It's getting light, angel. And I think the rain has stopped,' he said slowly. He pulled his inevitable flask out. 'Let's take a drink – to Mister Targo.'

The girl shook her head, covered her face with her hands. After a long time there were sirens.

10

The slim, tired-looking kid in the pale blue and silver of the *Carondelet* held his white glove in front of the closing doors and said:

'Corky's boils is better, but he didn't come to work, Mister Malvern. Tony the bell captain ain't showed this morning either. Pretty soft for some guys.'

Malvern stood close to Jean Adrian in the corner of the car. They were alone in it. He said:

'That's what you think.'

The boy turned red. Malvern moved over and patted his shoulder, said: 'Don't mind me, son. I've been up all night with a sick friend. Here, buy yourself a second breakfast.'

'Jeeze, Mister Malvern, I didn't mean –'

The doors opened at nine and they went down the corridor to 914. Malvern took the key and opened the door, put the key on the inside, held the door, said:

'Get some sleep and wake up with your fist in your eye. Take my flask and get a mild toot on. Do you good.'

The girl went in through the door, said over her shoulder: 'I don't want liquor. Come in a minute. There's something I want to tell you.'

He shut the door and followed her in. A bright bar of sunlight lay across the carpet all the way to the davenport. He lit a cigarette and stared at it.

Jean Adrian sat down and jerked her hat off and rumpled her hair. She was silent a moment, then she said slowly, carefully:

'It was swell of you to go to all that trouble for me. I don't know why you should do it.'

Malvern said: 'I can think of a couple of reasons, but they didn't keep Targo from getting killed, and that was my fault in a way. Then in another way it wasn't. I didn't ask him to twist Senator Courtway's neck.'

The girl said: 'You think you're hard-boiled but you're just a big slob that argues himself into a jam for the first tramp he finds in trouble. Forget it. Forget Targo and forget me. Neither of us was worth any part of your time. I wanted to tell you that because I'll be going away as soon as they let me, and I won't be seeing you any more. This is good-bye.'

Malvern nodded, stared at the sun on the carpet. The girl went on:

'It's a little hard to tell. I'm not looking for sympathy when I say I'm a tramp. I've smothered in too many hall bedrooms, stripped in too many filthy dressing-rooms, missed too many meals, told too many lies to be anything else. That's why I wouldn't want to have anything to do with you, ever.'

Malvern said: 'I like the way you tell it. Go on.'

She looked at him quickly, looked away again. 'I'm not the Gianni girl. You guessed that. But I knew her. We did a cheap sister act together when they still did sister acts. Ada and Jean Adrian. We made up our names from hers. That flopped, and we went in a road show and that flopped too. In New Orleans. The going was a little too rough for her. She swallowed bichloride. I kept her photos because I knew her story. And looking at that thin cold guy and thinking what he could have done for her I got to hate him. She was his kid all right. Don't ever think she wasn't. I even wrote letters to him, asking for help for her, just a little help, signing her name. But they didn't get any answer. I got to hate him so much I wanted to do something to him, after she took the bichloride. So I came out here when I got a stake.'

She stopped talking and laced her fingers together tightly, then she pulled them apart violently, as if she wanted to hurt herself. She went on:

'I met Targo through Cyrano and Shenvair through him. Shenvair knew the photos. He'd worked once for an agency in Frisco that was hired to watch Ada. You know all the rest of it.'

Malvern said:

'It sounds pretty good. I wondered why the touch wasn't made sooner. Do you want me to think you didn't want his money?'

'No. I'd have taken his money all right. But that wasn't what I wanted most. I said I was a tramp.'

Malvern smiled very faintly and said: 'You don't know a lot about tramps, angel. You made an illegitimate pass and you got caught. That's that, but the money wouldn't have done you any good. It would have been dirty money. I know.'

She looked up at him, stared at him. He touched the side of his face and winced and said: 'I know because that's the kind of money mine is. My dad made it out of crooked sewerage and paving contracts, out of gambling concessions, appointment pay-offs, even vice, I daresay. He made it every rotten way there is to make money in city politics. And when it was made and there was nothing left to do but sit and look at it, he died and left it to me. It hasn't brought me any fun either. I always hope it's going to, but it never does. Because I'm his pup, his blood, reared in the same gutter. I'm worse than a tramp, angel. I'm a guy that lives on crooked dough and doesn't even do his own stealing.'

He stopped, flicked ash on the carpet, straightened his hat on his head.

'Think that over, and don't run too far, because I have all the time in the world and it wouldn't do you any good. It would be so much more fun to run away together.'

He went a little way towards the door, stood looking down at the sunlight on the carpet, looked back at her quickly and then went on out.

When the door shut she stood up and went into the bedroom and lay down on the bed just as she was, with her coat on. She stared at the ceiling. After a long time she smiled. In the middle of the smile she fell asleep.

*Some other
Penguin crime books
are described on the
following pages*

THE NEW SONIA WAYWARD

Michael Innes

Colonel Ffolliot Petticate's predicament begins in the first glorious paragraph, and then knots and tangles itself up with humour, irony, and devastating suspense right up to the comically shocking finality of the end. Michael Innes surpasses himself in this novel with the subtlety and wit of the characterization – ranging from the savagely incisive to the delicately affectionate.

'A gem. How rare an item this is. A polished, urbane, and funny thriller. Wonderfully written. On no account to be missed' – *Evening Standard*

'Has everything. From the stunning opening paragraph ... it presents a plot packed with wit, irony, and varied characterization. The constant succession of new twists and turns, causing something to be happening on each page, never fails to amaze. It is an intriguing book and definitely the author's best' – *Manchester Evening News*

'Written with all the skill that has placed its author among the greatest crime novelists of the world' – *Birmingham Post*

A CASE OF TORCHES

Clark Smith

Just a case of torches – that's all there is missing when Nicky Mahoun, investigating accountant to a large industrial combine, starts his inquiries. But the research chemist with Communist leanings, whose report on the quality of the torches can influence the placing of a major contract, has also disappeared. Neither his chronically jealous wife, nor his mistress, the fascinating Valerie Brown, have seen him for days. Mahoun's investigations are carried out in defiance of his superiors against a background of boardroom politics, where power is the prize and the in-fighting is traditionally non-physical. But violence intrudes: pathetic suicide and brutal murder. Before the joker is revealed in this pack of scheming executives, Mahoun faces acute danger, and is made to face questions about himself and the ethics of a way of life he has accepted, until the catalyst is provided by . . . a case of torches.

Here, in fine form again, is the author of *The Speaking Eye* and *The Deadly Reaper*.

Also available:

THE DEADLY REAPER
THE SPEAKING EYE

OR BE HE DEAD

James Byrom

In delving into records of the 1890s, Raymond Kennington finds a fascinating case of murder and blackmail which he uses in the latest of his much-bought crime stories. But just before publication there is the awful realization that one of the men acquitted through lack of evidence may still be alive and would certainly sue for libel. Author, together with publisher's secretary, set themselves up as sleuths and get embroiled in a particularly exciting manhunt through London and the Paris underworld.

'The writing is admirably crisp and intelligent, and that difficult blend of past with present and violence with ratiocination is smoothly achieved' – Maurice Richardson in the *Observer*

'It is a great pleasure to welcome a crime novelist so lively and literate and undonnishly urbane' – Julian Symons in the *Sunday Times*

'James Byrom has most successfully combined a light-hearted, rather wry wit with a clever plot. This is an intelligent, amusing book' – *Birmingham Post*

THE MAN WITH THE CANE

Jean Potts

Murdered with his own cane; that was the cops' verdict on the corpse – a simple mugging. But Val Bryant, who found the body, had premonitions of even greater disaster. The dead man exactly fitted the lighthearted description that his six-year old daughter Arabella had given him of her 'imaginary' friend Cane.

When the other easy-going members of Val's family clam up tight as drums and mutual suspicion is the order of the day, Val refuses to put his fears under wraps and sets about unearthing the truth. The events which follow, from blackmail to suicide and kidnapping, menace the whole family and lead up to a climax which leaves nerve-ends jangling like a modern symphony.

'Has an impressive talent and exercises it urbanely and brilliantly. Cast of New Yorkers and not a cliché among them' – *Sunday Times*

'Excellently written. Miss Potts most skilfully integrates characterization and crime with her story-telling. Plenty of suspense and complete conviction' – Maurice Richardson in the *Observer*

Also available:

GO, LOVELY ROSE
DEATH OF A STRAY CAT

NOT FOR SALE IN THE U.S.A. OR CANADA